HIGHLY SUSPICIOUS
and *unfairly cute*

ALSO BY TALIA HIBBERT

THE BROWN SISTERS TRILOGY

Get a Life, Chloe Brown

Take a Hint, Dani Brown

Act Your Age, Eve Brown

THE RAVENSWOOD SERIES

A Girl Like Her

Damaged Goods

Untouchable

That Kind of Guy

STANDALONES

The Princess Trap

The Roommate Risk

Work for It

HIGHLY SUSPICIOUS

and

unfairly cute

TALIA HIBBERT

joy revolution

Text copyright © 2023 by Talia Hibbert
Jacket art copyright © 2023 by Mlle Belamour
Birds used under license from Shutterstock.com

All rights reserved. Published in the United States by Joy Revolution, an imprint of Random House Children's Books, a division of Penguin Random House LLC, New York.

Joy Revolution is a registered trademark and the colophon is a trademark of Penguin Random House LLC.

Visit us on the Web! GetUnderlined.com
Educators and librarians, for a variety of teaching tools,
visit us at RHTeachersLibrarians.com

Library of Congress Cataloging-in-Publication Data is available upon request.
ISBN 978-0-593-48233-9 (hardcover) — ISBN 978-0-593-48234-6 (ebook) —
ISBN 978-0-593-48235-3 (paperback)

The text of this book is set in 12.5-point Perpetua MT.
Interior design by Ken Crossland

Printed in the United States of America
10 9 8 7 6 5 4 3 2 1
First Edition

For Sam,

my very own

high school sweetheart

AUTHOR'S NOTE

This story involves parental abandonment and a portrayal of living with obsessive compulsive disorder. I hope I have handled my characters' experiences with the care they, and you, the reader, deserve.

This story also involves highly fictionalized portrayals of existing forests. I am very sorry for all the geographical inaccuracies. In my defense, I did it for the feels.

GLOSSARY

Bradley and Celine's story is set in England and Scotland because I, the author, am British and don't get out much. While working on this story with my American editor, we stumbled across a few colloquialisms and cultural references that don't directly translate. So we've put together this handy-dandy glossary for anyone who needs it. Enjoy!

A*: The highest achievable grade in the UK. (The letter system was recently replaced by a number system, which is a travesty for overachievers everywhere, but at least in this book A*s will live on forever.)

academy: An educational provision that is run like a nonprofit company.

AS results: AS Levels are a qualification Bradley and Celine studied last year. This year, they will study for A Levels. (There are numerous different qualifications students can aim for after they turn sixteen, depending on their career plans.)

barrister: A lawyer who marches into court and says things like, "Objection!" and "I rest my case, Your Honor." (Not really, but it would be fun if they did.) Not to be confused with a solicitor, i.e., a lawyer who writes documents that say things like "pursuant to subsection A."

Bonfire Night: Also called Guy Fawkes Night; a celebration of the time a guy named, well, Guy, tried to blow up parliament. We set off fireworks and burn stuff to remind us all that we're . . . not supposed to blow things up or burn stuff.

Boots: A Nottinghamshire-based international pharmacy and beauty retailer. Go there for your prescription, your makeup, hair products, photos, baby stuff, lunchtime snacks, Christmas gifts—everything but the kitchen sink, really.

buskers: Absurdly confident individuals who make music on the street for cash.

"Drop me in it": A colloquialism that describes getting someone else in trouble. "For God's sake, Mason, you've really dropped me in it."

face like thunder: A frown. A scowl. A glare. A generally Celine-like countenance. A warning of arguments to come.

football: The beautiful game, obviously. Helmets are not involved.

head of year: A teacher who's been given official responsibility for a particular year group. If you fail, they get in trouble. (The resulting anxiety is what inspires so many of them to make dramatic speeches about your penniless future.)

Maccies: A delicious and nutritious meal from the noble eatery officially known as McDonald's.

maintenance loan/grant: Money the government lends or gives to university students so they won't starve to death. This is (1) separate from tuition loans/grants, and (2) not to be confused with child maintenance, which is money your secondary caregiver gives to your primary caregiver after a divorce or separation.

Midlanders: Those who live in the middle of England, as opposed to Northerners (perfectly acceptable) and Southerners (. . . southern).

needs must: A phrase that allows you to get away with essentially anything ("Oh, well! Needs must.") but also allows people to make you do essentially anything ("Get on with it. Needs must.").

Oxbridge: The words Oxford and Cambridge smushed together; convenient for those who have applied to both highly prestigious universities. Equally convenient for those who are slagging off said universities and don't want to waste their breath on extra syllables.

pillock: A donkey. A plank. A regrettably dim lightbulb. A dull tool in a box of sharp ones. I can't tell if this is helping, but I am enjoying myself.

plaster: A little sticky bandage designed to protect paper cuts or skinned knees or gaping emotional wounds.

plummy: Say the word "plum." Now pretend there's a plum in your mouth and say it again. That's how posh people sound.

shit-hot: Excellent. Fabulous. Hot as shit. This is, perhaps, a slightly outdated term, but Celine is middle-aged at heart.

sixth form: An educational provision for students aged sixteen to eighteen (or nineteen, or twenty, depending on how well you cope with exams) that exists as part of a secondary school—i.e., you have to share with younger kids. Brad and Celine attend Rosewood Academy sixth form.

slagging off: To slag someone (or something) off is to speak badly about them, typically behind their back but potentially to their face. (This usually causes trouble, so please do proceed with caution.)

SEPTEMBER

CHAPTER ONE

CELINE

It's the first day of school and I'm already being forced to socialize.

"I'm dead serious," Nicky Cassidy says, his eyes wide and his acid-wash shirt stained with what looks like tomato sauce. "Juice WRLD is *alive,* Celine. The planet needs to know."

My TikTok account has 19,806 followers—@HowCeline SeesIt, feel free to take me to 20K—so God knows how I'm supposed to inform the entire planet of anything. Besides, I make videos about UFOs and vaccines (conclusion: I believe in both) and that guy who hijacked a plane and literally vanished with the ransom money. I don't make videos about people's tragic deaths because it's rude and tacky.

Also, I don't take requests. For God's sake, I am a conspiracy theorist. There must be some glamor in that, or else what's the point?

"Sorry, Nicky," I reply. "Still no."

He is appalled by my lack of sensitivity to his cause. "You're joking."

"Almost never."

"Fine. If you don't want to tell the truth, *I'll* do it. Your Tik-Tok's shit anyway." He storms off, leaving me to cross campus on my own.

So much for Mum's hope that I'll make more friends this year.

Oh well. I inhale the warm September air and stride through the school's higgledy-piggledy pathways alone. Rosewood Academy is a rambling maze, but this is my final year, so I know it like I know Beyoncé's discography. It takes five minutes to reach the Beech Hut—aka our sixth-form common area/cafeteria, a tiny, musty building that begs to be knocked down. I snag my usual table by the noticeboard and get on with the very important business of ignoring everyone around me.

I'm on my phone stitching together some footage of cows that I filmed this weekend for a video about the possibility of cannibalistic bovine overlords running the beef industry when my best friend slides into the chair beside me and waves a glossy leaflet in my face.

"Have you seen this?" Michaela demands, her pink curls vibrating with excitement.

"I haven't," I say, "and if you put my eye out with it, I never will."

"Don't be miserable. *Look.*" She slams down the flyer and crows, "Katharine Breakspeare!" Then she clicks her tongue piercing against her teeth, which is Minnie's personal version of a mic drop.

It works. I fall all over that shiny piece of paper like it's a plate of nachos.

There she is: Katharine Breakspeare, her wide mouth severe

(no ladylike smiles for Katharine, thank you very much) and her hair perfectly blown out. They did a whole article in *Vogue* about that blowout, which is ridiculous considering Katharine's famous for her trailblazing career in human rights law. Commentators call this woman the James Bond of the courtroom because she's so damn cool; she's won at least three internationally significant, high-profile cases in the last five years; she bought her mother an entire compound back in Jamaica to retire to. And *Vogue* is talking about her *hair*. I mean, yes, the hair is gorgeous, but come on, people.

Katharine Breakspeare is the blueprint and one day I'm going to be her, building my mum a house in Sierra Leone.

My eyes narrow as I study the leaflet. "'Apply for the Breakspeare Enrichment Program,'" I read. "Her nature bootcamp thing? But that's only for undergrads."

"Not anymore." Minnie grins, tapping the words in front of us. "'Award-winning enrichment program now open to those aged sixteen to eighteen—'"

"'—for the first time ever,'" I finish reading. "'Set yourself apart from the crowd, nurture early bonds with prestigious employers, and be in with the chance to win a *full university scholarship*. . . .'" My mouth is numb. My throat is dry. My nerves are fried. "I need a drink."

Michaela is a dancer; she never goes anywhere without a disgustingly heavy two-liter flask of water. "Here ya go," she says brightly, and causes a small earthquake by slamming it on the table.

"Where did you get this?" I demand between desperate gulps, shaking the Golden Leaflet of Opportunity.

"Mr. Darling's office."

"Mr. Darling's— *Minnie*. It's the first day of school. How are you on his shit list already?"

"I'm not," she says primly. "It was a preliminary warning. You know: *Focus on school this year, Michaela, or you'll die homeless under a bridge by twenty-five*. The usual morale-boosting stuff."

"Oh, babe. That's not true. He's just jealous of your fabulous hair and giant brain."

"Stop. You know I don't listen to him. I have bigger plans." It's true. She's going to be like Jessica Alba in my older sister's favorite film, *Honey,* except much cooler and actually Black. Then she winks and taps the paper. "And so do you."

No, I don't: focusing on school *is* my big plan, because that's how you get into Cambridge, which is how you get an excellent law degree and take over the world.

But I've done the research and read the forums: companies— including law firms—fall all over themselves to hire Breakspeare Enrichment Program alums because the program produces uniquely driven and capable candidates with work ethics and abilities worthy of Katharine's own reputation. It's not like other enrichment programs where you memorize textbooks and complete work experience. In this one, you're put out into the wilderness where you try to survive and, ideally, thrive, for what I'm sure are completely logical reasons. (It is true that I'm hazy on details, but I trust that Katharine knows what she's doing.)

Nature isn't really my thing—not anymore. But I would gargle pond water to get within three feet of this opportunity for the clout alone, never mind the *scholarship*. So it turns out this is it: my new agenda for the last year of school. Goodbye, Latin Club, and farewell to volunteering at the animal hospital.

It's time to make space for camping with Katharine.

Apparently, anyone interested in the details can attend a meeting in Nottingham later this week. I flip the leaflet over, searching for a map, but instead I see a QR code labeled "RSVP" and the logos of all the companies involved. The list is long. Some are huge, like Boots; some are small but powerful, like Games Workshop; and I see plenty of law firms, too, which is—

Oh.

My dad's firm is a sponsor.

Minnie sees my face, then follows my gaze. "What? What?" She squints at the page.

"Wear your glasses, Michaela," I mutter sharply.

"Not with these lashes." She bats her falsies at me (I think I feel a breeze), then reads "'Lawrence, Needham and Soro, corporate law, established 1998.'"

I swallow hard. My throat is dry again. I chug some more water.

"Whoa, whoa, whoa," Minnie says. "I do need that, you know. You want me to dry up like a prune?" She reclaims the mammoth bottle and says, "Soro. Why does that sound familiar? Soro, Soro—"

"My dad works there."

Minnie winces. She's my best friend, so we know stuff about each other's families. As in, I know her gran's a lesbophobic cowbag and she knows my dad ditched us for his second family ten years ago and I haven't seen him since. The usual girl stuff. Grimacing, she squeaks, "Maybe the sponsoring firms won't be super involved?"

"I honestly couldn't care less." I'm not lying. He's the one with something to be ashamed of. I'm the one who's a credit to my family name.

Which is Bangura, *not* Soro, thank you very much.

I slip the leaflet into my bag, pressed between the pages of a textbook to keep it fresh and uncreased. "I'll think about this. Thanks, Min."

She blows me a kiss as the bell rings, and we get up for class. Only then do I realize who slunk into the Beech Hut while Minnie and I were talking.

Bradley Graeme is here.

Alongside, you know, a ton of other people, but he stands out as the King of Uselessness. He and his breathless fan club are ensconced at their usual table, miles away from the admin office, which allows them to get away with breaking all kinds of rules.

Case in point: Bradley Graeme is currently bouncing a Completely Illicit Football off his head. His short, shiny twists are jumping, and his grin is wide and carefree the way only a truly terrible person's can be.

Minnie leans in as we walk by. "Do you think Brad's applying to Cambridge?"

"Of course he is," I mutter. When does he ever miss a chance to show off?

"So, you might see him at interviews and stuff. Right?"

Ugh. God forbid. "I don't care, stop looking at him."

She arches an eyebrow. "You started it."

Yeah, well. Who can avoid looking at Bradley? His sheer annoyingness creates its own gravitational pull.

His fan club—consisting of 70 percent boys' football team and 30 percent girls whose parents pay for their mammoth Depop wardrobes, which equals 100 percent skinny, glowing people who practice TikTok dances unironically and spend their weekends being bland and hooking up at house parties—is absolutely entranced by his tomfoolery like they've never seen a ball before. Except for Jordan Cooper, who rolls his eyes, snatches the ball out of the air, and says in his flat American accent, "Cut it out, or Mr. Darling will rip you a new one."

(Mr. Darling is our head of year, a tightly wound geography teacher who hands out detentions like he gets paid by the hour.)

Bradley just laughs as if he fears nothing in the world—which is an absolute lie. But then, I've always believed he is fake and false and entirely made of earth-destroying *plastic,* so . . . that tracks.

I'm in the process of looking away with withering disdain when he—inconvenient down to his very soul—glances up and catches my eye. Great. I give him my filthiest look, but his grin doesn't falter.

In fact, it gets wider. He raises his eyebrows, and I can practically read his thoughts: *Watching me again, Bangura?*

I glare. *You wish.*

His smile turns into a smirk.

Ugh.

• • •

BRAD

September's supposed to be fresh and crisp like the empty pages of my brand-new notebook, but so far, it's murky and hot as balls. When Max Donovan drags the gang up to the field at lunch and asks, "Five-a-side?" I look at him like he's off his nut. What, does he want me to sweat through my first-day-of-school outfit?

"No thanks," Jordan says while I'm still contemplating the horrors of unplanned exercise. *He* doesn't mind sweating out of uniform; he just has this thing about treating his Yeezys right.

Donno rolls his eyes and chucks the ball my way. "Bradders. You in?"

I'm not, but I can't resist the urge to keep it off the ground. A quick tap with my right foot, my left, then my knee, then my chest. "No thanks," I say, and do it again.

"Show-off," Jordan murmurs.

I stick my tongue out at him and kick the ball back to Donno, who snorts derisively. "Christ, you're a pair of wet wipes." He's our team captain, in possession of a killer left foot, floppy golden hair, and sparkling blue eyes. His smiles are always wide and mocking, barely hiding his fangs. I used to have the most unholy crush on him. "What about the rest of you pillocks?"

The guys milling around this makeshift pitch practically stand to attention. I imagine rigid salutes and a chorus of *Sir, yes, sir!* to match their worshipful looks. Donno has an ego problem—I'm qualified to point this out because I also have an ego problem—and the team really doesn't help.

Jordan and I leave them to it. There's a weeping willow at the edge of this field creating a pool of cool, green shade that's calling my name.

Five minutes later, we're curtained off from the rest of the world by a veil of leaves. I lie back, head on my rucksack, and crack open my well-loved copy of *All Systems Red*. I'm rereading the Murderbot Diaries again, mostly to torture myself with the fact that I'll never write anything this good.

Or possibly anything at all.

But I don't entertain defeatist thoughts. Dr. Okoro taught me not to invite them in for tea.

"Hey, Brad," Jordan says out of the blue. "What do you think of Minnie Digby?"

I study him over the top of my book. "Minnie Digby?"

"Yeah." He looks down, probably hoping his mop of curls will hide the blush on his light brown cheeks. "You know, the one who hangs around with—"

"I know who Michaela Digby hangs around with."

He smirks again. "Oh yeah. Of course you do."

"I'm a good friend, so I'm ignoring that comment." Jordan has a twisted mind that contains batshit theories about me and persons I will not stoop to name. (Okay, fine: her name is Celine Bangura, and she is my archnemesis. Happy?)

I shut my book—which is a real sacrifice, considering Murder-bot's currently deciding whether or not to rip someone's arm off—and try to answer his question. "I think . . ." *That Minnie Digby keeps poor company. That if she ever dares to disagree with her glorious leader about literally anything, ever, she'll be dropped on her arse at the speed of light. That—*

Uh, Brad? Mid-conversation?

Oh yeah. I put my completely reasonable amount of righteous Celine-hate aside and say something relevant. "I think Minnie's gay."

"What?" Jordan squawks. "Like, you have a *feeling* she's gay, or—"

"As in, I heard she was gay." Also, my gaydar is excellent and she's giving solar-powered rainbow strobe lights, but I won't mention that.

"Oh." My best friend droops.

"Hey, I could be wrong. How do you know her, anyway?"

He sighs. "She's in my Lit class this year. She said something this morning about, like, toxic canon and how literary gate-keeping being intertwined with heartless cisheterosexist white supremacist capitalism has poisoned Western creative culture." Jordan's usual monotone is ever so slightly animated, which means he's foaming at the mouth with fascination.

"All right, Minnie Digby. I bet everyone loved that." This school is not the most progressive. By which I mean: this school sits at the edge of a conservative borough and half of our class-mates parrot everything their posh parents tell them.

"Mrs. Titherly wanted to strangle her," Jordan says dreamily. Maybe he's in love. Maybe Minnie's bisexual like me, and he has a chance. After all, Jordan's cute—I know some girls don't like short guys but I'm hoping Michaela is too enlightened for that. In ten years' time, I could be at their wedding telling a story about this moment.

I can see it now: my suit is impeccable and all my best-man jokes land perfectly. Celine is the maid of honor but she's sadly absent because I snuck into her room and turned off the alarm on her phone. And then I locked her door from the outside.

I snort discreetly and tell him, "If you like the girl, say some-thing."

"Like what?"

"Like, 'Hey, Minnie, I also hate Dickens. Let's get pancakes.'"

"Bruh. Not Dickens. Everyone loves Dickens."

Well, that can't be true. I had to read *A Tale of Two Cities* last year and almost clawed my own eyes out.

"Anyway." Jordan is back to gloom. "I don't know if I like her. I just wanna know what you think of her."

"And then what? You write a letter to her parents asking if you can take her to a museum?"

He laughs. "Screw you." The school bell shrieks, and we groan in tandem. "What d'you have next?"

"Philosophy." Which it's too damn hot for. Existential crises should be saved for rainy days; happy sunshine just undermines the whole vibe. "You've got a free period, right?"

"Yep."

I beam at him. "Walk me to class, bestie."

"Nope. I'll see you at soccer practice."

Ugh. "Jordan. We've talked about this. You *cannot* keep calling it soccer."

He snorts. "Well, I'm not about to call it—"

As if on cue, a football whips through the weeping willow's leaves and slams between us.

"Pack in the gossip, ladies," Donno calls, jogging after it.

"Hey." Jordan scowls. "Don't call us that. You're supposed to be the team captain."

"Yeah, and I'm using motivational language to get you off your arse." Donno holds out a hand to help me up. Being friends with him is like having a poisonous pet snake who loves you so much they only bite you once a year. When I was thirteen, he saved me from feeling like I was completely alone. Now I'm seventeen and he gets on my damn nerves, but he's got my back, so I've got his. Even if he occasionally makes it difficult.

"You in Taylor's philosophy class?" Donno asks as he hauls me to my feet.

"Yeah, why?"

"Me too." He claps me on the back and jogs off to the rest of our group.

"I thought you were in different classes?" Jordan asks.

"We were last year." Apparently, the schedule's changed.

Even knowing that, I don't put two and two together until I've trekked across campus and reached Mr. Taylor's room. If Donno's tiny Philosophy class has merged with mine, guess who I'll be discussing Voltaire with this year?

Celine Bangura.

I stand in the doorway and stare at her like a creep. She doesn't notice me because she's talking to Sonam Lamba, so for once, I'm watching her smile instead of scowl. There's some kind of rose-colored makeup on her chubby cheeks which stands out against her dark brown skin. Her braids are long and fine and pool on the table, almost black with a few neon-green strands that frame her face.

Basically, she looks the way she always does—like a terrible, horrible person who I absolutely can't stand.

"Sorry," she's saying to Sonam, "I can't. I'm busy Thursday night. Actually, you might want to look at this." She riffles through her bag. "It's for an enrichment program run by Katharine Breakspeare. Do you know her? You should come."

Now, Sonam is a very cool girl, so I've never been able to figure out why she and Celine are friends. Celine's judgmental; Sonam's infinitely chill. Celine wants to be superior to everyone; Sonam is a violin genius with epic purple glasses who stomps around in these incredible goth boots, which makes *her* superior to Celine (who just stomps around). And finally, Celine thinks she's the queen of the universe, which is why it's pretty funny to hear Sonam tell her, "Nah."

"But it's going to be great," Celine insists. "The BEP has an excellent reputation. If you get in, you could add it to your uni applications—"

Trust Celine to bring up university applications on the first day of school. I bet she's only applying to Oxford or Cambridge or, like, Harvard, and she's convinced she's going to get in because she's *so* smart and *so* special and—

"Ah, Bradley!" Mr. Taylor notices me, his apple cheeks flushed pink by the heat. "I do believe you're the last passenger on our most noble voyage of philosophical discovery."

Everyone looks up at me. I snatch my eyes away from Celine like she's the sun. "Er, yeah. Hi, sir."

"Well then," he booms in a Shakespearean voice that doesn't match his bony frame. "Come in, come in, don't delay! Sit down, and let's get started."

Mr. Taylor's a great guy, so I would love to do as he asks. But the only open seat is right next to Celine.

CHAPTER TWO

CELINE

If I'm going to study law at Cambridge next year (which I definitely am), I need at least an A in Philosophy. That's the only reason I don't climb out of Mr. Taylor's window when I see Bradley standing in the doorway.

He looks at me and visibly winces, like I'm dog poo or something. His mate Donno, who is deeply annoying but usually easy to ignore (much like a gnat), snickers from across the room. "Bad luck, Bradders."

My cheeks heat. With the burning hellfire of rage, obviously.

People like them—"popular" people who think sports and looks and external approval are a valid replacement for actual personality—ironically don't have the social skills to deal with anyone outside their golden circle. I should know. Once upon a time, back when I was young and clearly going through some stuff because my decision-making matrix was severely *off*, I used to be best friends with Bradley Graeme.

Then he threw himself headfirst into the gelatinous beast that is popularity and was sucked away and transformed. Now he might as well be a slimy, shiny alien. I look him in the eye and let him see all my disdain.

Bradley discovers the tiniest fragment of a spine somewhere within himself, storms over, and sits down next to me. Actually, he throws himself resentfully into the seat and smacks me in the face with his deodorant. Or his aftershave. Or whatever it is that makes him smell so strongly of just-cut grass. School chairs aren't wide enough to cope with my thighs, and he manspreads like a walking stereotype, so our legs bump for a literally sickening second before I snatch mine away.

"Celine," Sonam whispers, leaning into my left side. "Stop *looking* at him like that."

"Like what?" I whisper back, but I already know what she means. I have this small problem where my feelings leak out of my face, and my feelings are often intense.

"If he turns up dead tomorrow, you're going to be arrested." Considering Sonam's permanently solemn expression, black-on-black fit, and the way her lanky limbs barely fit under the table, this is like receiving an ominous tarot reading from a goth spider.

"You guys are crap at whispering," Bradley butts in, "just so you know."

I jerk in my seat, appalled that he would have the gall to speak to me so casually. For God's sake, we are *enemies*. There are *rules* to this sort of thing. He's not supposed to address me unless he's calling me a know-it-all or challenging me to a duel.

"Don't blame me," Sonam murmurs back. "It's Little Miss Lungs over here."

My jaw drops. "What is this *betrayal?*"

Bradley grins and ignores me completely. "Hey, Sonam."

"Hey, Brad."

Amazing. I have precisely 2.5 friends (Sonam's mate, Peter Herron, says hi to me sometimes) and here Bradley Graeme is, bantering with one of them right in front of my face. Is nothing sacred?

Mr. Taylor adjusts his glasses and claps his hands, interrupting my thoughts. "Right! The gang's all here. We know each other, yes?" He points around the square of tables. "Brad, Celine, Sonam, Peter, Shane, Bethany, Max."

"Donno, sir," Donno corrects.

Mr. Taylor laughs in the face of this pretentious rubbish and moves on. "This is a small class, so I assume those of you who chose Philosophy are extra dedicated. Well, you'll need all that dedication to make it through the year!"

Hardly. Philosophy isn't difficult; just dull.

I slide a look to my right and watch Bradley twirl a pen between his long fingers. I can see the hint of a tensed bicep, half hidden by the short sleeve of his white shirt, and there's a distinctly mulish set to his obnoxiously sharp jaw. If I hadn't been forced to watch him go through puberty, I would assume he'd purchased his bone structure.

"We've a lot to cover today, but first things first." Mr. Taylor puts a stack of papers on the table. "This is our syllabus! Take one and pass it round. As you can see, we're beginning with arguments for and against the existence of the god of classical theism." He natters on about omnipotence and the problem of evil and suffering with great enthusiasm. I would pay attention, but Bradley slaps the papers down in front of me like the table just insulted his mother.

It's funny; I once read that the smell of fresh-cut grass is actually a chemical the plant releases when it's in danger, which reminds me of this theory I'm researching about how veganism might be as bad as meat-eating because of the exploited migrant workers (valid) and the totally viable possibility that plants feel pain. So, long story short, Bradley Graeme smells like murder.

I lick my thumb, take a copy of the syllabus, and murmur, "Is everything you do a calculated display of masculinity, and if so, aren't you afraid the constant pressure of performance will lead you to snap?"

He murmurs back, "One day you're going to leave education forever, and you'll have to face the fact that memorizing a thesaurus doesn't make you interesting."

I pass the papers to Sonam. "Fortunately, you will never be faced with that moment of reckoning because, after inevitably failing to accomplish all of your life goals, you will return to education as a teacher who harasses students in the hallways with wildly embellished stories of his glory days."

Bradley's eyes never leave the twirling pen in his hand. "I didn't realize you looked down on teachers. Does your mum know?"

Ten years ago, our family fell apart and my mum worked two jobs to keep us afloat while she finished her teaching degree. "That is *not*—You know I don't—"

"Settle, class," Mr. Taylor orders, which is as close as he ever gets to *Shut the hell up and listen.*

"Yeah, Celine," Bradley whispers. "Settle."

Across the table, Donno snickers again. I grind my teeth. *Don't care don't care don't care don't care.*

Mr. Taylor tells us all about C. S. Lewis's *Mere Christianity.* The clock ticks on. I take deeply intelligent and wonderfully concise notes while Bradley highlights his textbook to death. I suppose that's better than Sonam, who is doodling moths on a piece of scrap paper and writing absolutely nothing. Clearly, I'll be sending her copies of my binder again this year.

"Off you go, then," Mr. Taylor says with Teacherly Finality, and I realize I've missed something. Crap. I'm never going to get all As and a place at Cambridge and a first-class degree and an amazing job at a prestigious corporate law firm if Bradley Flipping Graeme doesn't stop failing to take proper notes right next to me. I bet he's doing it on purpose. He knows I can't stand indiscriminate high-lighting.

I go to glare at him and find he's already staring at me. "What?"

He squints. "We can all leave once we discuss this passage in pairs."

Well, that was a quick two hours. "Discuss in pairs? What, us?"

"Yes, *us,* Celine," he says snippily. "Do you see anyone else sitting next to me?"

"I wish," I mutter. Then a horrific thought hits me, or rather, a memory—what Minnie said this morning. "Where are you applying to uni?" I demand, admittedly out of the blue.

He taps the textbook. "Passage. Focus."

"Just answer the question." His mum and mine are unfortunately best friends, so I have been made aware—entirely against my will—that Bradley wants to study law too. And if I'm forced to spend three extra years in his presence while dealing with the pressures of my demanding degree, I'm liable to snap and push him off a bridge.

He flicks a dark look at me. "Applications aren't due for ages."

I should be relieved, because, no, most of them aren't, but Oxbridge applications are. Except . . . "Why aren't you applying to Cambridge?" I don't *want* him to, obviously. But he could almost certainly get in, so why wouldn't he try?

Bradley rolls his eyes. The sun is low and the windows in this room are massive, so he looks like the human embodiment of whiskey and woods and an ancient sepia Instagram filter. It's honestly atrocious. "Why would I?" he asks. "Just to spend another three years being the only Black kid in the room?"

I scowl. "Hello, I'm literally sitting right here."

"Hello, it's a turn of phrase. There are six of us in the entire year. What, do you like that or something?"

"I'd like it better if there were five." The worst thing about being a minority is occasionally needing to back Bradley up in public. Like that time last year when someone from a rival school said something vile to him during a football tournament and I had to throw a bottle of Coke at the guy (as a matter of principle). "Nothing changes if we don't make it change."

"It's not my job to change their minds," he says, which is all right for him. He has a soon-to-be-successful scientist for an older sister, and his little brother, who's signed to the Forest Academy, will probably end up playing for England at the World Cup or some such rubbish, and *both* of their parents are useful human beings with a sense of duty and loyalty. Brad can afford to go to a second- or third-rate university and have a second- or third-rate career because he has a perfect family and zero single-parent pressure and no shitty absent father to shame into oblivion.

My older sister swears up and down she's going to be the next Georgia O'Keeffe, but who knows how long that'll take? Until then, I'm the only one who can prove our worth. I'm the only one who can pay Mum back for years of blood and sweat. (Bangura women don't do tears.)

But all I say is "Hmm," and then I focus on my textbook.

"Hmm?" he repeats. "What's hmm?"

As if I'm about to explain. I needle him instead. "You don't think you could get in?"

He scoffs at the ceiling. "Of course I could *get in*—"

"Well, it's not exactly *of course,* is it?"

"If you can get in, I can get in," he says stonily. "We got the same grades last year."

"Almost," I correct lightly. Like I said, our mums are best friends, so I know *exactly* what marks Bradley got last year.

And I know mine were better.

Clearly, he knows it, too, if his stormy expression is anything to go by. Good. He can take his shiny new friends and his star position on the football team; I'll take my average exam score of 98.5. He left me behind in the hellhole that is secondary school, but when it comes to real life—when it comes to the future, when it comes to *success*—I'm leaving him in the dust.

"Celine," Sonam says, nudging my shoulder. It's a surprise, when I turn, to find her and Peter packing their stuff away. "We're done. You coming?"

I glance at Mr. Taylor, who is studying a book almost as thick as my arm, the word *DISTRACTED* written on his forehead. "Yeah." I'll do the reading at home and discuss it with myself.

But Mr. Taylor marks his page with a bony finger and pipes up unexpectedly. "Hang on, Celine. Bradley." His gaze pins us to the wall like bugs. "Since the two of you didn't manage to discuss one word of your passage, so far as I could hear—"

Oh. My. God. Did Mr. Taylor hear that? I run back the entire conversation, decide it was, at best, utterly juvenile, and attempt to crawl into the earth.

"—you may stay on after class and write down your thoughts for me," Mr. Taylor continues.

Oh, for God's sake. I clench my jaw, and Bradley's nostrils flare so hard I'm surprised he doesn't whip a tornado into being. Mr. Taylor doesn't care.

"Go down to the Little Library, please," he says serenely. "Lower Student Council has booked this room for the next hour."

"But, *sir*," Donno whines from across the table, "we have practice! We need Brad. He's our best striker!"

Mr. Taylor peers over his glasses, unimpressed. "Then I suppose he'd better work quickly."

• • •

BRAD

We walk through the building in mutinous silence.

I want to say this entire thing is Celine's fault, but let's be honest: I just spent the last two hours behaving like a ten-year-old and, surprise, surprise, it instantly came back to bite me.

I'm still pissed at Celine, though.

God, she's so full of it. Maybe I'm not my older sister Emily studying biomechanics, maybe I'm not my younger brother

Mason on a path to play professional football, but I'm just as smart as Celine. And clearly just as childish, because I can't resist murmuring, "Hope you weren't expecting Taylor to write your Cambridge recommendation."

She hugs her textbook tight against her Metallica T-shirt, her expression half boredom and half effortless arrogance. "Mr. Darling is a Cambridge alum, actually, so he's writing mine."

Of fucking course he is.

"Who's writing your recommendation?" she asks innocently, as if she *knows* I haven't gotten that far yet, *knows* I didn't email any teachers over the summer to help with my application.

And, yeah, she does. I can tell by her face, by the barely there smirk waiting to spread.

God. If Mum doesn't stop spilling all my business during Sunday tea with Neneh Bangura, I'm going to . . . well, I'm going to have very stern words with her about it.

"Haven't decided," I say flatly.

"You should get a move on," Celine replies, all bossy and superior as we skirt around a noisy pack of year eights. "Or the teachers will be too busy——"

My back teeth click together. "I know."

"And contrary to popular belief, they don't all wait around for the school's *football stars* to find time between *super important training sessions* to request a favor. They have actual jobs and a ton of students to write for, so——"

"Celine?"

She swings narrow eyes in my direction.

"Shut up."

Her jaw tightens and those eyes get even sharper. I look away.

So, I haven't got around to considering recommendations yet. It's not a big deal. I want to go to uni in Leeds or Bristol—somewhere good but, like, normal, because I can't imagine anything worse than memorizing tort case law in a class full of stuck-up Celine-a-likes. I'm not worried about my application: my grades are perfect, I can memorize almost anything, and I argue well enough to quiet Celine at least 50 percent of the time. Screw uni; they should call me to the bar right now.

I mean, it wouldn't be my *dream* job but . . . it makes sense. What's the alternative? I spend the rest of my life trying and failing to write a book, my parents finally kick me out by my thirty-fifth birthday because I'm still unemployed, and I die cold and lonely under a bridge like Mr. Darling's always ranting about? No thanks. Practicing law is the sensible option.

Celine opens the door to the stairwell, and I scowl reflexively. The Little Library is a cramped, windowless room down in the basement filled with the books only Philosophy, History, and Latin nerds give a damn about. She goes down without hesitation, but my legs falter.

The stairs are made of concrete and they're laughably uneven. My brain helpfully informs me that I could easily fall and crack my head open and die right now. (My brain, in case I failed to mention this before, is kind of a dick.)

Yeah, okay, thanks, I tell it. Then I kick away the mental image of my own unfortunate demise and finally head down.

The bannister is metal, painted a cheerful yellow, but overuse has left thirty-six tiny chips in the paint, and I count them as they pass under my hand. Celine's waiting for me at the bottom, but she doesn't say a word. Not until we reach the hallway that leads to the Little Library's closed door, the fluorescent lights harsh and the blue-gray carpet threatening to unravel. "Do you think someone's already in there?" she asks. "A class or something?"

"Why would there be a class in there?"

"Well, why's the door shut?"

I don't want to admit it, but that's a good question. Rosewood Academy has an open-door policy, so either something serious is going down in the Little Library, or a group of year elevens is camped out in there doing homework, eating Kit-Kats, and getting crumbs all over the Bible. There's only one way to tell.

I step forward and put my ear to the door. Celine moves at the exact same time and I freeze—but I'm not about to jump away from her like I'm scared. Which is how we end up both pressed against the door, basically face to face. Straight away, I realize she's . . . shorter than me.

What the hell? Celine Bangura is taller than me. She always has been. But now I'm close to her for the first time in almost four years and it turns out she stopped growing a few inches ago.

Weird.

"Move," she mutters.

"You move." I'm not usually this annoying, but she's infectious. Like the flu.

Celine rolls her eyes. "Your grace and maturity continue to astound me."

"Give me five synonyms for *hypocrite,* and yes, you're allowed to use your own name."

Watching this girl screw up her face before she insults me is like watching a striker run up to take a penalty. "Has anyone ever told you—" she begins with more acidity than the average lemon tree.

But she's interrupted by a raised voice through the door. "I'm sorry," someone says crisply, "but you can't be serious right now."

"What's that supposed to mean?" a second voice demands. This one I recognize: it's Coach, who is totally sweet and makes us Rocky Road on game days whether we win or lose. She's also what Dad would call *emotionally unyielding,* and her biceps are so huge she could crush your skull like an egg, but I think that's part of her charm.

"What, exactly, are you confused about?" the first voice asks, accent bobbing up and down like the actors on *Derry Girls.* "We can't make the children do *push-ups* as a *punishment*—"

"Of course we can! They're an able-bodied class! It's motivational! Find your arsehole, Gallagher." (There's that unyielding thing I mentioned.)

"Mr. Gallagher's my Economics teacher," Celine whispers. "Is that Ms. Morgan with him?"

I blink. "Ms. . . . ? Do you mean Coach?"

Celine rolls her eyes so hard, her optic nerve's in danger of snapping. "You don't even know your football coach's *name?*"

I swear she jumps on my every slipup like they contain her daily requirement of vitamins and minerals. "Obviously I know her name. It's Coach." (It's Stacy.)

"You're a parody of yourself, Bradley Graeme."

"And you are *so* in love with the sound of your own voice—"

"Says you." She snorts like a five-year-old.

"—I bet you fall asleep listening to your own TikToks as a lullaby!"

"Shhhh!" Celine hisses.

Maybe I was a bit loud there. Oops.

There's the sound of a scraping chair, and before I can react, the door we're leaning on swings open. We both fall in. Crap.

I grasp the door frame to stop myself going down, but Celine's still holding her textbook with both hands. I catch her automatically—as in, I kind of don't remember doing it? Suddenly, I've just got an arm around the soft width of her waist and she's staring up at me, her brown eyes so wide she looks like a cartoon insect. Self-awareness hits me like an electric shock. I come back to my senses and let her go.

A split second later, my brain tells me letting go was the *wrong* thing to do. But it's too late: she's falling. I watch in horror as she lands on the floor with a yelp, her book slamming to the ground beside her.

There's a moment of wintry silence.

Then she glares up at me with buckets of menace in her eyes and announces, "You *absolute* living demon!"

My mouth opens. "I—"

"You *dropped* me!"

Shit. "I didn't mean to." My voice creaks with uncertainty, which is annoying, because I'm serious: I didn't mean to.

"Yeah, right," Celine mutters as she goes to stand up—and hisses in pain.

Coach, who's been frozen in confusion since opening the door, springs into action. "Hold on there, young lady," she orders, kneeling and taking Celine's wrist in her hand. "Oh dear." She shakes her head, blond ponytail swinging.

My stomach drops. "What? What's happened?"

Coach gently presses Celine's wrist. "Does that hurt?"

Her reply is a stifled squeak.

"And this?"

A nod.

Mr. Gallagher, who is small and twitchy and pink, peers over Coach's shoulder. "Hmm. I think a trip to Student Support may be in order."

"What?" I repeat. You only go to Student Support if you're having a total breakdown or if you're sick and you need them to call your parents. "What's wrong? I'll take her—"

"No," Celine says, so quick and sharp I'm almost hurt for a second, before I remember that I don't like her, and she doesn't like me, and we are enemies.

Coach gives me a grim look as she helps Celine to her feet. "I'll take her. Brad, tell the team I'm going to be late for practice."

"Yes, Coach." Oh, wait a minute. "Um, actually, me and Celine were supposed to stay here and do some work for Mr. Taylor?"

"Well, Celine won't be doing any work this afternoon, so you can run and let him know about that too." She puts an arm around Celine, and they head for the stairs. Mr. Gallagher follows behind them.

I run my hands over my hair. "Shit, shit, shit." Did I just break Celine's arm or something? The possibility rolls around in my stomach like a concrete ball of anxiety. Acid climbs up my throat. Why the hell did I drop her? I stare down at my hands and whisper, "What the fuck?"

They don't reply.

I sigh, then crouch down to pick up the textbook she dropped. There's something sticking out from between the pages. I flick them open, and a vaguely familiar woman with brown skin and long hair stares back at me.

Breakspeare Enrichment Program, the glossy leaflet says.

Breakspeare. Katharine Breakspeare. That's where I've seen this woman: on the inspirational pinboard Celine used to keep in her bedroom. Back when I was welcome in Celine's bedroom, which I'm certainly not now.

I close the book.

* * *

Mummy♥: Keep me updated please.

Giselle✦: doc's sent us for an X-ray, in the waiting room now

Celine: sorry mummy

Mummy♥: Your wrist is broken and still you're on this blasted phone??? I bet that's how you fell.

Celine: it's not!

Mummy♥: talk to the hand little girl

Giselle✦: skdhfjsjkfhs MUM

CHAPTER THREE

BRAD

It's a good thing Celine's addicted to technology and that I have a finsta for the express purpose of stalking people without embarrassment. By the time I pull up outside my house, her Instagram Story tells me she's going to Queen's Med with her sister Giselle, which is not exactly home safe and sound, but also isn't completely terrible.

My brain decides this would be an ideal moment to present me with images of Celine suffering various life-changing complications from her arm injury, all of which would be my fault. It's basically a slideshow. If my OCD had a feedback form, I would write *Could do with a jaunty soundtrack next time.* Instead, I get out of my car and head inside.

"Brad?"

I lock the front door and glance up to find Dad wandering out of the kitchen, a smile on his angular face and a mixing bowl in his arms. Supposedly he's a family law barrister (that's how he met Celine's dad, which is how we know the Banguras in the first place), but in reality, all he seems to do is bake cupcakes and ferry my brother Mason to and from football practice.

"Hey, Dad," I say, kicking off my shoes and slotting them neatly into the rack. Did I lock the door? Not a big deal, since we're both home, but I turn back to check anyway. All good.

"Thought you had practice today?"

I skipped because I am in emotional turmoil, obviously. "Er . . . starting next week. First day back, you know."

"Got you. How was school?"

"It was fine," I lie, trying really hard not to think about Celine and catastrophically failing. Did I take my keys out of the door? If they're in there when Mum gets home, she won't be able to unlock it. I turn around and spot my Adrax Agatone key ring in the onyx dish on the console table. Oh. Well. Good. Patting it a few times, I look up to find Dad rubbing his short beard in a way that means he's worried about me.

"Heard about Celine?" he asks sympathetically.

I magically transform from a boy to a plank of wood. If Dad finds out I dropped a girl, especially *Neneh Bangura's daughter,* I am so dead. "Hmm," I grunt.

"Your mum just texted. Apparently she had an accident at school? Hurt her wrist, think they'll get an X-ray."

So, Celine told her mum and her mum told mine. That's all perfectly normal—except for the part where no one is mentioning my name? Or gazing at me accusingly? Or shaking their head in deep disappointment? I tread carefully and grunt again.

Dad laughs, tipping his head back. He's tall like me, so he

very nearly brains himself on the kitchen door frame. "Ah, Brad. I know you two are 'enemies'——" His free hand, the one that's not holding a mixing bowl, makes obnoxious air quotes. "But it's okay if you're concerned for the poor girl."

It's official: somehow——*somehow*——Celine has restrained herself from exploiting this valid opportunity to drop me in it. Which can only mean one thing: her mind is completely addled by agonizing pain. I've shattered every bone in her arm. In her entire body. She might be in a coma.

I force a hopefully innocent expression and say, "Well, I wouldn't want anyone, enemy or not, to be in hospital on the first week of our final year." This is 100 percent true. I am so mired in guilt, it's a wonder I even found my way home.

"I know, bless her." Dad blows out his brown cheeks and shakes his head. "Oh well. She's such a good girl. She could get into Cambridge with both hands broken——"

"BOTH HER HANDS ARE BROKEN?"

Dad stares at me.

Understanding hits a second too late, because of course it does. "Oh! Right. You meant . . . You were . . . being . . . hypothetical," I say. "Obviously. Haha! Ha." Could someone please tell me why the same brain that gets me the (second) highest grades in school is so slow on the uptake during normal human conversations? Is it some kind of system error, or . . . ?

"You all right, son?" Dad finally asks.

"I'm fine! Fine. Just. Busy day. You know what? I'd better go. Lots of . . . homework. Uni, er, stuff. You know." I nod awkwardly toward the curving staircase down the hall.

"Ahhh! That's my boy." Dad grins and reaches out as I pass, his hand landing on the back of my head. Even though this always frizzes up my hair, I wait patiently while he wiggles me around like a puppy with a favorite toy. (Don't ask, it makes him happy, okay?) He drags me closer and smacks a kiss over my left eyebrow. "You know, Mrs. Mulaney was asking about you this morning."

Mrs. Mulaney is an older lady down the street whose dog I walk sometimes. She finds herself around our front garden freakishly often, probably because she's in love with Dad. "Oh," I say, staring longingly at the staircase that leads to sweet escape. So near, and yet so far. "How is she?"

"Right as rain, bless her. She asked how you're getting on, and I told her you'll be studying law next year. You know what she said?"

Probably not *What a waste. That boy was born to win a Hugo Award.*

"She said, 'Whatever magic you and Maria are doing on those kids, you should bottle it and make a fortune.'" Dad beams. "I told her, it's all you. Hard work and commitment! You're all determined to succeed." I know exactly what he's going to say next—it's been his favorite phrase ever since I showed a vague interest in following in his footsteps and studying law. "But *you* are a chip off the old block, aren't you?"

Aaaand there it is.

I manage a smile. "That's right." The words are dry and crumbly in my mouth like stale biscuits.

Dad squeezes my neck and releases me, humming happily. "Go on, then, I won't keep you." He stirs the chocolate-brown batter in his mixing bowl and wanders back into the kitchen. I basically sprint to the stairs.

When I was younger, before we got the right combination

of therapy and meds, before I learned how to manage my OCD . . . I know my mum used to cry because of me. I know the gray in my dad's hair didn't come from nowhere. But I'm doing way better now, and they're proud of me, and I've gotten used to that pride.

It flares in my dad's eyes every time he remembers I'm going to be just like him.

(If I thought I could make them proud with my writing, I would, but unfortunately, *everything I write absolutely sucks*. So. Here we are.)

I make it up the stairs and past Mason's room—his door is open and the smell of farts and sweaty socks wafts gently into the hall. Emily's room is closed up and mostly empty, since she's studying in the US; then there's the family bathroom, followed by my parents' room. My bedroom is at the very end. It's the master. I have an en suite. Not because I'm a spoiled brat (okay, maybe I am) but because I went through a phase where sharing a bathroom with my clinically disgusting brother would have quite literally stuffed my mental health into the toilet and flushed.

Which Mason, by the way, often forgets to do.

I shut my door behind me, hang up my bag, and consider my options. The sun is sinking and the rays spill across my pale carpet and blue sheets. I could lie down in that light and do nothing, except I'm kind of wired. I could start my university applications, except I'm definitely not doing that. I *could* work on the latest terrible draft of my terrible book. . . .

Next thing I know, I'm sitting at the white desk beside my window, opening my laptop. My John Boyega screensaver squints purposefully at me. The book is on my desktop, currently titled

Draft M VI Take 3. In this version, I reached a scene where our hero, space cowboy Abasi Lee, faces down a local dealer of VetRo (a mind-control drug that is decimating the community of his tiny desert planet) in the hopes of extracting information on a bigger fish in the supply chain. Then I got stuck because presumably they have to fight? But I'm bad at fight scenes. Also, I can't tell if VetRo is a genius name or a really bad one (it's short for *Velvet Ro*—okay, yeah, I've just decided it's bad), and I think Abasi should go off-world soon or the story's going to get boring, but how? He's just a humble space cowboy, and his planet is so far from the Cosmotropolis Collective, how would he hitch a ride?

No, this whole thing is honestly a wash. I move it into my GRAVEYARD folder and open a shiny, clean new document. *Draft M VII Take 1.* Then I sit back in my chair, exhausted, and check Instagram.

No update on Celine's story.

Yet.

· · ·

CELINE

Giselle pokes her head into my bedroom. She can tell by now when I'm recording something, so she waits patiently.

Today I'm examining the possibility that plaster casts are a con by the medical community because they don't want us to realize humans are self-healing with the right amount of will-power. Not the most interesting theory I've ever discussed, but I spent way too long in Accident and Emergency today and my exhaustion inspired the bland choice in topic.

"Conclusion," I say, which is how I end all my videos. "Yes, most healthy people can heal simple breaks on their own—*eventually*. But if willpower had anything to do with healing, my bones would never dare fracture in the first place." I cut the clip, flip the camera, focus on the cast on my wrist, and start filming again. "Sorry, medical truthers, you lost me this time. The cast stays for at least six weeks." Cut, flip, film. "Stay safe, stay weird."

I turn off the little ring light attached to my phone, set it aside, and make a few quick, one-handed edits. "Yeah?"

"Yeah?" Giselle repeats, gliding into the room (she glides everywhere, not like a debutante but like a supernatural creature) and flopping onto the bed. "Is that how you speak to the greatest sister of all time?"

"Apparently," I say.

"Teens today. You're a disgrace." But there's a dimple in her dark brown cheek that says she's trying not to smile. Giselle is taller than me, which is fairly tall, and unlike me she's very thin. Combined with her shaved head and the way she rubs her cheek against my soft, forest-green duvet, she looks like a hairless cat.

I know I should stop drafting hashtags and have an actual conversation with her, or at least say *thank you* after she ditched her shift at McDonald's to take me to the hospital. But I am in a foul mood because my left wrist is fractured (like, it's in a cast! For six to eight weeks! Positive thinking hasn't helped at all!) and *that* is not an item on my Steps to Success board. Quite the opposite, in fact. My Steps to Success board, which is pinned up by the side of my bed, has pictures of Katharine Breakspeare, advertising CEO Karen Blackett, and management consultant Dame Vivian Hunt—three of the most influential Black businesswomen in the UK—as well as a life plan that should take me from age seventeen to twenty-one:

1. Maintain flawless school record.
2. Keep up with TikTok (unique extracurricular, will stand out on applications, also someone in admissions might be a genius who understands the joy of a good conspiracy).
3. Finish PERFECT Cambridge application and receive conditional offer.
4. ACE EXAMS AND GET THE GRADES.
5. Charm all Cambridge law staff members with sparkling wit and joie de vivre (also: find YouTube tutorials on sparkling wit and joie de vivre).
6. Secure training position with Sharma & Moncrieff.

Sharma & Moncrieff is the second-best corporate law firm in the East Midlands. My dad's is the first, but that will change when I rise as a giant in the field and Luke Skywalker his arse with the spiked heel of my Louboutin. It's going to be epic. Boardrooms will crumble. Empires will fall! He'll—

Oh, sorry, back to the point: clearly, a broken wrist is absolutely nowhere in my plan.

I should sue Bradley for this because he definitely did it on purpose. I mean, I know I'm a hefty babe, but he's supposed to be some kind of super sportsman and his biceps are the size of grapefruits. He had me. He *did*. And then he didn't. Plus, I landed harder than I would've without his oh-so-helpful momentary pawing of my T-shirt because I was too stunned by his audacity to concentrate on falling well.

In short, I would be well within my rights to demand blood.

Or his firstborn. Or whatever I wanted, really, except his integrity, because he doesn't have any.

Giselle unfolds a never-ending arm and presses her finger between my eyebrows. "Stop scowling, baby. Or the wind will change, and you'll be stuck like that."

"Good. It would suit my personality."

She rolls onto her back and laughs at the ceiling. My sister is twenty-four—seven years older than me—and when I was a kid, I wanted to be her. Maybe that's why, even now, whenever she laughs, I do too.

We're still giggling when someone knocks on my door. I wait a second for Mum to breeze in without permission, plonk herself on the bed, and steal my phone to scroll through TikTok.

When that doesn't happen, I frown in confusion and Giselle grins in response. "Oh yeah. Forgot to mention: Bradley's here."

"What?" It's supposed to come out frosty and disgusted, but I accidentally squawk like a bird.

Giselle snickers and taps my forehead again. "Deep breaths, Cel." Then she gets up and saunters to the door. I don't quite believe her until it swings open and, yep, Bradley's standing right there.

I haven't seen him framed by my doorway in . . . years. He looks different but the same: taller and older, sure, but wide-eyed and nervous like he used to be. My bedroom lamp is weak and warm, so he's mostly shadow. Shadowed expression, except for the gleam of his dark eyes; shadowed hands, clutching and releasing the strap of the satchel over his shoulder. Maybe he's not Bradley at all. Maybe he's something strange and familiar that crawled out of the past.

But, you know. Probably not.

We stare at each other for a second in what seems to be mutual shock, although I'm not sure what he's shocked about since he presumably carried himself over here on his own two legs. Then Giselle flicks him on the head and says, "Brad," as she leaves, and he jolts like a toy coming to life.

"Um." He clears his throat. "Hi, Giselle. Bye, Giselle." My sister's already thundering down the stairs, probably desperate to gossip about this with Mum because they are both nosy cows.

Bradley hovers awkwardly in the doorway.

I remember, belatedly, that I am sitting in bed wearing pink pajamas with little red lobsters all over them. Dropping my phone, I pull the duvet over my legs and adjust the pillow propping up my left wrist. Bradley's eyes follow the action, and he winces.

Winces! As if he's got anything to wince about! Then he looks away. His gaze wanders from my dark green walls, to the collection of candles on my bedside table, to the lights set up in the corner where I film my best videos. I bristle. "What are you looking at?"

He starts. "Er . . . nothing. It's. Just. Different in here."

Well, yes. The last time he was in my bedroom, the walls were lilac, and my bed had a heart-shaped headboard. But then, the last time he was in my bedroom, I was fourteen and quite clearly an idiot.

Maybe if I'd been cooler then, instead of an unapologetic weirdo, he wouldn't have ditched me for his glossy new friends.

Then again, I am still a weirdo (just, you know, a very gorgeous and stylish one), so the point is moot. Only boring people give a crap what everyone else thinks, and Bradley Graeme is the most boring human being on earth.

But I'm not.

"What do you want?" I demand.

"Can I come in?" he asks, the words slow and squeezed, like his throat's a near-empty tube of toothpaste.

He wants to *come in*? This situation is highly suspicious. *Highly* suspicious. "What for?"

He rolls his eyes, which is more familiar and relaxes me ever so slightly. "To talk, Celine, what do you think?"

"Fine." It feels like someone's stitching my stomach together. My voice comes out tight.

He treads lightly, as if the cream carpet might be booby-trapped. "I . . . er . . . brought you some stuff." He unzips his satchel and goes to sit down on my bed.

I make a noise like a game show buzzer. "Nope."

He straightens with a huff. "Well, where am I supposed to *sit,* Celine?"

"Who said you could *sit,* Bradley?"

His cheeks are too brown to show a blush, but his throat is turning splotchy red. "Jesus," he mutters, and kneels (*kneels!* I should make a note of the date and time) beside my bed. Then he produces a little plastic box and unclips the lid. "Dad made you these."

My heart calcifies and sinks down into my stitched-up stomach. "Oh . . . er . . . great." Tucked neatly into the box are four chocolate cupcakes decorated with silver sparkles—my favorite. And they'll be delicious because Trevor Graeme made them, but for that very same reason, I really don't feel like putting one in my mouth.

It's not that I don't like Trev. In fact, it's the opposite: he's basically a caricature of a perfect father who was put on this earth to taunt me with what I don't have. He and Bradley are *best buds*!!! And they go *fishing*!!! And Trev *loves and admires his wife*!!! Back when Brad and I were friends, the hardest part of our relationship was not drowning in mortifying jealousy every five seconds.

I know that's childish and ridiculous and pathetic. I'm just feeling sensitive because my wrist hurts. I put my dark feelings carefully away and say: "Tell your dad I said thanks." Now that I'm being mature, I could probably choke down a cupcake (or two, I deserve it), but eating dinner one-handed was a bit of an adventure and I'm not about to make a mess in front of Bradley. So, I put the box aside.

He nods. "I brought this too." He pulls my philosophy book out of his bag. "Your, um, leaflet's in there."

I press my lips tightly together.

"How's your arm?" he asks.

"Screwed."

He has the absolute gall to look upset. "That's not a real answer, Celine, come on."

"Fine, it's fractured. Happy?"

"Of course I'm not happy!" he says hotly, his face sort of crumpling. For so long, he's only looked at me with smugness or irritation, but now he's giving actual human expressions that change every five minutes and it's—

I don't know. It must be the fading painkillers that are making my internal organs jump around like this.

"You don't think I did it on purpose, do you?" he demands. "You know I didn't. Right? Celine. Do you?"

I'd almost forgotten the way he talks nonstop when he's nervous. "Shut up. You're giving me a headache."

His jaw tenses. "You do. You think I did."

Christ, what is he, a mind reader?! "I don't *know,* Bradley. You had a perfectly good grip on me and then you pulled away—what, completely by *accident?*" Disbelief drips from my words like candlewax, but at the same time, I'm not certain what I believe. His eyes are pure kicked puppy right now, and surely he's not that good an actor.

Instead of arguing, though, he just says, "Why didn't you tell your mum?"

"Why didn't you tell yours?" I toss back.

He grimaces. "Don't want them to fall out, do I?"

"They wouldn't fall out. They'd both be on my side and you'd be grounded for a century."

For some reason, he grins. It's so bright, I see dark spots like I've been staring into the sun. "Why didn't you tell, then?" Before I can stammer out a reply, he almost murders me by adding, "Look, Celine, I'm sorry."

I choke. *"Pardon?"*

"It's shit, I know it's shit, I realize we're not friends or anything, but I didn't mean . . . I didn't want to hurt you. Of course I didn't want to hurt you."

I absorb this tangle of words with my mouth hanging wide open. Seriously. A passing bird could build a nest in here.

Bradley's still talking, so disturbingly earnest it's like his current body has been taken over by his twelve-year-old self. "I'll make it up to you, I promise. I know I owe you. God, I *fractured* your *wrist.*" He props his elbows on my bed and looks down at the leaf-printed duvet, his dark eyelashes casting shadows on his cheeks. I should spray him with water like a misbehaving cat but I'm too busy having conniptions.

"Are you possessed? You are, aren't you?"

He looks up with a frown. "What?"

"*Something's* off. I don't trust this at all. Quick, list your allergies." It's a trick question; he doesn't have any. I squint at him, searching for evidence of ectoplasm.

All I can see is the faintest hint of stubble (stubble! How old is he, forty-five?) on his jaw, and familiar irritation as he rolls his eyes. "Give it a rest, Celine."

Thank God. I pull back. "For a second there, I thought you were a victim of Monarch mind control."

"God, you do my head in," he mutters.

"That's the spirit."

Bradley huffs. "I read your leaflet, by the way."

"Of course you did." He's just as nosy as our mothers. Honestly, I'm the only person in both our families who knows how to mind my own bloody business.

"How are you getting to the meeting on Thursday?"

"How do you know I'm going at all?"

He arches an eyebrow, looks at the picture of Katharine Breakspeare on my Steps to Success board, and remains silent.

I bite out, "I'm taking the bus."

"With your arm in a cast?"

What, is he here to gloat, or something? "Yes, with my arm in a cast, Bradley. I can't just take it off." Mum works late on Thursdays, and Giselle has to cover an evening shift because she ditched today—the bus is all I've got.

Unlike Bradley, who has a car. Bradley, who has his license. Bradley, who rises to his feet, sighs and says, "People might bump into you. I'll drive you."

Aaaand I'm choking again. This can't be healthy. "You'll what?" I rasp.

"I'll. Drive. You. Pay attention, Celine." He grabs his bag and heads for the door.

"Wha—Where are you going?"

"I *do* have better things to do than hang around here, you know." He falters, then looks over his shoulder. "I'll meet you outside the Beech Hut after school, okay?"

I open my mouth to say, *Um, no, not okay. What are you up to, you sneaky, slimy snake?!* But the thing is . . .

Well, I hate the bus. And I don't want to be all sweaty and tired when I see Katharine. And he does owe me, and shockingly, he is decent enough to know that, which is the bare minimum, so . . .

"Fine," I say.

Just like that, I agree to voluntarily share a space with Bradley Graeme for the first time in almost four years. I am still dazed and confused by this series of events ten minutes later when Mum wanders into my room and sits on the edge of my bed.

"Has my room recently been declared a public thoroughfare?" I wonder aloud.

"Mouth," Mum says in a tone that would terrify most of my friends but is only a 3 out of 10 on my mother's annoyance scale. She must be tired. I focus on her face and strongly dislike what I see.

"Hard day at work?"

She tuts. "Isn't it always? Those children are trying to kill me. So is my daughter, apparently." She slides a reproving look at my cast. "What, are you doing parkour at school now? Consider my blood pressure, Celine."

"Nobody does parkour, Mum." And my mother doesn't have

high blood pressure, which is a miracle, considering what my dad put her through.

We look very alike, by which I mean, neither of us smile easily because we don't have the time or the patience. People would be so shocked if they knew that, when my parents divorced, she let Dad off easy with the settlement and the child maintenance payments. At the time, I didn't really understand what she was doing. I was confused by the arguments she had with Bradley's mum, the ones I overheard by lurking on the staircase.

"He has twins now, Maria. Babies aren't cheap."

"That's his problem! All of his children are his problem, so make him pay."

"We don't need that much——"

"Don't be proud, Neneh."

But that's how Bangura women are: proud. So, she proudly accepted the absolute minimum from my so-called dad, and she proudly worked herself to the bone while studying full-time. She proudly bulk-bought our necessities with carefully cut-out coupons and she proudly worked her way up from a trainee teacher's salary to her school's assistant head. We're not poor anymore.

But it's too late. She looks tired in a way rest can't fix and it's because of us, because of me and Giselle and . . . him.

I can tell Mum's extra exhausted today; her usually glowing skin is dull, and she's thrown a green and blue headwrap over her hair instead of styling it. Glasses sit on her broad nose in place of her usual contacts. When I'm an adult, when I'm successful, when I'm rich, she can lie in bed all day eating Godiva chocolates instead of dragging herself to work.

But I'm not rich yet, so all I can say is, "What time did you go to bed last night?"

"Bed?" She blinks theatrically. "Oh! After a lifetime of sleeping, I forgot it was necessary. Must be my old lady brain acting up again."

"Isn't there something in the Bible about sarcasm being a sin?"

"No," Mum says primly.

"There should be."

"Pot," my sister shouts from across the hall, "meet kettle."

"Go away, Giselle," I shout back.

Mum snorts, then arranges her features into a carefully neutral expression. "So. Bradley was concerned about your health, I see? How nice. He is such a sweet boy. You know——"

Ah. Here we go: the *What happened to you and Bradley being best friends?* spiel. "He was just bringing me my textbook," I cut in, nodding to where it sits on the bedside table.

Mum practically pouts. "Oh. Well." She has this sick and twisted dream that Bradley and I will get married so she and Maria Graeme can be even more like sisters. I'm trying not to vomit at the thought when Mum says, "Oh, what's this?" and pulls the leaflet out of my textbook.

"Private property," I tell her, "that's what it is."

"Not in my house." Mum snorts. Light bounces off the back of the shiny paper and hits the printed logo of Dad's firm. My heart drops into my stomach.

Crap.

"Katharine Breakspeare," Mum says, skimming the page. "You're going to do this?"

Awkwardly, I squeak, "I'm . . . going to apply." How the hell do I get that leaflet out of her hand? She can't see Dad's name. She'll get the wrong idea and assume I'm interested in the program because I'm, like, upset about his abandonment or something cringey like that when, in reality, I just want to grind my future success in his traitorous face and possibly ruin his life a little bit. Which I can do without ever bothering her with the details.

"Well, I'm sure you'll get in, baby," she says fondly. "You're so clever. I told Mr. Hollis at school about your AS results and he was not surprised. You were the highest-achieving pupil Farndon Primary ever had. I still remember your year-four parents evening. . . ."

Year four was just after Dad ditched us. Her hand lowers to the bed as she waxes lyrical about a project I did on the water cycle. Gently, soooo so gently, I ease the leaflet out from between her fingers while *mmm*-ing in all the right places.

"Tea, Mum?" Giselle asks, popping her head into the doorway just as I shove the paper under a pillow. Her eyes narrow on the movement of my hand. I run it casually through my ponytail, and she looks away.

That was close.

· · ·

BRAD

Was I moaning about the heat on Monday? I want to go back and smack myself because by Thursday evening, the weather's cold and miserable. Autumn is officially here.

So is Celine, striding up to meet me outside the Beech Hut with a face like thunder and a jacket that's angry scarlet. It contrasts with the neon green in her hair and the tiny black love hearts she's drawn under her eyes (don't ask, she does it all the time) but . . . annoyingly, it suits her. The problem is that almost everything suits her because her skin is all glowy and—

"What are you looking at?" she demands, peering up at me from under her hood. There are raindrops clinging for dear life to the tips of her eyelashes.

"Nothing," I say flatly, and stalk off, trusting she'll follow. On second thought, the scarlet coat is way too flashy and makes her look a bit sick.

We're climbing into my car when someone shouts across the car park, "Bradders!" There is precisely one person who calls me that, because everyone else knows I don't bloody like it. I find Donno leaning out the window of his yellow VW Golf, waving an arm as if I could possibly miss him.

With a tight smile, I wave back.

He shouts, "Do you need a rescue, mate?" then screws up his face like a toddler rejecting broccoli and gestures dramatically in Celine's direction.

What the fuck? My cheeks heat at his rudeness and my gaze flicks to Celine. She doesn't seem as surprised as I am—or upset, for that matter. She looks bored.

"Charming as always, *Max,*" she calls back, and rolls her eyes as she gets in the car. I stand there like a lemon for a second or two before following her lead, turning my back on Donno entirely. He's really starting to get on my nerves.

I mean, he always gets on my nerves a little bit, but we're sharing more classes this year and it's . . .

He's . . .

"Sorry," I say, my eyes on the dashboard, *not* because I'm

avoiding Celine and her pointed eyebrow raise, but because I am preparing to drive and safety is my priority, thank you very much.

She snorts, the sound half swallowed as I start the engine. "What are you apologizing for? Compared to you, all your little friends are deeply polite."

Little friends. She always says that, like they're not real or they don't count just because they aren't Celine-approved.

Or possibly because they're dicks?

My friends are not dicks! Donno's just a poor representation of the group today. "Maybe I'd be polite to you," I say, "if I thought you were even physically capable of being polite back."

She raises her left hand, flashing the cast beneath her coat. "There's a lot I'm not physically capable of doing right now."

The *and it's your fault* part is silent. I click my teeth together and drive.

The meeting is being held in the Sherwood, a fancy hotel about twenty minutes away from school, in the center of Nottingham. I get nervous on busy roads, but if I let nerves stop me, I would never leave the house, so I do it anyway.

Celine doesn't comment when it takes me three tries to get into our parking space because I want to be perfectly central. But when I switch off the engine and open my door . . . she pipes up. "Where are you going?"

I turn to find her eyeing me with alarm, her arms crossed over her chest. "What," I say incredulously, "you want me to wait in the car?"

"That was the plan, yes."

"What do you think this is, *Driving Miss Daisy*?"

"Oh, get a grip, Bradley," she mutters, as if *I'm* being unreasonable, and slips out, heading toward the hotel.

I lock up and follow.

"You're not even interested in the meeting," she says briskly.

"I'd be bored in the car!"

"God forbid, you absolute five-year-old. You don't know how to entertain yourself?"

"Do you enjoy pissing me off?" I ask. "Would you consider it, like, a hobby?" This week is the most time we've spent together in the last four years, and if I didn't know any better, I'd think there was a zing of satisfaction beneath all her dry insults.

The worst part is, I'm starting to think I feel that same zing. Which is ridiculous because I'm a nice person! I don't *enjoy* snapping at Celine. It just . . . happens. This girl would provoke the Pope.

"Don't flatter yourself. You are not nearly interesting enough to be a hobby," she says with this scathing hint of amusement, and I find myself making a mental note of that exact tone so I can replicate it next time I tell her—

Wait. No. Arguing with Celine is not a competitive sport. Instead, I focus on my surroundings as we move through the hotel. This place—the Sherwood—has pillars of gleaming, unsmudged glass, and puffy brown chairs all over the lobby, and tropical-looking flowers stuck in posh gold vases everywhere. The signs directing us to a conference hall where Katharine Breakspeare will be speaking are subtle but clear.

We're ten minutes early—that's kind of my thing—but there's a healthy trickle of teenagers heading in the same direction as us, and I find myself scoping them out. Most people are easy to categorize as private school kids with plummy accents and designer clothes, or grim-faced loners with color-coded binders (aka Celine's people), or sporty types with confident grins and rain-soaked hoodies. What's interesting about this group is the varied mix.

I'm wondering about their motivations. I probably should've read that leaflet properly, but I almost choked to death halfway through when I realized that Celine's hero's enrichment program involved camping in the woods. She hates team building, and she's always avoided the outdoors, which I didn't understand until she let slip that her dad used to take her and Giselle camping. (God knows how he found the time, since he was so busy being a slimy, two-timing twat, but clearly he kept on top of his schedule.) She must be hating this and desperate for it at the same time.

I saw that arsehole's name on the back of her leaflet.

But when I sneak a glance at her, she looks the way she always looks: completely unbothered.

The conference hall is a wide-open space crammed with rows and rows of chairs, most of which turn out to be messily and noisily occupied. "Come here," Celine says suddenly, and grabs the sleeve of my coat. There's that *zing* again, that crackle like a sparkler on Bonfire Night. I thought I understood it, but now I'm officially confused.

I don't have time to overthink, though, because Celine is dragging me to a pair of chairs at the edge of a back row. There's more space in this section, probably because the view of the room's stage isn't great. "Here?" I wrinkle my nose. "How are we supposed to make friends and influence people if we sit all by ourselves?"

I think Celine shudders in disgust. "We're here to listen, not to talk."

Actually, I'm always ready to talk. "If you say so." We sink into our seats and I squint at the stage. "Can you see?"

"Do you care?" she shoots back with faux sweetness.

Honestly, it's like blood from a stone. "No." I turn firmly away from her bullshit, craning my neck to see past the hair of the guy in front of me. There's a blank screen above the stage, and as I watch, the lights lower and the words *Breakspeare Enrichment Program* rise. Then a lady in a slick, peacock-blue suit strides onto the stage, all swishy hair and piercing dark eyes. She raises the mic and says, "Good afternoon, guys. I'm Katharine——"

There's a cheer. A literal cheer, like she's a rock star. I slide a look at Celine; she's not making a sound, but she is watching Katharine Breakspeare with a bright nervousness I haven't seen in years, all her attention (and let me tell you, Celine's attention is *intense*) trained toward that stage like a spotlight. She sits up straight like there's a rod against her spine.

I used to think it was cute, how she took everything so seriously. Until I decided I wanted to make new friends and do new things and be someone other than *Bradley of Bradley-and-Celine,* and she very seriously dropped me like a hot potato.

I really need to change seats in Philosophy. Celine's always smelled like vanilla cocoa butter, and scents trigger memory.

"Wow," Katharine is saying with a muted aw-shucks vibe that feels a bit too on-the-nose, "I take it you've heard of me."

A completely unreasonable amount of laughter floods the room. I roll my eyes and glance at Celine, Queen of Interpersonal Skepticism. She analyzes every single thing *I* do and say with grave suspicion, but right now, she's eating this crap up. Katharine Breakspeare must be a wizard.

"But this isn't about me," Katharine goes on. Then she clicks something in her hand and the slide behind her displays a list of her latest and greatest accomplishments, plus a giant picture of her face. "Or rather," she corrects, "it's not *just* about me—it's about all of us. Everyone, past and present and future, who dares to dream bigger than the world around us. When I was at school, no one ever believed I could make something of myself."

Yeah, yeah, yeah. I wonder what she gets out of this, besides the PR philanthropy points. Maybe she's aiming to be made a baroness in ten years, or something like—

"I'm dyslexic," Katharine says simply. "As a child, that one difference in the way my mind works convinced teachers I was incapable. So they gave up on me, and I gave up on my dreams."

I blink and sit up straighter. Since I'm here, I might as well pay attention. I mean, the woman is providing kids with this opportunity out of the goodness of her heart; of course I'll hear her out. I'm not a monster.

"My journey to the legal field was long and difficult, just because I'm different. But those differences make me damned good at my job—and I have other qualities, too, ones that I believe all trailblazers have in common, that so many examinations just can't capture." Katharine wanders back and forth across the stage as she speaks, gesturing at the presentation behind her. The slides keep changing, but I barely notice.

"That's why I started this enrichment program for undergraduates three years ago, and that's why—this year—I've adapted it for pre-university students for the first time ever." There's another cheer. She grins and shakes her head at us rowdy but adorable fans. This woman is what Mum would call a "magnet," like a team captain or a cult leader. I was determined to hate her, since Celine likes her so much, but unfortunately, I'm feeling the pull.

"You're all at a crossroads in your lives," she tells us. "You know you want to make something of yourselves, to succeed, but so many professions have high barriers to entry—especially in this economy. You might study law or accounting or market- ing at university, qualify, and find your only option is to move to London if you want to earn enough to pay off your loans."

I notice she doesn't mention anything about being a writer. Probably because it doesn't matter what you study or where you work—you can only write the book by *writing the book*.

Spoiler alert: I still haven't written the book.

"You might even be hesitant to study at all—not everyone wants to start their adult life with mountains of debt," Katha- rine says, and I know that's right. Would you believe when my parents went to uni it was *free*? Injustice stalks my generation, I swear to God. "Maybe you dream of a certain professional future," Katharine goes on, "but you're well aware that you're rarely the highest flyer in your academic cohort, and thus you might secure a degree by the skin of your teeth and struggle to find employment as a result. The BEP," she says with relish, "is here to help you with that. This program is sponsored by a diverse range of employers within *our* region—why should Midlanders have to move south just to succeed?"

There is a ripple of agreement across the crowd, which, yeah, okay. She didn't lie.

"Being a BEP graduate *means* something, both here and across the country," she says, and the slide changes again. I'm not a numbers person, but she's got graphs illustrating the career trajectories of BEP alums that look impressive. "You'll distinguish yourselves to potential employers just by finishing the program, and you won't be doing it by swallowing textbooks and regurgitating them in an exam hall. Our unique enrichment program combines outdoor education with the patented BEP Success Assessment Matrix."

The slide switches to an image of a dark, dramatic forest. "Two outdoor expeditions," she says, "each taking place during a school holiday. The first is a training session, intended to teach you the necessary skills to survive and weed out those who can't hack it. The second is the real deal, independently executed by yourselves in the Scottish woodlands. Both expeditions are an opportunity to show you've got the skills elite employers desire."

The new slide tells us these skills are:

1. **Resilience**
2. **Commitment**
3. **Creative thinking**
4. **Relationship building**
5. **Leadership**

I smirk and glance over at Celine. Maybe she predicted my reaction, because our eyes meet, and she scowls.

"Relationship building?" I whisper.

"Shut up," she mouths.

"Tell me the last relationship you built. Quickly."

"I could build one right now, between my foot and your arse."

"Shh," I tut. "Don't talk over Katharine. I'm trying to listen."

Very, very quietly, Celine screams.

It's drowned out by Katharine's microphone boom. "Can you *commit* to the rules needed to survive out in the wild, and think of *creative* ways to apply them?" she asks. The next slide shows a woodland with the words *SHERWOOD FOREST: THE EDUCATION EXPEDITION* written over the top.

She keeps going. "And do you have the *determination* and *teamwork* skills to combine all you've learned and complete a miles-long trek independently, hunting down Golden Compasses along the way? You'll have the opportunity to prove it here. . . ." *Click.* A new slide appears with a picture of a forest. *GLEN FINGLAS: THE FINAL EXPEDITION.* "During both expeditions," she says, "trained supervisors will be scoring you from zero to five against each matrix indicator, then averaging your score for the week. After your education expedition in Sherwood Forest, you will meet *personally* with *me* to receive advice on how to improve ahead of the final expedition in Glen Finglas."

I think Celine's head just exploded and rainbow confetti flew out.

"In the end, your scores from *both* expeditions will be used to calculate your final marks. For context," Katharine goes on, "the highest score ever achieved through our matrix is 4.88."

Um. No one's ever gotten a five? What the hell kind of competition doesn't allow a perfect score? I slide a glance at Celine and find her just as outraged as I am, which is unnerving, to say the least. We really shouldn't agree on anything, ever.

"But first—only those of you whose applications are unique

and compelling enough will make it into the BEP at all. We'll begin with a twenty-person cohort."

Twenty people? There's at least ten times that in this room. The general hum of excitement turns into a low buzz of apprehension, of competition, as everyone eyes their neighbors.

For some reason, I find myself eyeing Celine. Not that we're in competition for *this*. It's just habit.

She glares back. "What are you looking at?"

"Not my competition," I say, "that's for sure."

Her mouth forms a perfect little O. "Bradley! Have you finally accepted that I'm fundamentally superior to you in every way? Bravo. I knew this day would come."

"Oh, Celine," I say, flashing the sweetest smile in my arsenal. "Some might say it's cruel to let you live in this fantasy world you've created. But if it keeps you from sinking into the depths of despair, I'll let you dream."

She scowls. I bet she'd scowl even harder if I got into her precious BEP and won the whole thing (surely someone gets to win? I would definitely win.), but that would be beyond petty and probably a waste of time. I'm not trying to take over the world like Celine. I do want to work in law—I'd get to help people, and I'd be good at it, and I wouldn't completely die of boredom—but I don't sit around daydreaming about *elite employers*.

I don't daydream about the future at all. (Unless you count the one where I'm a bestselling sci-fi author, but obviously that's not going to happen because I can't even finish a bloody short story, so—)

". . . fifty percent of the cohort," Katharine is saying, and I blink back to the room around me in time to see her latest slide. My jaw drops. On average, around 50 percent of the cohort—Breakspeare Explorers, she calls them—usually *quit* or are thrown out before finishing the program? What the hell does she have people doing out there, ice bathing and making blood sacrifices to the gods? It's just two expeditions. I mean, scrubbing about in the dirt and wilderness isn't my idea of fun—when I was sixteen, the football team camped in Bavaria for a tournament and I spent the whole trip peeing in bushes so I wouldn't have to use a public bathroom—but even *I* could complete two expeditions if I had the right motivation. Then again, I'm kind of a badass. I could do anything with the right motivation.

"But those who succeed will attend the Explorers' Ball to receive their coveted Explorer Awards and mingle with our sponsors, who'll be searching for students to offer internships. Oh," Katharine says, like a parent "finding" one last surprise present for their kid under the tree. "And of course, the three Explorers who score the highest on our achievement matrix—who become our Ultimate Explorers—will win the grand prize: a *full scholarship* to study any undergraduate degree at the British university of their choice."

The room cheers so hard and so sudden, it's like sitting on top of an explosion—but I barely notice. I'm too busy absorbing what she just said.

A full scholarship. No tuition debt. My parents have to contribute to Emily's studies in the US, so I'm determined to handle my own uni fees. I wasn't going to apply for the maximum maintenance loan—I was planning on cheaper, shared accommodation to reduce my debt. But if I don't have any *tuition* debt . . .

I could request a full maintenance loan. Instead of sharing with strangers, I could get a little apartment by myself, where everything is clean and tidy and proper and right and other people won't be showering wrong and messing up my kitchen cupboards and leaving *crumbs*—

If I can get this scholarship, the most nightmarish aspect of university will be dealt with up front. That sounds like motivation to me.

There are three scholarships. Only twenty people make it. Ten of them drop out. If I can just get through two expeditions, I'll have a decent chance of winning—and I know I could ace that matrix thingy. I'm resilient (you have to be when your OCD wants you to stay in a nice, clean, empty room for safety reasons, but *you* want to have a life). I'm committed (I did therapy for like five years even though it was really annoying). I'm a creative thinker (although you wouldn't know it the way my mind goes *blank* when I open a Word document).

My palms prickle with possibility.

By the time the presentation ends, I'm certain. There's electricity buzzing through my veins. I'm doing this.

"What?" Celine says, right next to me, and I realize I spoke out loud. She's staring at me with an interesting mix of horror and disbelief, the smile she wore as she listened to Katharine long gone.

I clear my throat. Might as well repeat it. "I'm going to apply. To the program."

Her jaw tightens, her mouth compresses, her eyes narrow. *"Why?"*

"Why not?" I snap back. She never wants me around. I never want *her* around either, obviously, but God. "You don't own the bloody BEP."

"Neither do you." She scowls, but it's not very intimidating. Celine's face is overblown and dramatically soft, like when magnolia leaves are about to fall. Someone should tell her all that glaring is a waste of time.

Won't be me, though.

Instead, I say, "Well, now we've established our complete lack of ownership—"

But she's not done. "You weren't even interested before I took you here—"

"Er, technically, I took you here."

"But now you think you can waltz into whatever you want and get whatever you want, just like you always do—"

That is so outrageously wrong that I laugh out loud. It's like a single, off-kilter yelp, halfway between amusement and astonishment. "Are you serious?" I always get what I want? Is she *high*? If that were true, I'd be doing literally anything other than arguing with Celine Bangura right now.

"Of course I'm serious," she snaps, but when I don't reply—when I don't bite back—a little furrow pops up between her eyebrows. "What?" she demands.

I don't speak. I can't. For once, I honestly have no idea what to say.

"You think you can waltz into whatever you want and get whatever you want, just like you always do—"

There's no way on earth she sees me like that. Not when I spend half my life memorizing textbooks just to scrape the grades she gets so effortlessly. Not when she has strangers on social media basically proposing marriage in her comments section. Not when a single, judgmental look from her makes me lose my composure.

There's just no way.

And yet I study her face, the firm set of her mouth and the certainty in her eyes, and I know: it's the only way she'll ever see me, because it's what she wants to see.

How else can she justify all the things she said to me four years ago?

How can you justify all the things you said to her?

Suddenly, I'm exhausted. But I'm also weirdly determined, the way I feel right before a match when I know the rival team is good but ours is better.

I'm doing this enrichment program. I'm running off into the woods, whether she wants me there or not.

"Cheer up, Celine," I say, rising to my feet. "Maybe you won't get in."

• • •

🐾**FAMILY CHAT**🐾

Brad: i want to do the explorer thing

Mason💘😊**:** LOLOLOLOL

Dad🐨**:** Okay. Want to talk more when you get home?

Brad: if Celine's doing it, i def can

Mum🕊️: I thought you said it sounded like a disgusting nightmare trail of doom and darkness?

Brad: that doesn't sound like me at all

Mason🎈💀: yes it does you DRAMA KING

Brad: i changed my mind

Brad: there's a scholarship

Dad🐶: A scholarship for camping in the woods?

Brad: a full one

Mum🕊️: Well, as long as you WANT to do it.

Brad: yeahhhh, now you're on my side

OCTOBER

CHAPTER FOUR

CELINE

I get in.

Obviously.

My application is shit-hot. I adapt the personal statement I've been writing for Cambridge, make more of a fuss about my social media channels because I know Katharine values entrepreneurial spirit, and have Mum check everything for me.

I'm still not telling her Dad's involved, though. It couldn't be more irrelevant. I mean, yes, there will be that celebration ball at the end of the program for Explorers and sponsors to mingle, but I doubt he'll be there and if he is, he'll be too busy vomiting with shame and regret to hold a conversation.

Giselle thinks I'm bonkers, committing to some experimental enrichment program in the woods, but there's a scholarship *and* career connections on offer, and only the best are chosen, so here I am: proving once again that I'm the best.

I bear that in mind as I sink—and sink, and *sink*—into the

saggy bed I've just been assigned at Sherwood Forest's Visitor Cabin. This place is basically an old and underfunded dorm with dingy shared bathrooms and decorative logs stuck to the exterior. Across the room, a girl whose name might be Laura, or Aura, or possibly Rory (to say she mumbles would be an understatement) flicks blue eyes at me from beneath her shaggy hair, then looks away.

"Be careful," Mum is saying on the phone. "Behave yourself. And stick with Brad."

Oh, yeah. Bradley got in too.

I don't groan at the reminder because I am very mature, but I do wrinkle my nose down at the dingy brown carpet.

"I know what you're thinking"—Mum laughs like she can see my expression—"but he's a good boy, and he's more cautious than you. Take care of each other. Especially while your wrist is still healing!"

Yeah . . . about that "wearing a cast for six to eight weeks" thing? Apparently, it's eight weeks for me. I'll be free next Monday, a week *after* this expedition.

Bradley's fault. Obviously.

"I mean it, Celine," Mum says, turning stern. "I guarantee Maria is telling him the same thing."

Not bloody likely. When we stepped off the coach twenty minutes ago, Bradley was already surrounded by people as always, grinning and relaxed, because he managed to make friends during the coach ride while I sat on my own listening to Frank Ocean's *Blonde* and texting Michaela. I bet he's chatting away to his little ginger roommate right now.

My roommate is glued to her phone with an expression that

suggests she's either Googling *How to kill your BEP roomie and get away with it* or reading really great fanfic.

"I'll be good, Mummy." By which I mean: I'll try my best not to get killed in the night. "I have to go now, okay?"

"Okay, baby. I love you."

"Love you too."

Laura/Aura/Rory glances up as I put the phone down and mumbles, "Five minutes till we meet outside."

I blink. "Are you watching the time for us?"

She shrinks into her gray hoodie. "Um . . ."

So she's not a murderer; she's just shy. Now I feel bad. "That's . . . nice," I clarify awkwardly.

Her smile has a lot in common with a wince.

The BEP has been a whirlwind so far. We hopped on a coach this morning, it took us basically up the road to Sherwood Forest, we were introduced to our supervisors (Zion is an Energizer Bunny with locs, and Holly is basically Kourtney Kardashian), and then we were told to pair off and given fifteen minutes to stow our stuff in our bedrooms and report for duty. I'm not sure how I ended up with Laura/Aura/Rory, but it probably has something to do with her being shy and me being . . . mutinously silent. In a very *confident* way. Obviously.

I try to make more conversation and, annoyingly, I find myself thinking of what Bradley would say.

Something obnoxious, probably.

But what comes out of my mouth is, "Cute nails."

She examines the chipped purple polish, and her razor-sharp nose flushes pink. "Oh. I can never make it stay. . . ."

"Well, who can?" I allow. "But it's a nice color."

Her nose blushes pinker. She smiles with a bit more warmth and a bit less terror. Success! I am practically a social butterfly.

"My name's Celine, by the way," I say, even though I already told her. I'm hoping she'll reintroduce herself, and—

Yep. She sits up straighter on her own rickety bed, despite the heavy-looking purple duffel bag planted in her lap, and says, "I'm . . . Rora."

Pretty sure I still did not hear that right. "Laura?"

There's more nose blushing. "Aurora? Like in, er, *Sleeping Beauty*?"

"*Ah*. Sorry. That's a pretty name."

She snorts. "I mean, it's . . . a name."

I grin. I think we're going to get on fine.

After some more chitchat about the lighting in here (fluorescent but still abysmal), the pillowcases (thank God we both brought our own), and the tiny desk crammed in under the window (that chair does *not* look stable; accidental injury is extremely likely), I tighten the silk scrunchie holding back my braids and we head out.

Unfortunately, we bump into Bradley in the hall.

"Celine," he calls, peeling off from his new group of adoring fans (seriously, how does he *find* these people?).

I sigh, not slowing my steps as we wind through the narrow and twisty corridors. The cabin should be called the Warren. "What?"

"Slow down," he says, practically skipping beside me. "I wanna talk."

Aurora, based on her wide-eyed alarm, has correctly identified Bradley as Shiny and Annoying. "I'll . . . see you outside," she manages, and hurries off toward the open front door. I watch her escape with utter longing.

Then I turn on Bradley and put a hand on my hip. "Now look. You've scared off my roommate!"

He blinks, all big brown eyes and pouty lips. "Why would she be scared of me?"

This is such a ridiculous question, all I can do is throw my hands in the air and splutter, "For God's sake. What do you want?"

"What's your room like?" he asks.

"Shitty. Why?"

He sighs, a little furrow appearing between his eyebrows. "I was hoping yours might be better so we could swap."

This is so outrageous it quite literally steals my breath.

He continues to talk while I quietly asphyxiate. "Anyway, I wanted to talk about your roommate. You guys made friends?" He doesn't wait for an answer, just nods. "That's good. She can keep an eye on you."

My breath comes back all at once. "I *beg* your pardon?"

He shrugs. He's wearing a Nike tracksuit, powder pink on the right side and baby blue on the left. "I made friends, too, so they can keep an eye on me."

Okay, that's making even less sense. "Once again," I say, folding my arms over my chest, "I am forced to beg your pardon."

"Aw, Celine," he replies sunnily. "You don't have to beg."

This is the thing people don't get about Bradley: he makes these earnest, slightly dim comments, and they genuinely do not realize he is being a total cow.

I narrow my eyes. "You know what? Since we're talking, let's make one thing clear."

"Oh good," he murmurs, "she's making things clear."

"While we're here, Bradley Graeme, I do *not* know you."

He arches an eyebrow. "Well, that's gonna be awkward. I already told Thomas you were my cousin."

"What?! Who the hell is—Why would you tell someone I'm your *cousin?*"

"He's my roommate," Bradley says, "and I told him that to explain why he should not ask you out."

"What?" The word is so high-pitched, it's possible I shatter my own eardrums.

Bradley winces. "What? We're supposed to be looking out for each other!"

"What the *fuck,* Bradley?"

"You basically are my cousin!"

"I'm not your *cousin,* Bradley!"

He has the audacity to look annoyed, with his arms folded and this crease between his eyebrows that says I'm being unreasonable. "Well, whoever you are, you don't want some guy chatting you up while you're busy impressing Katharine Breakspeare!"

He is technically right—I can't be bothered with distractions right now—but that just pisses me off more, because how *dare* he accurately guess what I do or don't want?! "You do realize Katharine isn't going to be here, right?"

"Fine," he huffs. "Then you don't want him chatting you up while you're impressing Katharine's holy representatives on earth."

"That is not funny." That was very funny. I hate him. "You are the most *unbelievably arrogant—*"

Someone clears their throat. Loudly. We both whip around

to find the Energizer Bunny, Zion, waiting for us by the door with a disappointed expression and a leather-encased tablet. "You're missing the introductory meeting, guys."

Oh shit. First day, first meeting, and one of the supervisors catches me wasting time with Bradley Goddamn Graeme. Perfect. Just perfect. I am going to eat at least five sticks of broccoli at dinner as penance.

"Gosh, sorry," Bradley says in the kind of sweet, genuine apology I have never managed to achieve (not since I turned ten anyway). My own voice sounds sarcastic at the best of times, never mind when following Bradley's Earnest Angel routine, so I just wince and follow them outside, where the wind is doing its best to inject us all with thousands of tiny ice needles.

Bradley, I kid you not, pulls out a pink woolly hat from somewhere and jams it on his head until his ears are covered, and the tips of his twists peek out like adorable bits of tinsel. I can't stand this boy.

We step into the short, midmorning shadows at the edge of Sherwood Forest, sidling over to the circle of Breakspeare Explorers who are listening avidly to an older, bearded white guy in a green anorak. I recognize the leaf-printed lanyard around his neck as part of the groundskeepers' uniform.

Sherwood Forest is close to home, but I haven't visited since . . . well. Since Dad took me and Giselle hiking here, a little before my ninth birthday. It was a weird trip. He was on his phone a lot and he got annoyed with us over the slightest things—Giselle's moodiness, my nonstop questions. At least now I know why. His mind was elsewhere.

You'd think the forest would seem smaller, now that I've grown, but if anything, it's bigger because I'm more aware of its darkness. The weather is bitter and gray; the forest is vast and stuffed with ancient trees I can't identify—trees whose highest leaves I could never reach and whose massive trunks I could never fit my arms around. From here, I can see a rugged path into the undergrowth that's for hiking, and I know there's plenty more scattered about. This cabin sits on the south side of the forest and a gift shop and restaurant sit to the north, but between those two spots of civilization there's nothing but wild and twisty woods that'll take a hell of a lot of trekking. That tracks. According to my mental itinerary, this week is for learning key survival skills—testing our resilience, our relationship building, maybe our leadership, all while not getting eaten by wolves. (Supposedly, England doesn't have wolves, but in my opinion, official sources of information are not to be blithely trusted.)

Brad and I try to slide into the circle without notice, but the bearded man stops whatever he was saying and pins piercing blue eyes on us. The wind whips his sparse hair upright on his head, and his upper lip wiggles like he's scenting the air. "*Ah,*" he says in a tone so pointed it's basically a health hazard. "These are our latecomers, are they?"

Every eye in this circle is burning into my forehead.

"You must be Bradley Graeme," he says, scanning a raggedy-looking bit of paper in his hand (no tablet for our friendly local forest hermit, apparently), "and Celine . . . Celine Bang . . . ?"

Bradley beats me to it. "Bangura," he says, sounding annoyed. Which, yeah. It's literally phonetic.

"Well." Beard Guy sniffs. "I'm glad we are all present and accounted for. As I said before, my name is Victor—"

Oh, good. Now I have an actual name to use when I mentally rant about how much I dislike him.

"—and I'll be guiding you through this training course. You will be expected to work *hard* and be *punctual*." Another pointed glare from good old Victor. Clearly he is a person of great subtlety. "You will also be expected to do for yourselves; nothing will be spoon-fed. Our first activity, therefore, will be an ice-breaking exercise in two teams of ten." He counts quickly, reaches a midpoint in the circle, and waves a hand to indicate the group should split in half. We do. It's all very organized.

"Within this sector of the forest are hiding spots that contain training booklets. These booklets will act as your guide to understanding the forest flora and fauna later this week, but first, you have to find them. Your supervisors have maps and compasses to give you. Using these tools only, each team must find their cache. The first to complete their mission wins a welcome party tonight!"

There is an audible hum of excitement. Apparently, we are all the competitive type.

"The losers," Victor continues, "will be on washing-up duty for the rest of the week, starting tomorrow. And I'll warn you; we've only the one Brillo pad left in the cupboard." He guffaws as if this is the funniest statement ever made.

I have no idea if anyone else laughs along; I'm too busy panicking about my crappy sense of direction and what happened that one time I tried orienteering in a year-eight PE class (I fell down a hill). I knew this whole thing was going to be hands-on, but this is, er, *quite* hands-on.

Also, teams of ten are huge. How are we supposed to

collaborate effectively? Do I establish myself as a leader early on, or is that bossy? Do I hold back and try to be a good teammate, or is that too meek? And, Christ, why am I standing next to Bradley? Now he's on my team!

As if things couldn't get any worse, the gray sky does as it's been threatening all morning and releases a gentle but miserable shower of rain.

I hope these booklets are laminated.

• • •

BRAD

I know as soon as the rain begins that I've messed up, clotheswise, but in my defense, this is a travel outfit. As in, a comfortable outfit *for traveling*. How was I supposed to know they'd throw us into the forest within five minutes?

"Excuse me," I call, raising my hand. "Sorry—can I change?"

Victor snorts. "No." Then he stalks off into the cabin, where it's *dry*. Ugh.

I suppose I could've changed when we arrived, but I needed that time for my social plan; I found some easygoing guys to talk football with, so I'd have a ready-made group for the week. Turns out that was a complete waste of time, though, because the only guy from said ready-made group who's part of my current team is my roommate Thomas, and he's already busy making eyes at Celine . . .

Who is busy glaring at me. God only knows what I'm supposed to have done now. Probably I caused the rain, or something.

"We should take cover," someone says—a short girl with

silky, straightened hair and a voice that reminds me of Coach, a friendly authority that'll steamroll you with its sheer enthusiasm. Maybe that's why we all follow her without question into the woods. Watching mud creep up the edges of my Nikes is severely pissing me off, my fingers are already aching in this icy drizzle, and I am definitely being contaminated by dirt and animal urine *as we speak*—but fear is the mind killer, so I kick that worry into a river and focus on the issue at hand. I wonder if our supervisor—Holly, I think her name is—will score me 5 out of 5 for creative thinking because I'm the best dressed Explorer here.

She is very sensibly wearing a raincoat, combat trousers, and walking boots, while my socks are already damp, so . . . probably not.

This little corner of Sherwood Forest smells like wet and greenery. It's fresh and cool and ancient, somehow, like we've traveled back in time and we're alone and Robin Hood might show up in a second. I take a lungful of clean air and tip my head back. The rain is struggling to reach us here between the trees, and the weak sunlight makes the thick ceiling of leaves above us all see-through and pretty. Maybe I should change my book's setting and plop the main character Abasi Lee onto a forest planet instead of a desert one.

A few meters away, I hear someone from the opposing team say, "Let's all take a picture."

"Oh—we can split up!"

"But we don't all have a . . ."

Here's my first strategy: don't mouth off as loud as them and give our techniques away.

My team huddles together, ten of us packed tight with Holly

standing off to the side. Then we stare at each other, apparently lost. Celine clears her throat, because of course she does. "Should we introduce ourselves?"

Thomas nods like a ginger bobblehead and says with completely unnecessary enthusiasm: "Absolutely! Cracking idea!"

I narrow my eyes.

To be clear, I have nothing against Thomas. He seems nice (even though his accent is so upper class, I wouldn't be surprised if he grew up riding his nannies around the garden like racehorses. Sorry, I'm being judgmental). But as soon as we sat next to each other on the bus, he poked me in the ribs and pointed between the gaps in the seats and said, "Look! Is that her? It is, isn't it?"

I blinked and followed his finger. "Who?" Then I laid eyes on my archnemesis, who was texting at the speed of light, devouring a Twix, and glaring at her fellow passengers every few seconds like clockwork, presumably to make sure no one came within five feet of her.

"@HowCelineSeesIt!" Thomas hissed. "You follow her, right? She's . . ." He trailed off and turned scarlet, which I took as a dangerous sign. Then he added, "She's basically famous. I'm gonna talk to her about, er, conspiracies and stuff," which I took as an even *more* dangerous sign because Celine hates talking.

So, in a fit of admirable charity and possibly feminism, I blurted out, "Oh, Celine? That's my cousin." Then I told him all about how I am on very strict instructions to *look after her.*

Clearly the warning didn't stick, because the guy is now gazing at Celine—not our *entire* group of *ten people plus Holly,* just Celine—and introducing himself like he's auditioning for the role of Mr. HowCelineSeesIt. "I'm Thomas! I'm almost

seventeen but I'm in my final year; I started sixth form early."
He's clearly hoping Celine will be impressed by that, which, in
fairness, she might. "I go to Nottingham High," he continues.
Private school. Maybe he thinks she'll be impressed by that too.

Instead, Celine flicks an alarmed look in my direction. For
some reason, it's really hard not to laugh. I bite down on the
inside of my cheek and say, "I'm Brad. I play football, and I go
to Rosewood Academy." The football thing is relevant because I
vaguely recognize a couple of guys here, and it's probably from
tournaments.

The silky-hair girl is Sophie; the wiry guy next to her is Raj;
the supermodel-looking dude at the head of the circle (so I
guess it's not exactly a circle anymore?) is called Allen, and then
I stop listening. I'm busy checking out the landscape so I won't
step on a snake or fall into any cleverly disguised quicksand pits.
(You might think quicksand would be unlikely in an East Midlands forest, but it seemed unlikely on *Dora the Explorer* too.)

"Is anyone especially good at reading maps?" Allen asks, the
command in his tone bringing me back down to earth. I'm
pretty sure he just interrupted Celine's shaggy-haired little
roommate, but I wasn't paying attention, so maybe I'm wrong.

Raj and a girl whose name I don't know both raise their
hands. Then Raj grins. "Look at us, putting our hands up like
we're at school."

Allen does not laugh. In fact, he must think we *are* at school
and he is the teacher. "*I'm* rather good at orienteering," he says
firmly, "so I'm thinking I'll hold the map and you guys can consult. Maybe someone else can be the compass person and the
rest can be sent ahead to scout, keep an eye on terrain, that sort
of thing?"

We all shrug at each other. Allen nods firmly—he has a very strong jaw and hair like thick wheat—and takes the map and the compass from our supervisor Holly like he is King Arthur pulling the sword from the stone.

I check Celine's expression, and it doesn't disappoint; she's watching Allen like he's the single most boring amoeba she's ever laid eyes on. I wish I was as easily disdainful, but I think Allen's kind of hot. (I have long come to terms with the fact that I have horrible taste.)

While our experts huddle around the (thankfully, laminated) map, I sidle over to Celine and obey our mums' wishes. "Let's stick together, okay?"

She looks up at me like I'm on drugs. "Why?"

"Because we're cousins," I reply, purely to get on her nerves.

"Please stop saying that," she murmurs politely, "before I vomit all over these lovely plants."

I've developed a little problem since school started: every week, I sit next to Celine in Philosophy, and we insult each other like always, but lately I find myself wanting to laugh. Really badly.

But I won't, because Celine talks to me like I'm a deeply suspicious stranger and if I make one wrong move, she will knee me in the balls for her own safety. It's annoying but what did I expect? Funny or not, she's still a judgmental know-it-all hypocrite.

Unfortunately, she's also still wearing that cast hidden under the sleeve of her coat. And if she trips over a stray twig and I don't catch her, my guilt will go from monumental to colossal and my spine might crack under the strain. So, "Whether you like it or not," I say under my breath, "I'm stuck to you like glue."

She scowls and asks again, "Why?"

"Why not?"

"Because I am committed to protecting my peace and you are so far from my inner circle you're basically a hexagon. Get thee behind me."

For God's sake. "What do you think I'm going to do, push you into a ditch?"

"I don't know what you're going to do, Bradley." She sends a weird, edgy look in my direction and all my hopes for a half-normal week land *splat* like an egg on the floor. "I barely know you at all."

My jaw tightens, but it's not as if she's lying. I barely know her, either. Because the Celine I once *thought* I knew would never have abandoned our friendship so easily, would never have ignored my honestly embarrassing apology, would never have been so determined to keep us apart for this long.

It's been almost four years now. And she's still not even *slightly* over it—

"Fine," I bite out, and go to stand with Thomas instead.

Allen and a few other people put their heads together over the only map, talking about keys and terrains and directions. I know I should be more active, and I know Holly is hovering around observing us, grading us out of five for each quality on Katharine Breakspeare's success matrix thingy. We've been reminded that we'll be graded every day before we receive an average for the whole expedition.

So when Allen asks who fancies walking a little ahead to keep an eye on the terrain, I volunteer immediately, and never mind the state of my trainers. See, Holly?! I'm literally leading the group. Please write that down.

Celine sticks with the compass people, which is ridiculous because I don't think she even knows her left from her right.

We scrabble around for about ten minutes before I realize I'm not hating this. It's a challenge, watching where I step, squinting through the faint fall of rain, listening to instructions from behind me and trying to stay alert—but the activity of it helps keep my mind on what I'm doing. The air feels good in my lungs. The space feels good around me. This is a bit like playing football—the way you get so present in your body, your head turns all empty and clean.

"You seem cheerful," Thomas drawls, managing to sound sarcastic even though he's panting a bit to keep up.

"We're almost there," I tell him. "I can feel it."

Raj pipes up from a meter or so behind us. "You mean you can hear Allen crowing," he says dryly, and Thomas snorts.

We find the marker a little while later, buried between the forked trunks of a big, twisty tree that I am determined to learn the name of. It has thick, dark leaves and crumbly bark and it gives off winning vibes to me. I spot the rain-spattered plastic bag tied to a low-hanging branch, but it's Allen who strides forward to open it and pull out . . .

A single, palm-sized little book, green and white, with *SHERWOOD FOREST GUIDE* stamped on the front and a silhouette logo of Robin Hood's pointed cap.

Allen stares, horrified. "This is just one book."

I hear Celine for the first time since we started searching. "Aurora said there's something else in the bag," she calls from the back of the group.

My eyes fly to her—her cheeks are wet with rain, her eyeliner slightly smudged, her chest rising and falling steadily.

Then I turn back to the bag and notice the little square of paper tucked in the bottom corner.

Allen screws up his face. "Who's Aurora?"

Okay, so I don't know *exactly* who Aurora is either, but come on, man.

Celine's big-eyed roommate—Aurora, clearly—blushes. Celine narrows her dark eyes in an expression that I know means *explosion imminent,* and says, "You must be hungry or tired or otherwise temporarily impaired. We should really hurry back." Then she steps forward to grab the note, apparently before Allen can decide whether or not that was an insult.

(It was.)

She has to stand between us—between Allen and me—to get the piece of paper. I stare at him over her head and wonder suddenly if she thinks we're the same.

He reminds me of Donno, which is a thought I do not enjoy.

Celine reads the note quickly and says, "Shit."

I glance over her shoulder, but Allen takes the paper almost immediately. Doesn't matter; I saw enough to get the gist.

"Shit," I repeat.

Allen's voice rings with disbelief. "'Step by step and line by line, places that hide each book, you'll find. From every clue, take letter and number—to start, what's small and strange and sweet, and in one bite appeases hunger?'" His voice rises at the end as if no one has ever fucked with him like this.

A little silence falls.

Then Raj laughs. "We have to find nine more books."

CHAPTER FIVE

CELINE

There's a very interesting vein pulsing in Allen's forehead. I catch Aurora's eye and she bites her lip on a smile.

"All right, change of plans!" Sophie says, patting her ponytail as it slowly frizzes into a curly puff. "First things first: what's the riddle mean? Is anyone good at that sort of thing?"

Aurora sidles over to me, leans in, and murmurs, "Petit fours."

Uh . . . is she hungry? "Pardonnez moi?"

Unfortunately, Allen finally regains his voice. "This can't be right," he announces, and strides over to our supervisor Holly. "Excuse me," he says all politely, which—it's a bit late for that, pal, she's already heard you mouthing off to everyone else, but okay. "Was there a misunderstanding earlier?"

Holly tilts her beautiful head to one side and says calmly, "No."

Allen waits for more information.

Apparently, none is forthcoming.

"It's just that we were told the books would all be together," he tries again.

Holly presses her fluttery fake eyelashes together and apart, very, very slowly. Her glossy mouth remains closed.

Allen is turning a lovely shade of pink. "So are you saying we now have to find ten books individually? Clue by clue?"

"No."

Allen starts to exhale in relief.

"You've already found one," she continues. "There are only nine left."

So Raj was right.

I should be annoyed that we have even more hiking to do, but I'm busy enjoying the barely restrained outrage on Allen's face. I bite back a smile, and by some unexplainable accident, my eyes meet Bradley's.

He's smirking. I'm smirking. For one impossible second, we're *both* smirking—at each other, but, like, not in the usual way. Then his smirk is replaced by a grimace of horrified realization, and he snatches his gaze away like I might give him fleas. God forbid someone like him make eye contact with someone like me, I suppose.

My jaw aches and I realize I'm grinding my teeth.

"But then . . . that's not . . ." Allen might be in the midst of a cardiac arrest. "Well," he manages, pulling himself together. "We've found *one* of the books. Shouldn't one person get to go back? Or . . . do we really need all ten? We can photocopy them, can't we? That would be smarter. We should work smarter, not harder." His gaze drills into Holly. "Is that what we're supposed to do?"

She looks incredibly bored. "I'm just your supervisor. I can't help you."

As entertaining as this is, I think the responsible thing to do is get on with our task now, so I reluctantly tear myself away and try to think.

Evidently, Sophie agrees, because she asks again—louder this time, "The riddle. Any ideas?"

"It talks about hunger," someone says, "so it's probably food, right?"

A discussion breaks out, one I could take part in if Bradley didn't choose that very moment to lean across me and murmur to Aurora, "Did you have an idea?"

I scowl. What is he on about? We haven't even—

But Aurora nods slowly, flicking a glance at me, then at him. "Do you two know each other?"

I say, "Absolutely not," just as Bradley laughs, "Unfortunately." His smile is warm and inviting and he has a dimple in his right cheek, all of which is directed with unwavering focus at Aurora. I have no idea what his game is, but there's definitely a game. Maybe he's noticed Aurora's smart and useful (because, you know, she is) so he's decided to latch on to her and look good by association. But I'm sure by the end of the day he'll be ignoring her and braiding Allen's hair. That guy's a substitute Donno if I ever saw one.

"It's petit fours," Aurora says. "Small and strange—as in foreign, right?—and it's a food. And there's a number, so it's probably . . . P4 on the map, or something, our sector is OPQ . . ."

Oh God. She's giving him all her ideas. I widen my eyes and shake my head but she's not paying attention to me because Bradley is luring her away with his annoying handsome face.

His smile widens and he says, "You figured it out that fast? You're some kind of genius."

Gag me.

Then he whispers, "Tell Sophie."

I pause, convinced I haven't heard him right. Why isn't he . . . ? Why would he . . . ? I mean, Bradley's way too smart to outright steal Aurora's idea and present it as his own. But why wouldn't he do some big pompous "I think Aurora has the answer!" moment to capture everyone's attention and prove what a Nice Guy he is? Why would he just quietly tell her . . .

"Everyone's talking," Aurora mumbles. "I can't just——"

"You can." He nudges her. "It's fine, they're all talking over each other. Might as well join in."

She blushes.

"Just blurt it out," he tells her. "Don't think about it, just go. Go on! Go."

Aurora is *giggling*. I am *appalled*. What is even *happening* in front of my *eyes*?

"Go on, say it, say it say it say it——"

"I have an idea," Aurora announces suddenly, her nose fire-engine red but her voice strong and clear.

I make a weird sort of *Gah?* sound. Bradley looks at me sideways. I snap my mouth shut.

"I think it . . . um . . . might be . . . petit fours?" Aurora croaks. "Maybe, I don't know, I was just thinking it might, because, you know." She has run out of steam, but it doesn't matter, because Thomas is nodding and saying *"Ohhhh!"* He explains the logic and Aurora agrees with this tiny, happy smile on her face, and the conversation races off. Sophie is asking about people's phones and talking about meeting points and efficiency. Raj is asking Aurora if he can call her Briar Rose. Bradley is examining a speck of mud on his hoodie and I am staring at Bradley because I just can't help myself.

He's supposed to be a different person now. He's supposed to be a caricature of a popular kid, towing Donno's maliciously drawn line, ignoring people he considers beneath him and pretending it's accidental, keeping himself apart as if he were *born* perfect. It's not that being hot and athletic and charming makes you a bad person. But *choosing* to put those qualities above everything else—above kindness and honesty and loyalty—that makes you a bad person. That made him a bad person when he used to be *my* person.

He's supposed to be someone I don't recognize.

But every so often he shows me flashes of a Bradley I *do* recognize, and I really need him to stop.

"Okay," Sophie says, "so that leaves . . . Brad and Celine?"

I jolt at the sound of my name. Next to me, Bradley does the same.

"One of you has a compass on your phone, right?"

I open my mouth, then close it. What am I going to do, admit that I have no idea what's going on? I doubt that would do my commitment score for the day any favors. "Yes," I say calmly, just as Bradley announces, "I have a pocket compass, actually."

I do a double take as he pulls out a little black plastic thing and snaps it open. Of course, Prince Perfect brought his own. I wonder if Holly's going to give him extra points for creative thinking—or commitment—or *leadership*. God. I really need to step up my game.

"Oh, great!" Sophie says. "Okay, everyone, come and take a picture of the map."

Subtly, I move closer to Aurora. "What's going on?"

"Relays," she whispers back. "We're setting up a group chat and going off in pairs."

"What? How does that make sense?"

"They have a signal booster out here," she says. "To make sure hikers can call for help, if they get lost."

"No, I meant, we need each clue to find the next book, right?"

"Yeah," Aurora says, "that's what the group chat is for. To share whatever we find. But this task takes part in the red-outlined section of the map—meaning there's only a limited number of sectors, right? It's not that big a surface area. So the other pairs will look around their sectors to see if they can stumble across anything while we all wait for more info. Going around in a big group of ten just seems like a waste of time. Most of us didn't even have a task when we were searching for this book."

That . . . is a terrible plan. I should really say som—

"Hang on," I hiss, realization thwacking me in the face like a tree branch. "So I have to go off on my own with *Brad*?"

Aurora winces, which is confirmation enough.

"Who are you with?!"

"Raj," she says. "Sorry!"

I fake-glare at her. She laughs. For the next five minutes, I completely ignore the impending doom staring me in the face. Then we all part ways, leaving Holly behind as a safety checkpoint, and I'm forced to approach Him.

The Utmost Pain in My Arse.

Stay zen, Celine. If we have to work together, we have to work together. I'm not a *complete* child. I take a nice soothing breath and rub my rain-damp palms over my thighs.

This is going to be fine.

I will make it fine.

Fine!

* * *

BRAD

Celine's being weirder than usual.

"This is honestly ridiculous," she mutters under her breath for the ten thousandth time as we trudge through the bracken. And no, her complaining is not the weird part; what's weird is that she's complaining to *me*.

Celine should be ordering everyone about like soldiers in her army, not meekly following Sophie's instructions. I keep waiting for her to say something bossy and annoying. The lack is starting to creep me out.

"What are we even looking for?" she demands, addressing a nearby tree.

"I don't know. A little plastic bag? A big flashing arrow?"

She whips around to face me, her eyes narrow and suspicious, like she has no idea why I'm answering her. Seriously? Come *on*, Celine. It's literally you or the undergrowth. Work with me here. We've been walking alone for like twenty minutes and I am so completely deprived of company, I'm actually grateful when she speaks again. "The chances of us finding either in this rain are roughly equal." She sniffs, shoving her hands into the pockets of her black puffer jacket.

The rain isn't heavy; it's fine like mist, clinging to your eyelashes, obscuring everything more than a meter in front of your face. So I suppose by "'equal'" she must mean "'zero.'" Instead of commenting, though, I say, "Hands out of your pockets."

She stares at me like I've lost my mind. "Suck a toe."

"If you want to fracture your other wrist," I say, "do it around someone else, because I'm not carrying you out of these woods."

"If I fractured my other wrist," she replies sweetly, "I wouldn't need anyone to carry me because I don't walk on my hands."

Fine; let her trip over a shrub and break her neck. Like I care. I catch sight of my mud-stained trainers and huff.

We move in silence for another five minutes before I realize Celine's done talking. If I want more noise, I need to wind her up again. "I don't think splitting up was that bad an idea."

Her eyes flash. She is wonderfully predictable. "Of course it's a bad idea! We split our resources and waste time stumbling around in the dark? Hardly the plan of the century."

Ooh, she's pissed. This is more like it. "Do you mean the literal dark, or the metaphorical dark?" I ask innocently.

Her jaw tightens so hard you can almost hear it pop. "*Obviously,* I mean the metaphorical dark, Bradley." Celine must really hate me because when other people annoy her, she gets bored and clocks out. When I annoy her, you can practically see the pulse pounding in her forehead.

"Well, if it was obvious," I say, "I wouldn't have asked."

She scowls. "Stop taking the piss. Listen, as long as we're in this together——"

"Did I hear that right? Did you just say *together*?"

"We need to keep an eye on these things," she continues, as if I haven't spoken. "I *know* you know how illogical this plan is. One of us should've been paying attention back there."

She knows I know? I keep my expression blank and my voice steady as I say, "Why, so we could speak up and undermine the whole democracy vibe?" But inside I'm vibrating like a confused Chihuahua, freaked out because Celine thinks I'm . . . smart? No, that might be too generous. Sensible? Or something like that? Basically, I'm astonished she doesn't think I'm an Allen-level idiot. I'm not, but she's never been reasonable enough to acknowledge my frankly impressive intelligence, so—

"Screw democracy!" she announces.

Er. "Okay, Comrade Celine?"

"Everyone's in a rush to win," she continues. "That's why they jumped on the first idea instead of talking over all the options."

She's not wrong, but then, she rarely is. It's one of her most annoying qualities. "I think you're being too harsh. The sector's small; we could stumble across some booklets out of order. There's a chance this'll make things more time efficient, and the group chat means we don't lose the teamwork element."

"We'd work faster if we used the strengths of every team member simultaneously, and I don't think a group chat is going to cut it. We're trekking through the forest, for God's sake; who's checking their phone?"

I don't mention that she has her phone out right now to check the pictures we took of the map. Celine's voice has gotten progressively higher in outrage and she's gesticulating wildly. I sometimes, occasionally, *accidentally* watch her conspiracy theories on TikTok, and she gets like this when she's talking about how the Loch Ness Monster has tragically died of old age but was, at one point, totally real.

"What are you smirking at?" she demands.

I wipe the illegal and unplanned smile off my face. "Nothing. Just . . . I knew your quiet and polite routine couldn't last."

She stops in her tracks, planting her (sensible, walking-boot-shod) feet in the earth and propping her fists on her hips. Her cast peeks out of one sleeve, poking me with the guilt stick. "What is *that* supposed to mean?"

I shrug, because staying casual when she's pissed always annoys her more. "What's with the shy and retiring bit you're doing in front of everyone else? Are you biding your time? Warming up your audience before you tie them in knots? What's the problem?"

"I told Allen to shut up," she counters with a scowl.

"I thought you were shockingly polite to Allen."

"Excuse me?"

"Well, for you. It was basically a gentle scolding. I hope you're not wasting all your energy on me, Celine. I need to see you scalp at least one other person while we're here."

"Funny," she bites back. "I thought you liked it when I kept my mouth shut."

All my amusement from making fun of her drains away like water down the plughole. She's said something like that to me before. Maybe she thinks I don't remember. Maybe *she* doesn't remember, and I'm the only one who's replayed that day in the cafeteria over and over in my head a thousand times.

Probably not, though.

When Celine was a kid, her dad went missing for a few days and she decided he'd been abducted by aliens. When he came back, announced that his mistress had given birth to twins, and divorced Neneh to go be with his new family, Celine concluded it was due to alien mind control. She had willful delusions and

I had obsessive compulsions—that's probably how we became best friends. Who was I to judge?

But as we got older, I learned to fold myself up nice and neat so no one would notice I was different. Celine never did. She talked about aliens to anyone who'd listen. Especially when she was nervous.

"I thought you liked it when I kept my mouth shut."

The quiet rush of rain against leaves fills the space between us like a swollen balloon. Her jaw is tight; I wish it wasn't. My chest is tight, but there's not much I can do about that. *Just ignore it. Don't say anything. There's no point—*

Except I've always struggled to let thoughts and feelings go. They gnaw at me until I give in. "I told you I was sorry."

She snorts, and just like that, I know there's nothing coincidental about this conversation. Celine hasn't forgotten why she hates me.

Maybe she sits beside me in Philosophy remembering things the same way I do.

"It's not my fault, you know," I blurt out, "that we got separated. Back then."

Her expression is incredulous. "Our classes, you mean?"

I shrug, already uncomfortable, wondering why I'm digging deeper instead of shutting this conversation down—

"Of course that wasn't your *fault,* Bradley," she says sharply. "Everyone's schedule changes eventually." Her jaw shifts as she bites some part of herself I can't see—her tongue? The inside of her cheek? She's talking again. "The problem was, you made it worse."

I have to put plasters over all my scabs because if I can see them, I'll pick them until they bleed. Maybe things would be easier if I could put a nice, beige tarp entirely over Celine, but I can't, so I ask, "How?"

"You had to go and . . ." She waves a hand. Her nails are glossy and black. "Make new friends. And join the *football* team, and—"

Righteous outrage roars to life in my chest. It turns out that after almost four years of quiet seething, I am so ready for this argument. "Because that was such a crime," I bite out. "Wanting to do new things without you. *I* was the bad guy for joining a new club and quitting Latin? Okay, Celine."

She presses her raindrop-studded eyelashes together, breathes deep, and says the last thing I expect. "Well, no. Obviously not. You were free to do whatever you wanted, and it was . . . it was unfair of me to question that."

Um. Did those words just pass through Know-It-All Celine's gritted teeth? I think I might be in shock. Thrown off course, I search for something to say and blurt, "My therapist said you were controlling."

Amazing stuff, Bradley. Team building to the highest power.

She winces and shoves her hands in her pockets. "Ah."

I'm clearly going through something because I feel bad. Maybe all this fresh air is poisoning my brain. I shift awkwardly and look around, like I'll find a guidebook carved into a nearby tree trunk. You know: *So Your Old Best Friend Admits She Was Wrong and Hating Her Is Getting Exhausting.* Something like that. But before I can find any handy-dandy instructions, Celine speaks again.

"You were . . ." She swallows hard, but her jaw is harder. "You were embarrassed of me. That was the problem. That's what makes you the bad guy."

Aaaand my stomach is on the floor again. "That's not true."

"You told me not to—"

"I apologized," I interrupt, because I know what I said, and I don't want to hear it again. "I *told* you I was sorry. I told you straight away."

"As if I was going to believe a word out of your mouth after *that*."

I know what *that* was. I can see it now: me dragging Celine over to the lunch table with all my new friends. The more she talked, the quieter they got, and the quieter they got, the more she talked. Nervous. A bit too loud. Repeating herself. About aliens, obviously—and how smartphones listen to everything you say and target political advertisements accordingly, advertisements designed to radicalize you into proudly destructive apathy or conservative extremism, and a load of other stuff pretty much no other fourteen-year-old was going to appreciate, and I wanted this to work, I wanted everything to work, so I told her after lunch that maybe the next day she should just—

Keep that stuff to herself.

And she said, *"But why?"* And I didn't want to say, *"Because I need them to like you,"* so instead I said,

"Come on, Cel. It's just . . . a bit . . . weird." I knew as soon as I said it that I'd made a mistake. *Sorry, sorry, sorry—*

Too late.

"I am weird, Bradley, and I don't care. Sorry I'm not pathetic enough to fake my entire personality. Some of us actually have integrity."

You know how things hurt the most when you're scared they might be true? *"I have integrity!"*

"Sure you do."

"Well, *sorry people like me but not you, Celine."*

"*One day they'll all find out how weird* you *really are, Brad. You know that, right?"*

Yeah. I knew. Just like I knew this whole fight was a mistake.

"*Will your new friends want you then?"* she'd snarled.

"*Of course they will!"*

Except it stung because maybe they wouldn't.

Things went downhill after that. And by *downhill,* I mean Celine called me a knock-off Ken doll with an inferiority complex, so I told her aliens weren't real and her dad was just a dick.

Jesus. Five minutes ago, we were wandering through the woods and suddenly, somehow, she's plunged me into a vat of the past and I feel like I'm drowning. I *knew* I should've stayed away from this girl. Around her, I am nothing but trouble.

"You realized you could fit in," Celine says now, "and you were gone. Like *that.*" Her fingers don't snap properly; they're too wet. "All you had to do was leave me behind, so you did it. It's not a big deal. I just wish you'd admit it."

"You're wrong." I don't like to think about this stuff—it's twisted and messy and I don't do mess—but the truth is, back then, I had a very clear plan: football, and friends, and still-Celine. Always-Celine. It's just, the closer I got to those first two things, the more she turned away from me. And I know it was deliberate. I know her. "I wanted you to sit with us at lunch—"

"What the hell was someone like me going to do sitting next to *Max Donovan? Isabella Hollis? Any* of them?" She laughs, like she can't even come close to understanding me. Like I'm on another planet.

"What's . . . what's wrong with Isabella?" I ask hoarsely. I mean, I know what's wrong with her from *my* perspective: she's my ex-girlfriend, and it was pretty brutal when she dumped me last year. But I always sort of hoped Celine would like her, and——

"You *knew* no one liked me," Celine says, and Isabella falls out of my head.

"I knew people *could* like you," I correct, "if you'd just talk to them! Properly! You never talk to anyone, not the way you did with me——"

"Piss off, Bradley."

I raise my voice over hers. "If you'd've just . . . If you could just be——"

"Well, I couldn't!" she shouts. "You could, and I couldn't! So you left me."

"I left *you*? You . . . you iced me out completely." I run a hand over the nape of my neck, my stomach lurching as if she's dragged me back in time. As if I'm in the cafeteria watching her eat lunch on her own with that bored expression and her head held high, like anything, absolutely *anything,* was preferable to me. "We were best friends for years and then suddenly that was it! Like we never even happened."

"Because you weren't *you* anymore. You were a completely different person like . . . like——"

"Like I'd been abducted by aliens," I say in realization, the words coming slow and flat. And it all falls into place: why she wouldn't accept my apology, why she wouldn't even let me try. Why we're standing here with nothing between us but an ancient argument.

She looks at me, her expression mutinous, her jaw tight. Like she's daring me to make something of the connection.

I don't even know what to say.

This thing we have, it's like throwing a tangled chain into a drawer, hoping one day it'll come out untangled again: the knot gets even bigger while you're not looking. I couldn't find the right piece to pull, couldn't get a good grip on the links, even if I wanted to. We're just too . . . done.

She takes a breath. Her voice sounds like the edge of a saw. "The way I see it, we weren't ever meant to be friends. Whatever we used to be was . . . accidental or circumstantial or . . ."

It takes me a minute to understand those words, just like if someone punched into your body and ripped out your kidneys, it'd take a while to realize you were bleeding out. So I let her get deep into her bullshit before I manage to interrupt. "What?"

She closes her mouth. The wind howls through the trees.

I repeat, "What did you just say to me?"

She lifts her chin.

Something in the middle of my rib cage snaps. "For fuck's *sake*." I. Am. Too. Hot. I rip the hat off my head and throw it toward the ground. "I can't *stand* you."

My hat hits her in the knee, somehow. She throws it back. Misses me. "Yes! I'm aware!"

"Don't throw my hat!" I shout, and pick it up from the mud, and then accidentally throw it again.

"Fine!" Before I know it, she's crouched down, scooped up a handful of wet mud and rotting leaves and God knows what else, and launched it my way. There's a visceral splat as it hits my chest, and I see satisfaction on her face for about 0.2 seconds before the expression vanishes like a snuffed-out candle. Her jaw drops. Her eyes are wide. She's a bit like that painting, the one with the scream.

I look very, very slowly down at my filthy clothes.

"Brad!" she says, like she doesn't know what *else* to say.

This outfit is pretty fucked now. From head to toe. It's not as if I've never been muddy before—you should see me at Sunday matches—but this isn't a wide-open, manicured field and I am not in uniform. God knows what's hiding in this forest. I've seen *mushrooms* in here. Mushrooms are *fungus*. I am fully contaminated.

"Oh my God," Celine breathes.

Accept the thought, my common sense reminds me.

Right. Yes. On it. I officially accept that I am tragically doomed to contract rabies from the poop-infected unidentified forest mud Celine just threw, and promptly die.

"I'm so sorry!"

Check for distortions.

Okay, fine: it's entirely possible that my imminent death is not a reasonable conclusion to this story. It's also possible that the rabies thing is inaccurate.

Technically. I suppose.

"Brad?"

Refocus.

I tip my head back and count all the branches above me. *I must not fear.*

"Brad, please say something. I'm sorry."

I breathe out once, deliberately, through my mouth. *Only I will remain.*

Okay. Okay. I'm fine.

But Celine looks a bit like she's going to cry. Or maybe that's just the rain. "What?" I demand.

Her eyes widen. "I . . . Do you need . . . Is it . . ."

I bend down, scoop up my own handful of mud, and throw it right back. *Splat.* Now her coat is a mess too.

She stares at me in astonishment for one second, two, three, before her shock fades and the mud fight officially starts.

We abandon the compass and the photo of the map as we chase each other—I don't know who's doing the chasing so don't ask—through the woods. Her aim is better than mine, probably because she played netball for so long. I'm faster than her. She's sneakier, but she has asthma and I'm worried she might run out of oxygen and die in the woods and I'll have to break the news to Neneh. By the time I bring myself to call a truce, we're both caked in mud and I'm really hoping there's a washing machine back at the cabin, or else we are absolutely screwed.

Maybe Celine's thinking the same thing because she leans against a tree and starts to laugh. A small colony of giggles is rushing to escape her chest; hiccups tumble over one another. It's so ridiculous, I laugh, too, and next thing I know we're propping ourselves up against an oak tree, side by side, and—

She runs out of giggles. She has a spot of dry mud just above her eyebrow and her face is so different now, but it's still the same.

I used to think Celine was the prettiest person on the planet.

Best not to think about that now, though.

"If we have to do this whole thing," I tell her, "together—"

She looks away from me when I say that. Tilts her head up to the sky. I keep going anyway.

"I can't spend days at a time fighting with you, Cel."

"Why not?" she murmurs. "It's not like they have TV at the cabin."

I really don't mean to laugh. She's not funny. Can't stand her.

"Bradley——" she says suddenly.

I interrupt. "You're never going to forgive me."

"I'm not the forgiving type," she replies calmly. "I have a dreadful personality."

"You're not supposed to just say that"—I scowl—"like it's okay. You're supposed to regret that you can't be the bigger person."

"Well, I don't," she murmurs. "By the way——"

"I'm not forgiving you either." It's important she knows that. And now she does, so I barrel on to the next part before I can overthink it. "Can we forget it, though?"

Celine blinks. Her face is unreadable. I keep talking, fast.

"I mean, just . . . when we're in places like this. Just act like we're strangers, or something . . . and then . . . it'll be easier," I finish. "When we argue, we distract each other. But we both need to do this, to focus, to succeed." I feel like I woke up in the middle of the night desperate for a wee, and now I'm feeling my way past furniture in the pitch-black with a serious sense of urgency. "Just . . . let's . . . normal?"

Just. Let's. Normal.

Amazing. Absolute round of applause. I will make an incredible barrister, standing solemnly before the judge as I ask: "Just . . . let's . . . innocent?"

"Fine," Celine says suddenly, shockingly. "Whatever. As long as you shut up about it. Now, would you listen to me?" Her *hand——*

Cups my chin.

She's touching me. She's touching me. She——

Pushes my head up.

Her fingertips are damp and freezing and my throat, my face, is on fire—

"See?" she says.

I blink hard.

There's a plastic bag hidden in the tree above us, with a little green booklet inside.

* * *

SUNDAY, 9:20 P.M.

Jordan🖤: Have you killed Celine yet or what

Brad: worse

Brad: much worse

Jordan🖤: YOU KISSED HER DIDN'T YOU

Brad: ????

Brad: no???

Brad: why would you say that?

Brad: Jordan

Brad: JORDAN.

Brad: TEXT ME BACK YOU COWARD.

CHAPTER SIX

CELINE

"That game was completely rigged," I huff.

"You might've mentioned that," Aurora murmurs wryly, "a thousand times or so."

"Yeah, yeah." It's a little past nine and we're holed up in our room trying to ignore the sounds of the other team's common room party. They got back *seven minutes before us,* which is apparently significant enough that they get music and party snacks and we get washing-up duty. Outrageous, if you ask me.

On the plus side, washing up dinner plates doesn't take long when there's ten of you to do it, so I'm already sitting here in my room, moaning while I watch Aurora journal. Analogue hobbies fascinate me. Why write stuff down when you could just film, record a voice-over, and throw some sparkles at it? Then again, Aurora does seem relaxed right now. I crane my neck to stare at the plain brown leather of her scrapbook.

"Does that say *emotional barometer*?" A moment after I ask, I realize it might be an awkward question. Emotions are private; everyone knows that. "You don't have to tell me," I add quickly.

Pink spreads across her nose—and her ears, I notice, because Aurora's ready for bed with her hair in a ponytail, tucked up under the covers. "No, I don't mind," she says shyly. "And yes, it does say *emotional barometer.* I like to track my moods."

Wild. I only have two moods: pissed and fine. "How come?"

She shrugs. "Hormone cycles and stuff. It's nice to know when I'm really sad and when I'm just PMSing."

Well, damn. I stare at her, impressed. "You are so wise. Can I read your palm?"

"Erm," she says. "No, thank you."

It's possible I pout. "Do you bullet journal? Like all those cute Instagram accounts?"

She nods.

"Do you use the pretty tape?"

She nods again.

I am torn apart with jealousy. "I tried to do one of those, but I couldn't choose a color scheme and my bubble writing looked drunk and/or deeply disturbed."

"Maybe you're naturally drawn to a more minimalist style," she says kindly.

I glance down at my pajamas, dark green with spooky yellow mushrooms all over them. "Um. Maybe."

She laughs. "So, what's up with you and Brad?"

At the sound of his name, the air turns solid and still—or maybe that's just me. I feel strange. What happened between us earlier, out in the woods, was weird. I don't want to think about it and I definitely don't want to talk. "Er . . ." I squint, searching for signs of a slight fold in the space-time continuum. "Am I losing time? Did I just slip past a whole conversation where we worked up to this?"

Aurora ducks her head. "No. Sorry. I just . . . I thought I'd ask before I could convince myself not to." She wince-laughs and it is annoyingly charming. I really do like her, even though my fight-or-flight instincts would love to tell her to back off right now.

But that would be immature, and while my mental age *is* stuck around twelve, I need to get better at hiding that if I plan to be a Fabulously Wealthy and Agonizingly Successful Legal Professional. So instead of ignoring her and going huffily to sleep, I arrange the raggedy, off-white duvet more neatly over my lap and mutter, "Just . . . Warm a girl up first, would you?"

Her laugh is cautious this time, like she's worried she's pissed me off. "You don't have to—"

"No, it's fine." I sigh, mostly because I think Aurora is like a cat—very sensitive to bad vibes. I don't want her to think I'm annoyed. I mean, I *am* annoyed, but not with her. Why is everyone bringing the past up today? Her, Brad . . .

Whatever. Who cares? "We go to the same school." But she already knew that after our introductions earlier. I pick at a loose thread on my pajamas.

"Have you known each other long?" She sounds interested, and not in a gossipy way, just a normal, curious way. It occurs to me that no one really knows the full story of Bradley and me. Our parents know the, er, parent-safe parts (you can't tell them *all* your feelings, or they'll get upset; that's just a basic of proper parent-care), and Michaela knows . . . the surface stuff? But I never got into detail with her because by the time we became friends, there wasn't any point. Brad and I hated each other;

everyone knew it; people barely remembered what we'd been before. It was the Mandela Effect; it was a mass hallucination. *Brad and Celine? God, they've been enemies since birth.*

That's not the truth.

I wonder if Brad tells his perfect, plastic friends about the way we used to be. I wonder if he tells his only likeable mate Jordan Cooper about me, and whether they talk about it seriously, the way they sit under that weeping willow on the field and talk about books.

"Our mums are best friends," I explain, "and we're the same age so we were best friends too. We applied to the same secondary school and stuck together, and I was . . . well." I take a breath and when I exhale it shakes. "In primary school, I was the kid everyone made fun of."

"That's rough," Aurora says wryly. "Obviously, *I* can't relate."

After a second of silence, we both burst into laughter. It's the kind that knits your stomach muscles together but releases something deeper. I speak again, and it's easier now. "When I made friends with Brad, I thought we were both . . . you know . . . He's really short-sighted. He got contacts for football, but he used to wear these Coke-bottle glasses, and he had acne." He still gets acne sometimes. He puts these star-shaped stickers on his face and everyone thinks it's mind-blowingly cool, but if I get a single spot (which I do, twice a month, like clockwork), I get comments on TikTok telling me to wash my face. My theory is, there's a special *something* that certain people just have, something that makes everyone around them breathless and witless with adoration. And he has it. He's always had it.

But I'm distracting myself when I should just get this over with. "I assumed we'd be bullied together," I admit, "and I thought we could handle that. We didn't need to, though, because it turns out when Brad is on your side, that stuff just doesn't happen." So guess what happens when he's not on your side?

Yeah.

Oh, well.

"Even back then, no one made fun of him because he was so beautiful——" Shit. I did not mean to say that. "——and charming," I add quickly, smoothly (I hope). "You know how he is. You *like* him."

She's blushing, appropriately shamefaced. "Well, yeah. He's . . ." She waves a hand. "You know."

"Sure," I say dryly. "I know."

"Honest!" she laughs, blushing harder. "He's so honest! You feel how much he means everything, like . . . like he cares about every single word he says to you."

Yeah, I do feel that. It's rocket fuel to the fire when he insults me. But four years ago, he squashed that quality, he squashed *himself,* to fit into a social box that wasn't made for him. Brad is so much more than the popular crowd's Nice Guy or the prettiest girl in school's boyfriend. (Thank God that thing with Isabella Hollis didn't last too long because watching him French-braid her hair in the cafeteria was honestly a gut-wrenching, nauseating *travesty of hygiene* and at one point I was on the verge of *shaving her head* for the good of the school *biosystem* and——)

Anyway. The point is: he was Bradley Fucking Graeme and he was too special to play a crudely drawn role in some tacky 2000s high school movie. But he didn't even know it.

I tried to tell him. But he didn't want to hear.

Silence rings in my ears and I realize I haven't spoken for a while. Instead, I've been sitting here glaring daggers at thin air while Aurora watches me with patience and a hint of alarm. "Sorry," I say, clearing my throat.

"It's okay." She shrugs. "If you went on much longer, I was just gonna push you until you laid down, then turn off the lights."

I snort. "We can go to bed if you want. I know I'm rambling."

"We're *in* bed," she says, stretching pointedly and punching her pillow. "Finish the story. I'll tell you one tomorrow, but it probably won't be half as interesting."

I roll my eyes and lie down, but after a second, I keep talking. I'm not sure if I can stop. I feel like a waterfall. "There's really not much more to say. He decided he wanted us to be normal more than he wanted me to be myself."

I didn't mean to phrase it like that. I always thought my . . . my disgust with Bradley was about his own choices, about principles, not about the fact that he'd wanted something better than me and left when I couldn't be it.

I remember what he said today, though: *My therapist said you were controlling.* I might've been more offended if I didn't think he was right. Sometimes—not so much now, but a lot when I was younger—I felt like one of those little kids who squeezes a doll so tight its head pops off. No one wants to be left, right? But I've always been OTT, so I don't want to be left *on pain of death.* I'm better now. But I do remember how I used to be.

So maybe it's a good thing Bradley ditched me before I could squeeze his head off. Maybe that's why I agreed when he asked me today if we could be kind of, sort of, temporarily okay.

"When did all this happen?" Aurora asks quietly.

"When we were thirteen or fourteen. It was snowing, so . . . just after my birthday, I think."

"Huh," Aurora says, thoughtful. She glances in my direction, eyebrows raised, her eyes big and reflective in the lamplight. "Capricorn?"

"Obviously." I squint at her. "Aquarius?"

"Scorpio," she says calmly, as if that's not the shock of the season. I'm so busy absorbing the implications that it takes me a second to ask, "Wait, when's your birthday?"

"Friday," she says. "You know, fourteen is such a—"

"Friday?! We're going to be *here* on Friday!"

She blinks slowly. "Yes, I know."

"You're turning eighteen *here*!"

"Yep. But we were talking about—"

"Who cares what we were talking about?" I yelp. "What are we doing for your birthday?"

She blushes as red as Rudolph's nose but stays firm. "You're doing a very good job of avoiding the topic," she says severely, "but not good enough."

I open my mouth, then close it. Surprise. Birthday surprise for Aurora. That's my plan, because no one should turn eighteen while stuck in the woods away from her friends and family, but especially not Aurora. She's so *sweet*. She's so *lovely*. She's like everything I wanted to be as a child before I grew up and realized I was an incurable cow and it might be genetic. A birthday surprise is happening because she *deserves* it—

But I need to lull her into a false sense of security. "Right. Er. What were we saying?"

"You and Brad," she reminds me, "being fourteen and stupid."

I snort.

"I would've given a lot to be normal at that age," she says pensively.

"You are normal."

"Not really. Which is fine, I know that now. But when I was younger . . ." She glances at me. "I have celiac. Did I mention that? No gluten. I was diagnosed a couple of years ago. But before that, I was always sick and sore and stumbling all over the place, and everyone thought I was a complete freak, and I thought they were right. I just wanted people to like me. Everyone else had friends. What was wrong with me?" She shrugs while my heart calmly shatters.

I've never minded people saying I'm annoying or weird or a bitch because I don't think those things about myself are bad. It never occurred to me that some people deal with the weight of everyone else's judgment *and* their own. That never occurred to me at all.

"But I have friends now," she continues. "And I know they're worth more than all the people who were . . . who were casually cruel to me, because they're deliberately kind, and that makes them better people. My kind of people. Except I had to *learn* that. Don't we all have to learn that?"

I huff and turn my pillow over. "So what are you saying—Brad was unfortunately deprived of his *learning* years because he's tragically gorgeous and charming?"

Aurora grins. "I didn't say that. You said that."

I throw my pillow at her. "Not buying it."

Because that can't be enough. *Surely* that can't be enough for the way he made me feel.

And the way you made him *feel . . .*

Was justified. It was.

But only if he's the enemy.

And apparently, out here at least, he's not.

* * *

BRAD

Our second day of the BEP is spent being lectured on the contents of our little green books (the short version is: DO NOT EAT 99 PERCENT OF THE PLANT LIFE AND DO NOT PLAY WITH FOXES) and learning all kinds of safety survival stuff we'll need to remember for our next expedition. I don't insult Celine. She doesn't insult me. In fact, we don't talk at all, nor do we glare holes into each other's skulls. It's all completely normal and healthy and very boring.

Success, I suppose.

On the plus side, freeing up the brainpower I usually spend on pissing her off has helped me think about my novel a lot more. On the minus side, I'm mostly thinking about how bad it is and how I'm never going to finish it, rather than useful stuff like, you know, working on the plot.

On our third day, rain falls again to match my attitude, and Victor gleefully drags us outside to perform manual labor. (I'm no therapist but I'm pretty sure he has issues.)

"Can you hold on to this?" I ask Raj, trying to hammer our final tent peg into the soggy grass.

He crouches down at my side and grimaces, which is basically all he's been doing since we were paired off and given our tent. "You're not gonna bonk my fingers, are you?"

"I might."

"I'm an artist, Brad. I need these fingers. Break them and I will sue."

"It's a soft mallet, Raj," I tell him. "Get a grip." Then I bonk his fingers on purpose.

He collapses into the mud (it's fascinating, really; he doesn't even seem to hesitate) and howls, "Betrayal!"

I bonk his head.

"Violence! Vicious, relentless—"

"Everything all right over here, boys?" Zion asks pointedly, looming over us like a tablet-wielding god when, in reality, he's five years older than us, max.

Raj pops up like a daisy, brighter than today's cloud-covered sun. "Yes, sir, Zion, sir. Tent's almost up. Pegs behaving. Everything's in order. If you ask me, I think we're doing a cracking job."

Zion rolls his eyes and taps at his tablet as he leaves. Shit. Did he at least notice what an effective leader I'm being today? Probably not, since I was leading via mallet attack.

"Oops," Raj says. "That probably wasn't very committed of us."

"Nope," I agree. My eyes flicker across the tent-dotted clearing without permission, and I catch a glimpse of Celine. Her tent's been up for ages. She's now helping everyone else put up theirs, showing both leadership and team-building skills.

If I don't get this scholarship and Celine does, I'm going to shave off my hair and eat it.

"Hey," Raj says, dragging my attention back to our sad excuse for a tent. He pushes the peg into the grass. "How's this?"

"Wrong. You're supposed to hold it at a forty-five-degree angle."

"I thought it was a ninety-degree angle?"

"No," I say patiently, "the *guide ropes* loop into the *pegs* at a ninety-degree angle. The pegs—"

"Come on, Brad," he interrupts, "just whack the peg for me. You can do it."

I wave the damp scrap of paper that passes as the instructions. "I know you read this, because you got muddy fingerprints all over it—"

"Ouch."

"—so you must realize the numbers were very clear. Forty. Five. Degrees. We have to do it right or it'll . . . collapse! In the night!"

"Brad, we're not sleeping in these tents tonight."

"No," I say seriously, "but it's the principle of the thing."

"Fiiiiiiine," he says, and takes the sheet, squinting at the diagram. I only realize I'm smiling when the rain streams around my cheeks instead of down them. "All right, how's this?"

I want to appreciate the effort, but mentally, I'm questioning his eyesight.

He catches my expression and adjusts his grip again.

I wonder if he's ever studied angles in his life.

"Bloody hell," he laughs, "*you* hold it, then!"

That's not a bad idea. We switch jobs, and he only bonks my fingers eight or nine times.

Once the tent is up, we crawl inside it to admire our handiwork. I eye his muddy walking boots, and he kicks them off before they can spoil our beautiful shiny plastic floor. "Not bad," he announces.

"Not *good,* either," I allow. The right side of our tent's inner lining dips drunkenly toward the floor.

"Rubbish. This is a feature, not a bug." Raj ducks under it and disappears behind a swathe of blue fabric. "Privacy compartment. Now I can get changed without you clocking my six-pack and getting jealous."

"Wow, thank God for that. Did we remember to hook all the

clips to the outer lining?" I ask, trying to sound unsuspicious and nonjudgmental.

His head reappears, brown eyes huge and innocent. "You must have forgotten, Brad. That's okay. I don't mind."

I laugh. A lot.

When we crawl out again, Celine's there. Okay, not *there*—she's a few meters away, being all perfect and impressive. I watch as she helps a sunny Irish Traveller girl named Mary wrestle a tent key into a pole.

"Don't be scared of it," Celine says firmly. "It's not going to break."

"It'll break my damn nose if I let go," Mary huffs.

"Then don't let go," is Celine's sweet-as-honey response. She doesn't seem bothered by the rain; she's taken her coat off and wrapped it around her waist. Her hoodie's unzipped and her collarbone is gleaming wet. A few braids have slipped out of her ponytail but her black eyeliner—two wings per eye, like a butterfly—is sharp and clean and as unbothered as she is.

"Mate," Raj says in this very weird tone of voice, "isn't that your cousin?"

"No," I reply, watching Celine corral tent poles as if they were rogue boa constrictors.

"Oh." He sounds relieved but still dubious. Relubious. "It's just, Thomas said—"

"No," I repeat. Sorry, Thomas, but the cousin lie is no longer working for me. I blink, realize I'm staring, and turn away.

"But you do know her?" Raj asks, watching me with this one-sided, flickering smile.

"No. I mean, yeah. Yeah, I know her. We go to the same school, remember?" And that's it. She's not even *talking* to me, so I'm definitely not thinking about her. I know I asked if we could be normal—which, in hindsight, seems like such a pathetic attempt at begging for friendship—and she said yes, but I bet she regrets it. I bet it didn't feel like her heart was a fist unclenching. I bet she's going to come over here and say—

"Bradley?"

My head jerks up. Celine.

"Can we talk?"

I ignore her butterfly eyes and nod. "Okay."

Raj grins as Celine and I crawl into the tent.

Inside, Celine headbutts the saggy part of our roof like a fault-seeking missile and looks at me. "Um."

"Don't judge."

She rolls her eyes, but the action is more amused than scathing. Weird. Very weird.

"I thought you were pissed at me," I blurt, then instantly regret it. Why would I mention that? I could honestly sink into a hole.

Celine blinks and echoes my thoughts. "Why?"

"We didn't talk. Yesterday."

Her brow furrows, like you could press a fingertip between her eyes and smooth the creases out. In this shadowy, raindrop-stained blue universe, she is very soft and dark, like falling into bed at night after a long, hard day. "I didn't think we needed to talk. You said . . . *not-enemies.*"

So she wasn't ignoring me—just being infuriatingly literal and pragmatic and other Celine-like qualities. "Typical. I put my pride on the line to negotiate an historic peace treaty and you can't even tell me good morning?"

"Do you hear yourself?" she asks me curiously. "Like, when you speak? Or is it just noise?"

I'm going to strangle her.

"Why do you look like you've got gas?" she asks.

I rub a hand over my face. "You know what I admire about you, Celine? Your class and sophistication."

She snorts. "Bite me."

"No, it's impressive. You're like a debutante, or something. If I didn't know any better, I'd think you'd gone to finishing school."

Her laughter is unexpected and tastes like treacle and it does not implode reality. I wait for something, anything, to come along and sour this conversation, making us utter and abject enemies again, but nothing happens. My palms start to itch.

Her smile fades. "Hey," she says awkwardly. "Um. So, I want your . . . advice?"

In my head, I collapse from shock and Celine holds smelling salts under my nose. Out loud, I say, "Makes sense. I am wiser and smarter than you and always knew this day would come."

"Would you like to see the pictures I took of my tent?" she asks sweetly, tapping her phone. "Holly poked her head in and said it was perfect. I assume she then emailed Katharine Breakspeare about how I'm a shining example of teamwork, leadership, and strategy."

"All right, Celine, give it a rest." I tut at my saggy privacy curtain. "Raj says it's a feature, not a bug."

"Raj says a lot of things. He's incurably positive."

"Just so you know," Raj calls, "I can hear you out here. Like, you do realize tents are not made of brick walls?"

We ignore him. Celine reaches up and starts fixing my saggy

tent. She seems to be hooking bits and pieces together through the fabric. If we were more than distant acquaintances, I might be impressed by her never-ending competence.

She turns her head and catches me staring. My cheeks feel flammable. What's wrong with me today?

But clearly Celine doesn't think anything of it, because she just jerks her chin as if to draw me closer. I crawl over until we're a foot apart. There's a tiny dot of mascara under her lower lashes, and she whispers to me. "It's Aurora's eighteenth on Friday."

I watch her mouth moving for a second before the words sink in. "What? Oh. Really? That's rough." Imagine turning eighteen out here, sleeping on a borrowed mattress in a room with very old carpet that probably hasn't been shampooed for months or even years. It's tragic. Like, literally Shakespearean.

". . . lovely," Celine is saying, "so I want to do something for her, but I'm not sure . . . I'm not really . . . My ideas all seem . . ." She fumbles her words in a deeply un-Celine-like manner, and I try not to smile. She's like a toddler who's still learning to verbalize feelings. The urge to squeeze her around the middle is therefore completely normal.

"Yeah?" I ask, still not smiling. "All your ideas seem what?"

She scowls in response. The tent is fixed and officially Celine-standard. "Oh, never mind."

"Go on."

"It's nothing," she snaps, turning to crawl away.

Well, now I feel bad. "Hey, hang on . . ." I don't realize I'm touching her until it's already done. My hand is on her upper arm and I only have a split second to shrivel inside with the sheer awkwardness of it all before I let go.

Her arm is really soft. Silk-soft. Cloud-soft. Honestly, who has skin like that?

I clear my throat and close my hand into a fist. "Just . . . what were you planning to do? For Aurora?"

She eyes me warily. "I want to throw her a party. On Friday. After curfew."

"Sorry, what?" I splutter. "A *party*? *You?*"

"Will you *lower* your *voice?*"

Good point. I continue winding her up at a lower volume. "An illicit, illegal, after-hours—"

"It's not *illegal,* Bradley, come on."

"We can't be in each other's rooms after curfew," I remind her.

"Yes," she says tightly, "I realize that. But Zion says they can get a cake from Tesco Express for after dinner, but anything more is out of the question because then everyone would need one for their birthdays. Obviously I said no because that sucks, and anyway, I don't want to invite everyone—"

Ah, the sheer Celine-ness of that statement. Some things never change.

"—so I thought we could just have a very small but very good *secret* surprise party, except I don't go to that many parties and obviously you do." Her tone implies that my regular presence at social gatherings is unspeakably disgusting, but I let that slide.

"Let me get this straight. You—*you*—are planning to break the rules to make sure Aurora has a decent eighteenth birthday. And you're asking me to help."

Celine is wary again, like I might laugh, or refuse, or bite her. I'm not going to do any of those things. I couldn't if I wanted to, because I'm too busy grappling with this unwelcome reminder of what a good friend she can be. She doesn't care about people easily, but once you've got her, you've got her.

Until you give her up.

There's a hollow space in my stomach that feels a lot like regret.

"Well?" she asks, eyebrows raised.

"I don't know," I say, folding my arms, drawing this out. She wants my help. She wants *my* help. "What'll you give me in return?"

"Here." She opens her hand and blows softly across her palm. I feel her breath against my cheek.

The hollow in my stomach sort of . . . hops, like a little kid on a playground. Am I breathing loud? Or is it just the trapped air in this tent? "What . . . what was that?" I ask. My tongue feels heavy.

She smiles, so sweetly. "Those were all the fucks I had to give, Bradley." Then she shows me her middle finger and goes to crawl out of the tent.

I'm laughing so hard, I can barely speak. "Of course I'll help. Celine! Come on, come back."

The miracle is, she does.

CHAPTER SEVEN

CELINE

What does *not-enemies* even mean? Clearly it's a matter of opinion, but I know my stance: there's a lot of people in this world, and you can't just categorize them as yes or no, friend or foe. There must be shades, gradients, in-between phases, because absolute trust leads to absolute heartbreak. You can't pull the rug out from under me if I've barely stepped on it in the first place.

All of which is to say, Brad and I might be not-enemies, but that doesn't mean we're *friends.* I should keep him well beyond arm's length.

Instead, I asked him to arrange a party.

> **Minnie:** . . . You asked WHO?

> **Celine:** Well he's the only person I know here!!!
> I had no choice!!!!!!

Minnie: FT me it's urgent

Celine: NO. I will see you next week Michaela

Minnie: WHAT IS IN THE WATER OVER THERE

I don't know! It just happened! The last party *I* organized was Michaela's seventeenth and all I had to do was get us tickets to an under-eighteens night at Rescue Rooms and buy her some birthstone jewelry. I think she had a good time at the club, but there's no Rescue Rooms in the woods, and I don't have time to buy Aurora a birthstone—

And Brad goes to parties constantly, according to a few clips I might have accidentally seen on a friend of a friend's Instagram Story, so asking for his help made sense. Letting him take over the entire thing completely, however, makes no sense at all.

Now it's Friday night, I have no idea what the plan is, and I'm trying to explain to Aurora why she shouldn't take her makeup off yet even though we're both in our pajamas and it's way past curfew.

"But I'll get foundation on my pillow," she says doubtfully.

"So don't lie down," I advise.

She looks at me like my head's fallen off. "It's bedtime, Celine."

Well, yes, it is. And she seems pleased enough with the card I made her and the gluten-free cream cakes I managed to trade off of Mary (RIP to my sparkly chili-shaped hair slide), so perhaps the whole party idea is way OTT and I've made a mistake. I'm wondering how to tell Brad this entire thing is off when someone knocks very, very quietly at our door.

Crap. It's too late. I cast a nervous glance at Aurora as I tip-toe to answer it. She *is* a Scorpio; I know she has hidden depths.

Hinges squeak, carpet sticks, and I grunt as I wrestle with the ancient handle. Then Sophie and Raj pop their heads into our room. I have very little idea what Brad's planned (he's been annoyingly secretive), but I assume these two are part of it, because Raj cranes his neck to look past me, lays eyes on Aurora, and grins. "All right, birthday girl?"

"What are you doing here?" Aurora whispers, getting up. "It's well after curfew. We're supposed to—"

"Live a little," Sophie advises firmly. Her hair has given up on the sleek and glossy vibe, and her pajamas have Lilo and Stitch on the front, but nothing else has changed since we met during orienteering—she's still intimidatingly athletic and exudes bad-bitch energy, and I love it. "Aurora, come on," she says with authority, and after a moment's pause and a questioning glance at me, Aurora does indeed come on.

I ignore a tiny wobble of rule-breaking anxiety and follow.

The corridor is dark, dashes of moonlight jumping through the infrequent windows. I can't hear anything but the standard, ghostly howl that deserted woodland locations do so well. We creep and crab-walk through the halls, coming to a dorm near the back of the building, where Raj gives a soft, rhythmic knock like we're sneaking into a speakeasy. The door creaks open to reveal a slice of warm light and Thomas's thin, freckled face. "What's that knock for?"

"It's code," Raj says.

"*Code*." Thomas snorts like a very cut-glass-sounding horse. "Hey, happy birthday, Rory."

"Erm," Aurora says.

"Hi, Celine." He grins at me.

I wince and attempt a wave. Then the door opens fully and . . .

For a second, my jaw drops and my heart rises. This is . . . this is so cute I might die. There's a purple HAPPY BIRTHDAY banner strung up on the wonky curtain pole, blankets and pillows piled on the floor, pink and purple paper butterfly confetti everywhere. One of the beds is covered in cans of Coke and Sprite and packets of popcorn, and on the desk, there is a single can of gin and tonic beside a Tupperware box. Brad is perched on the second bed in blue, button-up pajamas and a beaming smile. He did this. Because I asked him to.

"Oh my God," Aurora says, her voice a whisper. "Is this for *me*?"

Correction: I meant that Brad did this for Aurora, obviously. Well, good. She looks so happy, I raise my phone and take a picture—which, yeah, Celine, what a great idea: document your rule-breaking with photographic evidence. I honestly can't stand myself sometimes.

But she's really pretty when she smiles, so I take another one and then I take one of the whole bedroom for good measure.

"Is that *alcohol*?" Sophie demands.

"For legal reasons," Brad says, "I can neither confirm nor deny."

Raj says, "I had no idea Aurora's birthday was an issue of legal contention," and Aurora giggles.

Then Brad blurts out for absolutely no reason, "This was Celine's idea, by the way."

What? Why isn't he taking credit? I glare at him, suspicious. He smiles sunnily back. Aurora's nose turns fire-engine red and her eyes get very big and—

"Celine."

—she holds out her arms and emotes all over me. I bear it heroically and try not to panic about liking her so much after less than a week of acquaintance.

The truth is, I realize, as we all curl up on the floor and the snacks are shared out, that I like almost everyone in this room too much. And by the way they talk to me and hand me the Vanilla Coke when I ask and so on and so forth, I think they . . . maybe . . . like me too?

It's strange, because for me, building friendships usually takes a few months. And a great deal of exertion. And maybe a cappuccino or five to keep my energy up, and also, the people I befriend have to be okay with the fact that I am excessively sarcastic and frequently mean, which most people are not okay with at all.

So this whole situation? Way too easy.

"Celine," Bradley says from beside me. "It's a party. Stop glaring at the wallpaper."

I try not to jump—when did he get off the bed?—and take a sip of my Coke. Everyone else is focused on Aurora. No one's watching us. "This is . . . really great," I whisper. "You did . . . good. Th-thanks."

He leans in closer. He smells like the Dove soap my mum bought in bulk on sale last month. "What was that?"

I scowl. "What?"

"What you just said. It sounded like . . . th . . . thaaaa . . ."

"Thanks," I snap, knowing very well I am the most ridiculous person on planet Earth. There's nothing wrong with thanking him! He did exactly what I asked—more than, really—and he did it well, and I'm grateful, and I have no idea why acknowledging all that out loud feels like a slippery slope into a dark and dangerous forest, but I am not Little Red Riding Hood and he's no wolf. I'm not scared of him. So I lift my chin and repeat in a calm, mature manner, "Thank you very much, Bradley. You've done a wonderful job."

He squints at me. "Where's that G and T? Have you had it? You have, haven't you?"

I flick him in the ribs and stick out my tongue without hesitation. This is coming back to me like a dance I can't forget, but there's too many spins and I can't tell if I'm giddy or nauseous.

"Yeah, mate, how'd you get your hands on booze?" Raj interjects, grabbing the can off the desk. "And what's— Are these cupcakes?" He's peering into the Tupperware.

"Lay off," Thomas says, snagging the box, "they're for Aurora."

"There's six. What's she going to do, scoff them all down and laugh at our pain?"

"My dad made them," Brad says. "They're gluten-free."

Aurora sucks in a delighted breath and snatches the box faster than a seagull stealing a chip.

Meanwhile, I'm eyeing Brad incredulously. "Don't tell me your dad brought the G and T too." I won't believe it. I think I've mentioned before that Trevor is a Good Man. He's very like Bradley in that way: annoying.

"No," Brad admits. "I got Dad to make the cupcakes and told him Giselle would pick them up. Met her at the edge of the woods earlier. She brought everything else."

My jaw drops. "You engaged in a clandestine woodland drug deal with *my sister*?"

"It's not a *drug deal,* Celine. She gave me a *cocktail* for *free.*"

"Why?" I demand. "She doesn't even like you!"

"Newsflash," Brad says like an early 2000s TV script, "your entire family loves me. You're the only one who needs to get with the program." He looks at the others, and I realize with a stomach thud of embarrassment that I forgot they were there. "It's only for Aurora, though," he continues, deadly serious. "I crossed my heart."

"You're adorable," Sophie tells him.

He blinks rapidly, then smiles like a ditsy cherub. His neck goes splotchy red. Ridiculous, if you ask me. Why don't they just make out right here on the floor?

"Do you want it?" Raj asks Aurora. "It's okay if you don't. I'm eighteen too. I can drink it."

"Are you?" Thomas asks.

"In spirit," Raj replies.

"That does *not* count—"

"I want it," Aurora interjects, and we all whisper-cheer when she pops the tab and takes a sip. Then someone passes around the cupcakes, and from that point on, it's really a party.

• • •

BRAD

We stay up until my eyes feel gritty and everyone forgets to speak softly, lying on the blanket-smothered floor like sausages in an oven tray. Sophie is on my left. I have a crick in my neck because I haven't turned to my right in about an hour, but I know Celine is still there; I can hear her arguing with Thomas about Kanye West. Joking around. Or at least, she was.

Now she's rolling over, her body bumping into mine as she moves.

She flicks the back of my head. "Hey."

When I turn to face *her*, it is a very serious and stately roll in which zero part of my body touches any part of her body. She should take notes. It's deeply impolite to brush your elbow against someone else's back; that someone else might accidentally suffer a momentary but overwhelming neurological collapse. "Yes, Celine?" I ask pleasantly.

She eyes me like I demanded we fight to the death. "What's up with you?"

"Nothing's up with me."

"Then why are you being so quiet?"

"I had no idea you could hear my quietness over the sound of you and Thomas——" *Flirting,* I was going to say, but my brain remembers just in time that pointing out someone else's flirting is pretty much its own form of flirting, unless you're talking to a friend. Me and Celine aren't friends.

She arches a single eyebrow. "Me and Thomas what?"

"Geeking out over ancient hip-hop," I say, because my modus operandi is very simple: when in doubt, piss her off.

She is beautifully predictable. *"Ancient?"* Her eyes are wide with outrage and her nostrils flare. "We listened to *Yeezus* together. How ancient could it be?!"

"If you have to go back to 2013 to think of his last decent album——"

"I don't," she says hotly.

"Then what are we talking about *Yeezus* for?"

"What are you tormenting me for?"

I grin, genuinely amazed. "Celine. I think you've just reached a new level of social awareness. You *know* when I'm winding you up."

She punches me in the arm. Well, *punch* is a strong word, but the point is, her fist meets my bicep.

Then she props herself up on one elbow and leans over me, and I realize she's going to punch my other arm too. She's going to help me feel balanced, the way she used to. One of her braids brushes my neck. Something weird and tight and up and down happens in my chest. Her eyes meet mine. They're so dark I can see myself and I look winded.

"Um," she whispers.

"Is not a word," I whisper back.

Her hesitation dissolves into a reluctant tilt of the lips and she does it. She punches my other arm to even out the sensations. Then she lies back down beside me, and I try not to have feelings and monumentally fail.

Celine used to do anything I asked her to do. We're lying here like different coins, but for years of my life we were two sides of the same. She had my back and I had hers.

"I . . ." I clear my throat, fumbling for words. "I don't usually . . . need that anymore."

Her eyes shift away from mine to stare up at the ceiling. "Sorry," she says lightly, as if it doesn't matter, which means it does. She's embarrassed.

"No, I—" *liked it.* The words get tangled at the back of my throat, and then Sophie speaks to me, and the moment is gone.

"Brad, what about you?"

"What?" Her, Aurora, and Raj are all sitting up, looking at me expectantly. I sit up too. We all do. The too-soft, too-close feeling dissolves and this time, when she moves, Celine doesn't touch me again.

"What do you want the scholarship for?" Sophie asks, nudging my shoulder with hers.

"Oh. Er . . . law." Or rather, for solo housing while I study law.

Aurora seems interested. "Really? What field?"

Is that the sort of thing you're meant to know at seventeen? I haven't really thought about it. I bet Celine knows. I plaster on my best and brightest smile and hold up a hand. "Whoa, hold on a second—I want to know about you. What do you want it for?"

Aurora's nose turns red. "Oh, um," she says, "I want to go to art school. So does Raj."

"Graphic design," he says, "and marketing. Aurora's doing *fine art*."

"If I get in," she mutters.

"Of course you'll get in," Sophie says firmly. "You're very talented—"

Aurora blinks. "But you haven't seen any of my—"

"And you're a BEP Explorer. Done deal."

Have I mentioned how much I like Sophie? "What about you?" I ask her.

She smiles almost shyly and adjusts the scarf covering her hair. "Oh, well, I want to study politics and international relations. Not sure what I'll do with it yet, but . . ."

It's a good degree, I think. *Stable job opportunities.*

"The world is at a crossroads," she says. "Nation-states can't effectively combat global problems, but climate change and waning resources are some of the most pressing issues we have. I don't know. Just . . . someone needs to do something." She shrugs. "Lots of someones."

Well, spit in my eye and call me a shallow bastard.

"Celine?" Sophie asks.

Here we bloody go. "I'm studying law," Celine says.

"You're going to be just like Katharine," Thomas murmurs dreamily. I really wish he'd get a grip. (For his own good, obviously.)

Celine smiles, not in the cautious, begrudging way she does with me, but like a pageant queen humbly accepting her bouquet. "Nooo. Oh my God. I *do* admire her a lot. . . . That suit against Harkness Oil?" Celine shakes her head in worshipful awe. "But I have a long, *long* way to go before I could do something like that."

A crease forms between Thomas's ginger eyebrows. "Didn't she lose the Harkness Oil suit? Am I remembering wrong?" He is clearly tortured by the fact he's had to question the almighty HowCelineSeesIt.

"Oh, technically she lost it." Celine nods. "It was unwinnable. But that's not the point. The point is someone embarrassed them. Someone took a billion-pound company to task and drew the world's eyes to their behavior. And the victims did get settlements out of court. She helped people and she changed public perception—which has such a huge impact on long-term governance, you know?"

Sophie is nodding wisely. "It's all about chipping away at big structures."

"Exactly," Celine agrees, and the two have an eyeball-based communion of the soul right over my head.

"So, you want to go into human rights law like Katharine?" Aurora asks.

Celine's blissed-out expression shutters with a blink. "No. No, I'm . . . going to try corporate law." She studies her nails, and I think maybe I'm not the only imposter in this room.

"Huh," Sophie says after a moment. "So—" Her phone vibrates in her hand, three times fast, and she breaks off with a frown. "Shit. Guys."

"What?" I crane my neck to read over her shoulder. She tilts the screen in my direction.

> **Mary:** don't be mad but I told Allen about the party and I think he snitched

> **Mary:** just heard Holly & Zion in the hall

• • •

CELINE

If I weren't so busy panicking, I'd be flattered by the fact that Sophie turns to me first. "Do you think we have time to go back?"

Absolutely not. We are screwed screwed screwed, doomed to zeroes on the Matrix at best, and my stomach is sloshing around like an ocean of nerves. "No," I manage. *Why* did I think this was a good idea? WHY? I blame Bradley.

"All right." Sophie looks grimly around the room. "Everyone and everything under the bed."

"Seriously?" Thomas huffs. "Under the bed?"

"Got a better idea?"

"It's just a party!" He scowls.

"Cheer up," Aurora cuts in. "This is an experience. We're living life on the edge."

Raj shakes his head and points at her. "We'll talk about your secret daredevilry later." When she giggles—*giggles*—in response, he grins. "Or we could talk now. How do you feel about motorbikes?"

"I—"

"Guys," Brad says mildly. He has none of Sophie's authority, and he's not glaring at anyone the way Thomas is, but for some reason Raj and Aurora snap out of it and everyone gets their shit together. In a whirl of panic, we rip banners off the wall and stuff crisp packets into dark and dingy corners. Sophie drops a cupcake and mutters, "RIP, man. We barely ate ye." Then she brushes it, crumbs and all, under the bed, and Brad very quietly goes into cardiac arrest. Everyone's laughing and nervous and breathless right up until the moment we hear a door creak down the hall and a low, rapid-fire murmur that sounds disturbingly like Zion.

They're close. Too close. And I'm convinced this place is obviously occupied and smells like a gin factory. Raj is still wrestling with all the blankets we laid out. I'm stuffing chocolate out of sight and wondering if Brad brought any scented candles (I wouldn't put it past him; he's very particular about his space), when I notice everyone's finally leaping for their hiding places. And I realize that, duh—

I'm not going to fit under a bed.

They're already low to the ground, I'm pretty sure the mattresses sag when you sit on them, and we have to crawl under in pairs. Long story short, that narrow dark space does not look like a *Celine*-sized space and—

"Cel," Brad whispers.

I whip around to find him standing by the open window. "What are you doing? Get in bed—"

"Get out here," he says.

It's dark outside. Dark on dark on dark, in fact: black night, plus blacker shapes that could be trees but could also be seventy-foot-tall murderers; the jury is out. "Are you taking the piss?" I demand.

There's another murmur from the hallway, louder this time.

I jerk closer to Brad, closer to the cold-as-space window.

"I know why you're here," he says. "I saw your dad on the leaflet. You can't get thrown off the program."

"What?" The blood in my veins turns to liquid mortification. My pulse is slow. My tongue has weight. "I . . . don't . . . It's—"

"Get out," he says, pushing me through the window, his hand on my hip.

There's a knock at the door. My feet touch damp grass. Then the window snaps shut, and I very much realize that I am out-side. In the dark. Barefoot. *In my pajamas.*

He's locked me out here. He doesn't have to let me back in. I could lose toes to frostbite or . . . or have to walk around to the front of the building and get caught sneaking inside, and it would all be revenge for every time I implied Bradley was shallow or snide or just not good enough, and maybe I'd even deserve it. Maybe I'd deserve it because—

"Yeah?" I hear Thomas say, his voice thick with faux sleep. These windows must be paper thin.

Holly's voice is soft from the other side of the door. "Okay in there, guys?"

"Yeah," Thomas repeats.

"I heard you might be having a little shindig," Zion says lightly, as if a warm and encouraging tone will lead Thomas to confess all.

"Um, no," Thomas says with the perfect touch of bafflement, "I don't think so . . ."

Silent. Everyone, everything, is silent. I hold my breath for way too long before Zion replies, "All right, then. Night."

My heart rate begins to slow, despite the very creepy hooting going on in the MASSIVE GODDAMN FOREST BEHIND ME. I don't think Brad's going to leave me out here. Which is a strange realization to have, when I've spent so long thinking of him as evil incarnate.

I lean back against the roughly textured wall of the cabin. At least the star-studded sky is pretty. If I had my phone, I could film this for a video about spooky season folklore, but I don't, so I just stuff my hands under my shirt to keep them warm and wait for Brad to let me back in.

Thirty-six clouds have passed over the moon and I've thought about being dragged off into the woods by a hot werewolf nine times before the window clicks and eases open. I whip around and Brad's eyes are somehow bright in the dark, gleaming like ink. "Celine," he whispers, and I feel his breath on my cheek. Then the thirty-seventh cloud moves, and moonlight floods the space between us, and he realizes I'm standing approximately 3.2 centimeters away. "Oh." He pulls back hard. There's a pause before he's right there again—not his face, but his hands, and they're even warmer than they were before, red-hot. "Celine," he says, "you're freezing."

I bump my head on the window. "Shit."

"Shhhh," someone tells me in the dark.

Brad tuts over his shoulder. "Shut up. She's cold." He turns back to me. The way I clamber into the room is not exactly graceful. He catches me when I stumble. I tread on his toes. Instead of collapsing in agony, he says, "Your feet are wet."

"Um."

"Sit down." He pushes me toward the bed. I half land on Aurora—I can tell it's her because she's incredibly bony and because she squeaks "Ouch" like a little mouse.

"Sorry," I whisper, then jump out of my skin when Brad drops to his knees in front of me. "Bradley. What are you going to do? Dry my feet with your hair?"

"Shut up," he mutters, and drags a blanket from somewhere and *touches my feet*. Well, he pats them awkwardly with the blanket, but still. I think I am going to pass out. My stomach isn't in knots; it's in bows that loop and unloop with every heartbeat.

Okay, so I have a theory: Bradley Graeme isn't two people, two faces, a best friend and an enemy. He is just one person, just one face. The other is smoke and mirrors.

Time to prove which is which. And maybe prove myself a complete and utter monster in the process.

"Aren't you two cousins?" Thomas demands in the dark.

Solemnly, Aurora says, "They're a very close family."

"Aurora!" Raj is clearly delighted. "God, I enjoy you."

Sophie snorts. "That's one way of putting it."

Another cloud passes over the moon. When Brad looks up and grins at me, I smile back.

• • •

Brad: hey

Brad: 😔🎈

Brad: 👆 guess who that is

Celine: Why are u texting me rn. We are like ten feet apart and we're meant to be building a fire.

Brad: just guess

Celine: idk

Brad: it's Holly

Brad: on her birthday

Celine: I should never have given you my new number

NOVEMBER

CHAPTER EIGHT

CELINE

The Thursday after our first BEP expedition, I'm back in the Beech Hut (was school always this bland and gray?) trying to halt Minnie's meltdown. "I'm sure you did amazing yesterday."

"And I'm sure I *didn't*." Her voice is quiet because it's mid-afternoon and the building's at least half full, but she's shouting at me in spirit if not in volume. Her eyes are wide. Her hair is especially big today and vibrating with panic. "I was about as graceful as a newborn giraffe."

I blink. "Is that . . . bad, or . . . ?"

She throws up her hands and sinks into a patented Michaela Digby sulk: crossed arms and a toddler-like scowl. Not that it's unwarranted: Edge Lake is one of the best dance schools in the country, and Minnie's been nervous about her audition for months. "I'm doomed. Mr. Darling was right. They're going to reject my application, and I won't have the grades for a proper degree—"

"Dance *is* a proper degree," I say firmly.

"—and I'll die alone under a bridge. Probably *before* twenty-five."

I like Mr. Darling (kind of) but if he doesn't stop being so negative all the time, he's going to send us all into a collective depression. "Rubbish. You must be hungry. Do you want my emergency Mars bar?"

"I'm in turmoil, Celine," she growls. "How could anyone eat at a time like this?"

I shrug and take the chocolate bar out of my pencil case. "Suit yourself."

She snatches it out of my hand. "I didn't say *no*."

"Good. Now, Michaela." I'm supposed to be answering comments on my latest TikTok (reviewing a selection of mood rings from various questionable internet stores), but I lock my phone and put it facedown to show her I mean business. "I don't want to hear another Mr. Darling quote out of your mouth," I tell her seriously. "Okay? Is that the energy you want to sully your consciousness with? Mr. *Darling's*?"

Minnie shakes her head and takes a bite of the Mars bar.

"I should think not. No wonder you felt giraffe-like yesterday! His bad attitude was poisoning your mind."

She nods, a little more hopeful. "That's true. That's very true. I'm not a giraffe. It's all his fault."

"Exactly," I say. "You are a swan. A beautiful, beautiful swan. Like Normani."

"Yes," she murmurs. "It's okay, Michaela. You are a Normani swan."

I pat her shoulder. "Now, why don't we walk into town and see if Sonam and Peter are still at Starbucks?"

Minnie brightens up like a lightbulb. "Frappes?" she asks around a mouthful of caramel.

"Frappes."

"Celiiiiine. You're the best." She gives me a chocolatey kiss on the cheek. I wipe it off, pack up my things, and we head out, walking past my latest conspiracy theory.

Bradley Graeme is sitting at Top Table, as always. And he's flawless, as always, with his twists shining and his clothes immaculate but effortless, and an adorable (objectively speaking, I mean) furrow between his eyebrows as he highlights the crap out of what appears to be a history textbook. Since we got back to school, we've barely spoken because I no longer know how to speak to him. I should be desperate to prove my who-is-Bradley-really theory, but I'm not sure which outcome I want. If he's always been the best friend I remember, that means—

But if the way we were during the Sherwood expedition wasn't *real*—

My stomach churns.

So that's us these days: near-silent. No arguments in Philosophy, no bitchy comments in the halls. You'd think we were ignoring each other, but whenever our eyes meet, he gives me this tiny, tentative smile and says: "Hey."

And I reply, helplessly, "Hey."

And then we lapse into a silence I don't know what to do with.

Which is why I've decided to just focus on school.

Unfortunately, Minnie has followed my gaze and there's a speculative gleam in her glitter-adorned eyes. "Are you ever going to tell me how the forest thingy went?"

"I did tell you," I say firmly. I told her it was fine. "Are you ever going to tell me why you've been texting Jordan Cooper all day?"

She smiles sunnily, her earlier mood evaporated. "Well, he's in my English class. And since *his* best friend's been acting weird and *my* best friend's been acting weird . . ."

"Brad's acting weird?"

"*Brad,* is it?" she repeats, pouncing like a panther in sparkly Doc Martens. "I *see.* Fighting off bears in the woods must forge a powerful bond."

"There are no bears in England, Michaela."

"Then what's with the nickname?" she asks.

"Bears," I confirm. "There were so many bears. We were inundated."

"Yeah," she says dryly. "I bet."

I clutch the straps of my rucksack tight as we pass slowly by Top Table. I don't care if Brad says anything. I mean, I don't mind if he *does,* but if he *doesn't,* it's really no skin off—

He looks up from his textbook. "Hey, Cel."

If I smile, the way he does so naturally, people might infer something pathetic and needy that screams *ABANDONED EX–BEST FRIEND DESPERATE TO BE REINSTATED,* which is honestly light-years from the truth. I have a best friend and I love her. The way I was with Brad back then . . . I don't want it back.

But I don't want to brush him off, either, so I nod and reply, "Hey, Brad."

Unfortunately, he's not at his table alone. The popular crowd is largely present and accounted for, from Jordan Cooper to Max Kill-Me-Now Donovan. He sits at the head of the table like a king, one overbearing arm around Isabella Hollis's slender shoulders. When Brad talks to me, Donno's colorless lizard eyes narrow. He lets go of Brad's ex-girlfriend, turns in his seat, and says with a smiling earnestness that couldn't be more fake, "Hey, Cel. Are you okay?"

I falter. What's his game? Despite being a notable flea on the hide of the school ecosystem, Donno is usually sneaky when making his most obnoxious comments. "Yeah?" I say finally.

He pouts and touches his cheek, all curious sympathy. "Looks like you have some kind of rash there."

Ah. I can only assume he's talking about my freckles.

Yes, my fake freckles. I know, I know. They're cute, okay? Everyone does it. Isabella Hollis is sitting right next to him with cheeks bright pink like she's been slapped and brown eyeliner splotches across her nose that are nowhere near as artful as my (incredibly subtle and totally realistic) few dots, but I'm the one everyone's staring at. I'm the one Donno is sneering at. I straighten my spine—

"Fuck off," Michaela snaps before I can get there.

He holds up placating hands. "Whoa, whoa. What did I do?"

"Nothing," I tell him coolly. "Ineffectuality is your defining trait." Hardly my most scathing comeback, but Minnie snickers loyally. I should leave now; I should sweep out of here without a backward glance. It's what I usually do, because even looking at people for too long suggests you care, and I don't. I don't care about anyone or anything but the people I love and the accolades I'll win over the course of my life.

So why does my icy gaze wander across this table to Brad?

On the way, I see a few surprises. I was expecting a sea of snide faces to match Donno's, but half the people at his table haven't even glanced up from their phones. Of those who have—Isabella seems slightly confused, or torn, or something wishy-washy that I have no time for because she was *born* with a spine, she got it for *free,* why should I care if she pretends it doesn't exist? Jordan is throwing Donno a look so filthy I'm surprised no one in the vicinity has died, and Brad—

Brad has put down his history textbook and is saying, "Max. Don't be a dick."

· · ·

BRAD

When I was younger, I decided I would never lose a friend again.

Growing apart is one thing—but that gut-wrenching shift of loving someone today and hating them tomorrow? I couldn't do it twice. Couldn't even stand the thought. So I vowed to stick by the people who stuck by me, because life is about learning not to repeat your mistakes.

But the older I get, the more I realize mistakes are complicated.

Me and Donno have been mates for years now and I never thought of him as a bad guy. He always makes mean comments, yeah, but only to his *friends,* and we don't really mind because we all know why. We've been to his house. We've heard how his dad talks to him and we know that his mother is gone. So maybe Donno *is* a bad guy, but trust me; he could be so much worse.

The thing is, I wish he would be better.

He looks sharply at me after that dick comment. "What's your problem?" he asks, half laughing, playing it down. "It was just a question."

I remember what Celine said to me in the forest: *What the*

hell was someone like me going to do, sitting next to Max Donovan? I thought she was calling him boring. "What's *your* problem?" I demand. There are little sparks flying off the edge of my voice like a blacksmith forging a sword.

He rolls his eyes. "Brad. Come on. You can say whatever you want to her, but the rest of us have to stay quiet?"

"Pretty much." She's *my* enemy. He doesn't even know her. What's he got to complain about? "Don't—"

The subject of our conversation chooses that moment to walk out of the Beech Hut without a backward glance. Michaela throws an unreadable look in my direction and follows. I play back everything I just said and feel my stomach thud down through my chair and splatter on the floor.

Beside me, Jordan drawls, "Aw, Brad, don't mind Max. He's just jealous 'cause you're paying more attention to Celine than to him."

A snicker ripples around the table. Donno turns rage-red.

I wish I could enjoy it, but my thoughts are elsewhere. I get up and grab my bag. "Don't talk shit to her again. Leave her alone."

The frigid air outside smacks into me like a brick wall. I left my jacket, I realize; doesn't matter. Jordan will hold on to it. More important is following Celine's retreating back. She's a pop of scarlet in the November fog, her distinctive winter coat and Minnie's huge curls fading into the gloomy crowd of kids from lower school. I wind through little ones who are swamped by their bottle-green uniform blazers, step onto the bark that borders the school pathways—

Somewhere in the fog, a teacher blows their whistle. "Brad Graeme! I can see you, young man! Get off those flowerbeds!"

I sigh and step back onto the pavement. So much for that shortcut.

But up ahead, Celine and Minnie must hear my name because they turn around. Celine clocks me, even through all this mist—I can tell by the angle of her head, by the shift of her weight from one foot to the other.

Then she turns back around and starts to *walk away*.

"Celine Bangura," I bellow. "Do. Not. Move."

If I'd thought about what I was saying before I opened my mouth, those words are . . . not the ones I'd have chosen. A few kids giggle as they pass me, but it's worth it because Celine halts. Instead of flipping me off and leaving with Michaela, the two bend their heads together for a second before Minnie leaves. Alone.

I stride over to meet Celine before I lose my nerve. I feel like a wrecking ball headed for a skyscraper made of steel. The last trickle of schoolkids loiter on their way past, making themselves late to lessons, all for the chance to see a bit of sixth-form drama. Celine's skin is slightly damp with fog, gleaming like silk. I'd stare at her too.

"I'm sorry," I say when we're a meter apart.

She scowls. "What for?"

I blink. "Is this a test?"

Celine rolls her eyes, but she doesn't walk away. "Your friend was a dick. You told him to shut up. What are you sorry for?"

"You don't mind that I said . . . I mean . . ." I take a frosty breath and get myself together. "Listen, Celine, I've treated you like shit for the longest, and that's not me, and I'm sorry. And if . . . if it made other people do the same, then . . ." Then I will very shortly be flying myself into the sun because I'm too enormous an arsehole for this planet. "Then I'm even sorrier." I meet her eyes and I mean every word. "Like . . . the sorriest." With such a masterful command of the English language, it's a wonder my book isn't already published.

Celine's scowl intensifies, but it's focused on the floor rather than on me. "Whatever," she mutters. "That douche canoe has nothing to do with us."

Us is a real heavyweight of a word and it almost knocks me out.

"And you don't treat me like shit," she adds, chin up, eyes burning. Suddenly her glare seems less deadly and more self-conscious. "I treat *you* like shit, and you try really hard to reciprocate but ultimately fail to meet the high standards I've set."

The tension bracketing my spine slides away. My lips twitch at the corners but if I smile, she might whack me. "The . . . high insult standards?"

"Yes," she bites out.

"Right." A thought hits. "Hang on. If you aren't pissed about Donno—"

She rolls her eyes. "That amoeba wishes he could piss me off."

"Then why were you ignoring me just now?"

She blinks rapidly and assumes a vaguely innocent expression. "Um."

"*Um?*" I repeat. "Um, what? You saw me following you and you just kept walking?"

"How was I supposed to know you were following me?" she mutters. The self-conscious scowl is back. It's very cute, but it doesn't change the fact that I'm officially mad at her. She saw me and turned around! She was going to walk away! For no reason!

There's a question that's been biting at the back of my brain and I thought it was just paranoia but now, *now*, I set it free. "How come you've been weird with me since we got back to school?"

Her head snaps up. "I haven't—"

"You *have*."

"I haven't! You say hi, I say hi. You highlight your entire textbook; I keep my mouth shut. What do you want from me, Brad?"

"The . . . How . . . *Before!* I want before! How we were in the woods!" I didn't intend to say this, but the nagging urge in the back of my mind finally quiets, so I swallow my vague horror and keep going. "I know I'm not wrong about this, Celine. We were basically friends and you *liked* it." I point a finger like I'm accusing her of cannibalism.

"We were friend*ly*," she corrects.

"Yeah, and you're sooo friendly with people. All the time! Notorious for it."

"You didn't ask for everything," she splutters. "You didn't *say* we should be friends. You didn't *say* I should forgive you for . . . for back then. You said to forget it. Temporarily. While we were out there!"

"Yeah, well, I changed my mind." The words spill out before I can check them for contraband. "Forgive me. For everything. Please."

Silence falls. There are no more children lurking; just us and the fog and the buildings on either side of this path, windows filled with students and teachers who probably aren't paying any attention to us. I really hope they're not paying attention anyway, because I might've just lost my mind.

After a pause so long it almost murders me, a laugh bursts from her lips. "You're funny," she says, like I was joking.

"Oh, are we listing qualities? Here's one: you're avoidant."

She throws up her hands and sweeps away like a queen. "Piss off, Brad."

I follow. "You're avoiding a conversation about our friendship because you avoid your feelings."

She examines a nearby bush with apparent fascination.

"Way to prove me wrong."

Her focus transfers to a brick wall.

I put on my best clipped-and-impatient voice. "Look at me, I'm Celine. I want to be friends with Brad, but I would rather choke to death on a crab stick—"

Her braids whip my shoulder as she spins around to face me. "Why would I be eating a crab stick? I hate crab sticks!"

"I know," I explain patiently, "that's the point. Now shut up and let me finish." I clear my throat and start again. "I'm Celine and I would rather choke to death on a crab stick than admit I like Brad because I think I can replace all emotional conversations with power moves and epic stink eye."

"Oh my *God*." Her voice lowers to a hiss, like air rushing out of a hot-air balloon. "Fine! Okay! You're not so bad and I . . . I might understand why you did what you did when we were kids, and I . . . forgive you. Okay? So will you shut up?"

Did I just annoy Celine into saying we're cool? I think I might have. Funny how it's not as satisfying as I imagined. "Maybe." I shrug.

"*Maybe?*"

"Hey. You're not the only one who can hedge."

"*Ugh*. Can we just . . . talk for five minutes without you making me think about myself?" she asks, which is a sentence I never thought I'd hear come out of her mouth. She wrinkles her nose. "I'm not like you. I really don't have the whole emotional intelligence thing down."

I blink, and the tension in me pops like a cork. My smile is slow but this time I'm satisfied because she's talking to me. Actually talking, like we know each other again. I didn't realize how badly I wanted that until it happened.

We walk down the path side by side. "You know," I say casually, "I have a theory that everyone needs therapy. Like going to the dentist."

"Yeah? Tell that to the NHS." She snorts.

My parents paid for my therapist Dr. Okoro privately because, between Dad's job and Mum's dental practice, we're not exactly struggling. I scratch the back of my head.

Celine's grin is razor sharp. "Nothing to say, rich boy?"

"I could say that we're not rich," I mutter, "but I'm sure you'd have a field day with *that*."

She laughs. My heart thuds. "Thanks, by the way," she murmurs after a moment. "For. You know. Saying that. In there."

I have been on such a roller coaster since I left the Beech Hut, I'd almost forgotten Max Donovan even existed. Now it comes thundering back, and I wince. "Does he talk to you like that all the time?"

"Why?" she asks. "What are you going to do, fight him?"

Would it be bad to say yes? I think it would be bad. Violence is not the answer. Although, history suggests it is *occasionally* the answer—

She laughs. "*What* is going on with your face right now? I'm joking."

I roll my eyes. "You're the bane of my existence. Did you know that?"

She grins. "I hoped."

I really can't stand this girl. I wonder how long I get to walk with her.

"And no, Max doesn't always talk to me like that. He's usually less brazen. It's more of a he-whispers-snide-comments-which-I-pretend-not-to-hear vibe," she says.

I stare at her. "You mean he's been bothering you this whole—"

"I don't care." She meets my eyes. "I don't care at all. Trust me, okay?"

And by the way my anger slowly dissipates, I think maybe I . . . do? A second passes. "Fine," I say. "Okay. Fine."

"Good."

I study the path beneath our feet. "Where are we going, by the way?"

"Me and Minnie are meeting Sonam for frappes." If I didn't know any better, I'd think she's nervous as she asks, "Do you want to come?"

Yes, I really really really really do. But . . . "I have History next lesson, and I haven't done the reading." I could read at Starbucks, except no I couldn't, not if Celine is gonna be there. Saying things. With her mouth. She dropped History in year ten. Then again, maybe I could teach her—

"Walk me to the gate, then?" she suggests.

I know I say yes too quickly, but I can't make myself regret it.

As we wander down, she says, "I have a theory about you, Brad Graeme."

A theory. She has a theory about me. I am so fucking in.

Wait. What?

I clear my throat and ask, "Yeah?"

She hesitates, then says, "That you're exactly who you claim to be."

"And who's that?"

We reach the green gate and she fiddles with the lanyard around her neck, lifting up her student ID to open the lock. "A decent person," she says after a pause. "The person I thought I knew." She holds the gate ajar with her shoulder and finally looks at me. "I'm sorry, by the way." The words are so stilted, it takes me a moment to figure out what she's talking about.

And even when I do get it, I'm . . . not sure. I catch her hand to stop her from leaving. Her cast is off now, her nails are painted pumpkin orange, and fine brown lines are etched deep into her palms. Celine thinks there's life in those lines. I wonder what she'd read in mine.

"Sorry for what?" I ask, my eyes pinned to hers. I want every inch of this apology.

Her lips roll inward but she releases them again. "For . . . before." Her voice is scratchy. "For all of this, everything we've . . . But mostly, for what I said to you, back when we fell out."

I remember it. *Will your new friends want you then?*

"I shouldn't have said it and I didn't mean it," she says, holding my gaze, every word clear. "There's nothing wrong with you. Or with you having OCD, obviously. I just wanted to piss you off, but it was horrible and untrue and you're . . . fine. Better than fine. Anyone who knew you would want you, okay? So.

Yeah." Celine snaps her mouth shut and her eyes finally slide away from mine. I don't mind. I'm too busy slipping into a feather bed of *Yes, thank God* because I had no idea how much I wanted to hear her say all that. There was a last little ember of hurt in me, and she just blew it out.

"Good," I manage, my voice half a breath, a gasp. "Good, that's . . . great."

"So. Um. I'll stop being weird with you, and you stop examining the darkness of my soul, or whatever. Yeah?"

"Yeah," I manage. "Yeah. Okay." I let go of her hand. I watch her disappear into the shroud of fog that hides the road into town. Then I slump against the nearest wall and lurch back into my body, like when you're following directions on your phone and press the button to take you back to the little arrow on the map, and the perspective on the screen goes *zoom*. You know? Here's my new perspective: my mouth is dry, my heart is still thundering against my ribs, the difference between a smile and a scowl on her face is the difference between rainfall and drought and— Oh shit no no no no no . . .

I am so into Celine.

• • •

⚽ROSEWOOD MASSIVE⚽

Donno 🏆🍸 changed the group name to: YOUR STD TEST RESULTS HAVE ARRIVED

Brad 😜 changed the group name to: 🖤football🖤

Harley ✌ changed the group name to: ROSEWOOD MASSIVE

Donno 💰 🏆: all right lads here's next week's starting & reserve team

Donno 💰 🏆: <teamlist.doc>

Brad 😀: me and Jordan aren't on there

Donno 💰 🏆: play better then

Jordan 🤙: lol you so butthurt man

Jordan 🤙: tragic

DECEMBER

CHAPTER NINE

CELINE

Being friends with Brad again is weird.

Not *bad* weird. Just . . . you know when you were a little kid and you went to a birthday party and ate five times the amount of sugar your parents usually allowed, and you felt *dangerously* high? It's that kind of weird. And something in me is tense as if I'm waiting for the crash.

Like I don't have enough on my mind. Final year was always going to be a struggle—uni applications, exams, and now the BEP—but I can't stop thinking about Aurora's birthday. About the way everyone described their plans, like the future was dragging them forward instead of adding to the weight on their backs. I even texted her about it.

> **Celine:** how come you want to study art?

> **Aurora:** it's basically the only thing I'm good at

Celine: ??? wrong

Aurora: okay maybe not

Aurora: more like

Aurora: it's the only thing I CARE about being good at.

Well, I care most about law. I always have. So there's no reason for this weird, sloshing uncertainty in my stomach whenever I think about my glittering, corporate, take-over-Dad's-business-and-ruin-his-life future. I turn my back on pointless anxieties and snuggle deeper into my pillow, scrolling through TikTok and saving all the best sounds.

It's December, and I'm planning a theme: Christmas Conspiracies. Santa Claus sightings, capitalist manipulations of the workforce during the holidays, and anything else slightly bonkers and compelling and festive I can think of. I already feel my stress levels sinking. Who needs candy cane–scented candles when there's social media chaos?

A knock sounds at my bedroom door. "Hey," Giselle says. "How's it going?"

"Fine." I flash my sister a smile and switch over to my Notes app, typing out a potential idea about hot chocolate, lactose intolerance, and Santa's nefarious intentions. "What about you? How was work?" She's a crew member at McDonald's because, apparently, shift work suits her "creative cycle" better than a nine to five.

"Ugh. They're still refusing to put me in the kitchen. *But you have such a pretty smile, Giselle!"* she mimics, flopping onto my bed like a dying swan. Her never-ending arms knock my snuggly crocheted mushroom off his favorite pillow.

"Oi," I say, reaching over to restore him to his rightful throne. "Watch it."

"Don't shout at me, Celine. I'm nursing wounds of the soul. If one more football hooligan comes waltzing out of the Forest stadium to take out his pent-up aggression on me . . ." Her elegant features screw into an expression that can only be described as murderous. Combined with the smooth curve of her newly shaved head, she looks like a vengeful spirit crossed with Alek Wek. "Well, they'll learn." She sighs and changes the subject. "So, I read your leaflet."

This means nothing because I collect all kinds of leaflets. How are you supposed to learn about the different opportunities in the world if you don't comb over the appropriate literature? "Mmm-hmm?" I murmur, turning the sound down on my phone and scrolling through a few more videos.

"Did you know Dad's firm is partly sponsoring this Katharine Breakspeare thing?"

I drop the phone. It smacks me in the nose. *"Shit."*

"Smooth," she says.

"What? No. I . . . er . . ." My face hurts, which apparently inhibits my ability to lie. I rub my nose and give up. "How did you even find it?"

"Find what?" she asks. "Oh, you mean the leaflet you hid behind your bedside table? I just came into your room and thought, 'Giselle, if you were a shady little shit, where would you put your illicit materials?' And then I poked around."

"So you went through my stuff."

"I went through your dust and lies, yes," Giselle says brightly. Then she sits up, settling against my cushions as if she's planning to be here for a long time. My eyes flick toward the door, and she gives me a knowing look. "Mum's gone for a drink with Maria, remember?"

Well, thank God for that. I try not to seem too relieved, though; it will only imply guilt.

"Why do you want to see Dad?" Giselle asks, each word cautiously placed like steps through a land mine.

A little dirt devil of uncertainty whirls in my gut. "I don't."

She is clearly unconvinced.

"I mean, not like that. I don't want to *see* him, see him." I don't give a single solitary shit about the man. "I just . . . I'm going to be a BEP alum, you know? I'm going to be an *Ultimate Explorer*. I'm going to be up onstage at the Explorers' Ball receiving an award and a scholarship to Cambridge because I'm so bloody brilliant, and his firm will be clamoring to forge ties with me as an up-and-coming corporate star, and he'll have to . . . to see it."

That was a perfectly valid explanation, but Giselle sighs pityingly the way only an older sister can. "Oh, Celine."

"What? It's not . . . I'm not . . ." My face is hot, but I fold my hands together and force myself to speak slowly. "I didn't choose to do the BEP because Dad might—and it is, technically, a *might*—be at the ball. But if he is there, good." A lump rises in my throat. I swallow it. "I bet he never even thinks about us. We are a government-mandated direct debit, Giselle. Meanwhile, Mum has done everything for us, *been* everything for us, and you know what? She did an incredible job, because we are amazing human beings. He should see that."

Giselle snorts. "Amazing human beings? You're an emo nerd and I'm a ne'er-do-well with delusions of artistic grandeur. What's so amazing about that?"

"Shut up." I smack her arm. "What are you being a dick for?"

"Because it doesn't matter." Her hand rests on my shoulder. Her eyes are black like the ink of a message I can't quite read. "Even if neither of us ever did anything interesting in our entire lives, it wouldn't matter. You don't need to be special or significant to have value. You're just important, always, and people either see that or they don't. They either love you, or they don't." She bites her lip. "Dad's messed up, Celine. They should've given him an Unfit for Purpose stamp at the parent factory. But he is who he is—"

I'm nodding, vindicated, my plan rushing out like I've secretly been waiting for someone to tell it to. Maybe I have. "Exactly. Exactly! So when he sees me at the ball, he'll *feel* what a failure he is. I'm going to achieve everything he ever did," I tell her, "only *better*. And he'll hear all about it. I'll get the highest grades in my entire school and they'll put me on BBC News, and he'll spit out his morning coffee." It's true what they say about the power of intentions because every word I speak wraps around me like magic, reinforcing my bones with steel. "I'll dominate his field and in ten years' time he won't be able to move without hearing my name. I hope the shame suffocates him in his sleep. I hope he retires early with exhaustion. I hope he has the audacity to try and claim me as his daughter so I can tell him I have one father and her name is Neneh."

There should, by rights, be a mysterious wind whipping around my bedroom as I lay a dread curse upon my sire. Giselle should be glowing with admiration and adding her own deeply positive affirmations to this moment. Instead, for some reason, she seems . . . upset?

"Cel. Babe. No."

I stop. Blink. I have no idea what I've done wrong.

"Why do you care? Why do you think about him at all?" She stands up, hands on her hips, sadness on her face. "Do you even *want* to be a lawyer?"

"What?" I squawk. "Of course, I do. Like—" *Katharine,* I'm going to say.

"Like Dad?" Giselle accuses.

That's so ridiculous, I laugh. "Him? No. I don't want to be anything like him."

Giselle stares down at me. "Then why are you planning your whole life around him?"

"I'm not! God. You think you know everything—"

She snorts. "More than you."

"Just because you're, like, five seconds older than me. This is for *Mum,*" I correct. "Obviously. To prove how . . . how wonderful she is, and how she didn't need him, and . . . and that it was worth it."

Giselle's brow creases. "What was worth it?"

"Staying with us!"

My sister doesn't reply; instead, she studies me with narrow-eyed urgency, like she's only just noticed I have a third eyebrow and it's blond. Meanwhile, I'm having a minor internal freak-out because I know when I'm winning an argument. I know when I'm making logically sound points. And all this stuff made perfect sense in my head, but when I say it out loud, it sounds more like the conspiracy theories I analyze.

But . . . but that's okay because plenty of conspiracy theories are basically true. There's nothing wrong with wanting to restore balance and order and meaning to a messed-up situation. And there's nothing wrong with punishing someone who was supposed to love you but couldn't do it right. Isn't that basically what law's about? Crime and punishment?

I ignore the little voice in the back of my head saying, *Well, actually* . . .

My sister takes a noisy breath, her lips pressed together, and I realize with a jolt of discomfort that Giselle—whose moods are usually limited, much like a panther's, to sleepy, hungry, and bitey—seems worried. Serious. Uncertain. My heart twists. Then she destroys my sympathy by being a complete prat. "Contrary to everything you just said, Celine, I know for a fact that you are very smart."

I glare. Violently. "I will not deign to respond to that."

"I believe," she says, "that if you think about this situation, you'll reach a logical conclusion. I believe in *you*."

That would be a very nice speech if she wasn't technically insulting me. "Would you stop? This isn't a big deal. It's just a ball." I know I'm ignoring a huge chunk of the conversation we just had by saying that, but God. I'm exhausted. Sometimes talking to Giselle is like having an angel on each shoulder while the devil lives between your ears.

"Just a ball?" she repeats. "No, Celine. No, it's secret. It's a lie by omission. If it didn't matter, you wouldn't have hidden that bloody leaflet. You're sneaking around."

My throat cinches tighter with every calm accusation my sister throws. "That's not . . . I'm not . . ." I can't finish my sentence.

Giselle sighs. "And even if it *was* about the ball: aren't parents invited to this thing? How do you think Mum's going to feel if she shows up and sees him, and you could've told her, but you didn't?"

I . . . hadn't thought that far ahead, possibly because imagining that scenario makes the bottom fall out of my stomach. I was always going to tell Mum eventually. It's not that big a deal. I just haven't figured out how to, you know, phrase it, how to explain.

"Yeah," Giselle says flatly. "I want you to think about this *plan* of yours." Her expression sours on the word. "And about what you really want from your life. Because it is your life, Cel. No one else has to live it." She opens her mouth like she wants to say more, then shakes her head and leaves, closing the door behind her.

I curl up like a bug and roll onto my side, staring up at my Steps to Success board. Giselle doesn't get it, that's all. If she got it, she'd . . . well. She'd get it.

Except there's this annoying sickly feeling in my stomach that I'm desperate to turn away from. My phone vibrates, and when I glance at the screen, I see Brad's name. For the first time since we became friends last month, my mood doesn't lift in response.

Instead, I remember him calling me avoidant, and I remember that he's right.

• • •

BRAD

By December, Donno has kept me and Jordan off the pitch for so long, I've started to seriously consider jogging.

"Bruh." Jordan's disgust is loud and clear through my headphones. "*Jogging?* Not to be dramatic, but I'd honestly rather die."

"What?" I'm lying on my bed (wearing my inside clothes, obviously), studying the smooth, perfect white of my ceiling. Wintery, afternoon sunlight makes the whole room fresh and bright, and Jordan's cracking me up as always. "Come on, man. It's basically football, just fewer people and no ball."

"It's soulless and painfully boring," he announces.

"We have to think of our cardiovascular health!"

"That's future me's problem. I am too young and sexy for pointless exercise. Give me a trophy or get out of my face."

Incredible. "I hope you know how ridiculous you sound."

"Always," he assures me.

My smile fades. "I'm sorry, by the way, that Donno's taking this out on you. It's basically my fault he's pissed."

Jordan snorts. "No, it's *his* fault he's pissed, so let him stew. I could give a good goddamn about Max Donovan and his stank-ass attitude. I only joined the soccer team 'cause I needed to make friends over here, and look: I have friends."

That's a great point. Why did *I* start playing football?

Because Dr. Okoro said getting out of my head and into my body would be helpful, and she was right. So, who cares if Donno won't play me? Maybe I'll jog after all.

While I'm having Very Important Realizations, Jordan's still ranting. "Anyway, you had nothing to do with me finally telling him about himself. He can't speak to people like he speaks to Celine. You know, she's basically my homegirl now."

My eyebrows fly north. "How is Celine your homegirl? She barely says two words to you."

"Yeah, and? She's shy."

I want to bust up laughing at the idea of Celine as shy, only . . . she kind of is. In a really weird way. She'll cuss out a complete stranger if she thinks it's warranted, but it usually takes her thirty business days of acquaintance to feel comfortable with the question, *Hey, how are you?*

I catch myself smiling and realize that I find her suspicious nature dreamy and adorable. This crush is a sickness. A sickness, I tell you!

"Plus," Jordan continues, oblivious to the steady degradation of my brain cells, "she's best friends with Minnie, and I like Minnie."

Oh yeah; it turns out Michaela Digby is indeed gay, so Jordan has transformed his interest into general hero worship. The past month or so, it's usually me and him and Minnie and Celine hanging out between classes. Sometimes Sonam and Peter are there, chattering about a New Year's party; sometimes a few guys from the team come over and Celine glares at them like they might be hiding deadly weapons in their socks. It works pretty well.

"And then," Jordan finishes grandly, "there's the fact that *my* best friend is in love with her—"

I swallow my spit the wrong way and come very, very close to choking to death on a Sunday afternoon with my bedroom door wide open. My obituary would be tragic. "What?" I croak, sitting bolt upright. "I am *not*—What are you—"

"Man," he says. "Come on. What do you think I am, stupid?"

"Jordan," I say. "Jordan, Jordan, Jordan. I don't . . . It's not . . ." I glance furtively at the door because Mason's home, for once, and he has ears like a bat. "I'm not in love with—" *Celine,* I mouth.

"What?" Jordan says. "I think you're breaking up."

"I just . . . have the teeniest, tiniest crush on her," I say. "That's all. It's so small. Sooo small. It's microscopic!"

"Oh, really?"

"Yes," I say, relieved that he's being so reasonable about this. "Absolutely, yes."

"Huh. See, usually when you have a crush on someone, you're mad obvious about it," Jordan says, "and you tell me right away—you don't shut up about it—and then you spend a couple months spacing out while you daydream about your converted loft and your kitchen garden and your seventy-five adopted children—"

"Jordan," I groan, flopping back onto the bed. What is he, a bloody modern history book? "Stop dredging up the past. I'm very nearly a mature adult and I only did that with, like, five people."

"I know," he says. "That's why I thought this thing with Celine—you know, you trying to act like you're not into her at all, and being friends with her, and finally admitting that you watch her TikToks, meant you had real, big boy, serious feelings for her."

I don't say anything; I'm too busy freaking out.

"But, hey," Jordan says cheerfully. "What do I know?"

"Nothing. You know nothing, Jordan Snow." See, my strategy is: if I ignore this, it will go away. Which is literally the opposite of what Dr. Okoro would tell me to do, but she's not the boss of me, so there.

"Are you telling me you're not in love with Celine?"

"No," I say firmly.

"No, you're not in love with her, or no you're not telling me you're not in love with her because you are?"

"What . . . No, as in, no, I'm not in love with her! Obviously!"

Someone rings the doorbell. I pop up out of bed and plaster myself to my window because I'm waiting for my paperback copy of *Black Leopard, Red Wolf,* but instead of the postman, I see a familiar scarlet coat. "Crap."

"What?" Jordan demands.

"Celine's here!"

"At your *house*?"

"No, at the Eiffel Tower. Yes, at my house."

"The Eiffel Tower?" he echoes dryly. "Seriously, Brad?"

"Shut up! What do I do?" My room is a hideous mess and I'm wearing glasses instead of contacts and I have a halo of frizz around my head because I've been lazing around in bed all day without my do-rag. This is why people aren't supposed to just show up unannounced. "I haven't put my washing away!"

"Just . . . throw it in the closet and close the door."

"Jordan," I say, aghast.

"Okay, fine, put it in your sister's room."

Now, that . . . that could work. I snatch up the basket of washing and tiptoe across the hall. Downstairs, the front door opens, and I hear Dad's voice. Thank God. He can talk for England.

"Maybe she's not even here to see you," Jordan says as I sneak into Em's room. It's colder than the rest of the house and half empty. I put my washing down and get out of there sharpish. "Aren't your parents friends?" he asks. "Maybe she's come to pick something up."

Ohhh. "Maybe," I say, my heart slowing. And dropping. Stupid heart. Then I hear Dad say, "Brad's in his room," and it bounces back to life. "Nope," I correct, rushing back across the hall. "Definitely here for me!"

My brother Mason sticks his big, square head out of the bathroom door. *His* hair is in perfect glossy curls and he has a wax strip stuck between his eyebrows. "What are you doing running around out here?" he demands at foghorn volume.

"Shut *up*," I whisper.

"Did you go in Emily's room? We're not allowed in there."

"Celine is coming upstairs," I tell him, "so unless you want to demonstrate your monobrow management technique, get lost."

He gives me the finger and slams the bathroom door with all the force of his overdeveloped biceps.

Jordan is laughing in my ear, which is not helpful. "Stop snickering," I tell him sternly. "What do I do? What do I *say*—"

"Normal stuff," Jordan instructs, then corrects himself. "Brad stuff. The usual. You do know this girl, remember?"

Right, yeah. It's only Celine. I take a breath and plop back onto my bed. "Of course. Thanks, Jordan."

"You're welcome. By the way, I think she likes you too."

"Jordan!" That is not helpful, either, because it's ridiculous. Celine is . . . *Celine*. She doesn't *like* people. In her world, we've only been friends again for, like, five minutes, and I'm pretty sure she requires ten years of loyal companionship and smoldering eye contact and maybe a few deadly battles fought side by side (or back-to-back—that always looks badass in films) before she'd even consider developing a crush. I know she had a . . . *thing* with Luke Darker last year, but it was weird and aggressive, and I don't want that. I want something she's not going to give me. "That's not . . . She doesn't . . . Shut up."

171

"If you say so." Jordan snorts.

"I do say so!"

"Fine, whatever," he singsongs. "Let's pretend neither of you is remotely interested in the other, if that makes you feel better. Oh, and, Brad?"

"Yeah?"

"Get off the phone."

"Oh yeah!" I hang up.

CHAPTER TEN

CELINE

We've only just settled into December, but when I knock on Bradley's front door, a holly wreath frames my fist. Trev Graeme answers a few moments later.

"*Hello*, Celine!" He beams. (He's just like Bradley, smiling all over the place.) "Come in, come in. How are you? How's—" He breaks off, clocking the garden's wonky SANTA STOP HERE! sign with a scowl. "Oh, not again. This raatid wind. Excuse my French, sweetheart, one second." He tiptoes outside in his slippers.

When Brad and I fell out, I stopped coming around, so I haven't spent much time with Trev these last few years. He visits my house every so often—mostly when Mum needs help lifting things, and then they have a cup of tea in the kitchen. I tend to make myself scarce. It's not because I don't like him. He just reminds me how shitty I am.

Trevor Graeme, you see, loves his family quite a lot and would probably rather die than leave them. When I was younger, I went through this absolutely mortifying phase of envying Brad his good fortune.

I know. It's awful. Don't worry, I'm over it.

But maybe there are other, shitty dad-related things lurking in my brain that I'm *not* quite over. Maybe Giselle made a few teeny, tiny points yesterday. I can't stop thinking about that possibility, which is why I'm here. So I smile through a few minutes' chat with Trev when he returns, graciously accept a drink and a packet of biscuits, then scurry upstairs to find what I hope is still Bradley's room.

It is.

He must hear me hovering on the stairs because he comes over to lean against his door frame like a bouncer. His hands are in his pockets, his expression is amused . . .

And he's wearing his glasses. They're oversized circular frames made of pale gold and I don't think I've ever noticed how adorable his nose is until I see his glasses perched on top of it just now. This is mortifying. I think I'm already having heart palpitations.

Stop. Get ahold of yourself!

Brad arches an eyebrow. "You know you have my number now, Celine. You can text me if you're coming over. I could . . . unlock the door for you."

I try to sound unaffected by his presence. "And let me bypass your father like a mannerless heathen?"

He rolls his eyes and steps aside to let me in. But I notice him flicking looks back at me as I walk through his room, like he's nervous. "What's up, anyway?"

There's no easy way to ask someone if they think your entire life plan amounts to BIG FAT DADDY ISSUES, so I decide to subtly ease into things. "Nothing. I'm fine."

"Right." He snorts, then points at the pack of digestives in my hand. "Don't you dare eat those in here, by the way. I can't deal with crumbs."

"Ugh. You're tyrannical." But I already knew that, which is why I haven't opened the packet.

Brad's room has changed just as much as he has, but also not at all. There's still soothingly cream walls, a perfectly made bed, and his drawers and wardrobe are neatly shut instead of over-flowing with crap like mine. The desk under his window is new, but everything on its surface is set at perfect right angles. He's always neater when exams are coming up, and we're revising for winter modules right now.

The enormous bookshelf by his wardrobe isn't new at all, but the books on it might be. Although, judging from the spines, he's still into sci-fi and fantasy.

"You can sit down," he says, interrupting my thoughts.

"Where?"

"Wherever you want, Celine, come on." He flops down onto the bed, pointedly messing up his perfect duvet.

I tut and perch neatly on the corner of the mattress.

Brad grins. "You're so nice."

"What?" I am horrified. No one has ever accused me of this. "*Nice?* Do you realize how . . . utterly *bland*—"

"Don't have a cow, Cel."

"How disgustingly *milquetoast*—"

"Nice," he says over my conniptions. "Nice, nice, nice. Like pie."

"*Pie?*"

He's confident. "Pie."

Dear God. The fact that I'm enjoying this conversation—that it's a real struggle not to beam like an enthusiastic lightbulb—should be setting off alarm bells in my head. Unfortunately, I have been feeling this way around Brad for a while, and I suspect I know the issue.

He's wearing soft pastel clothes again, mint green, and his dimple is showing because he's smiling at me. He's obnoxiously beautiful and he calls me *nice* despite the sheer number of times I've succeeded in ruining his day. Something warm and nervous rises in me like the tide and before it can spill free and cause untold harm, I blurt out something else. "Am I a terrible daughter?"

His smile fades. "What? No. Why?"

I don't know why I'm happy he said no. He hasn't even heard my crimes. "Giselle knows about . . . my dad," I say stiffly, "being involved in . . . you know." That's why I'm here: Brad *does* know. He knows so well, he helped me climb out of a window.

"Hang on." Brad gets up to close the door because he's thoughtful and thorough—someone should tattoo those words on his forehead—and I hear Mason shout from down the hall, "Dad, Brad's shutting the door with a girl in his room!"

"It's only Celine," Brad calls back. "Grow up."

For some reason, my cheeks catch fire like two piles of dry, shriveled up leaves. Right! It's only me! His completely platonic friend! *Obviously,* Mason, get a grip.

The door closes without a word of complaint from Trev (so you agree, Trevor, that your eldest son finds me as dangerous to his virtue as a hunk of wood? Okay, that's cool, just checking). Then Brad comes back to sit on the bed with a serious expression, closer to my corner than before. His right knee is a handspan away from mine and he's leaning toward me, legs crossed, elbows on his thighs. It's a very comforting posture. His eyes are like a warm summer night. "What'd she say?"

I blink. "Hmm? Erm, she said . . ." I scrabble through my mental files to remember the distant history of yesterday. "She said I'm hiding things from Mum and I'm letting Dad rule my life when he's not even in it, and lots of other rubbish like that. All because I want to rub my eventual, inevitable success in his face. She's wrong." I pause, take a deep breath, and admit through gritted teeth, "But. Then again. Giselle is smart and she is technically in the same boat as me, parent-wise——"

"Technically," Brad agrees, far too solemn to be serious.

"Shut it." I whack him on the shoulder and try not to have heart palpitations at the fact that he is (1) warm and (2) solid. Like, duh, Celine. He is a living human, not an icy transparent ghost; obviously he possesses form and vigor. I put my tingly hand carefully in the pocket of my black Vulfpeck hoodie and continue. "I just . . . I have an intellectual duty to investigate accusations like that without bias. Right?"

Brad nods.

"So. I thought I'd ask you for an . . . outside perspective."

"Okay," Brad says. "Let me ask you something. Aside from the scholarship—is your dad one of the reasons you're doing the BEP?"

I shift uncomfortably and force myself to be honest. He called me avoidant but I'm the boss of my own brain and I'll face whatever's in there, thank you very much. Just like every woman on my Steps to Success board faces whatever's thrown at them. "Maybe."

He arches an eyebrow. "Does maybe mean yes?"

"No."

"So it means no."

"No!" I glare at him. "What are you doing?"

"Applying pressure," he says serenely. "I learned about it in therapy."

"Did you?"

"Nah." Before I can flick him between the eyes for being so deeply annoying, he reaches out and squeezes one of the pom-poms on my socks. (Yes, there are pom-poms on my socks. It's cold, okay?) I watch him pinch the soft red ball between finger and thumb. But when I look up, he's not focused on my socks; he's focused on me. "Tell me the truth," he says so, so softly, not like it's an order but like he's really asking. Like it really matters.

I swallow hard and admit it. "There's . . . something satisfying in the fact that my dad's going to see me win this scholarship."

The corner of Brad's mouth twitches.

"What?" I demand, self-consciousness creeping in like fog.

"Nothing." He lets go of the pom-pom and squeezes my ankle. I very nearly die. "I just like how certain you are, that's all," he says. "What else?"

My mouth is dry. "What else . . ."

"What else are you doing because of him?"

"Not *because* of him." I frown. "I don't want to be a lawyer because of him."

"But you want to work in corporate law," Brad says. "Is that because of him?"

My frown deepens into a scowl. Annoyance is easier and

much more familiar than whatever I feel about the weight of his hand, which is *still on my ankle, Jesus Christ, Bradley*. It's nothing, it's nothing, I see him touch all his friends. "How do you know what field I want to work in?"

"Because I was at that party where you announced it," he says mildly, "and I thought it was weird how the people you admire—like Katharine—work elsewhere, but you're not remotely interested in following in their footsteps."

"It's not that I'm not interested," I protest, then cut myself off because—

Well, what does it matter? These decisions, practically speaking, are years into the future. And yes, I am someone who plans her decisions in advance, but, well—

"For God's sake," I mutter, "what are you asking me all this for? You're supposed to tell me I'm great and Giselle's wrong and everything is fine."

"You're great," he says, and the tension in my muscles slides away. But it snaps right back when he adds, "Giselle's not wrong. Everything . . . may or may not be fine?"

I pull my ankle out of his grip. It immediately feels ten degrees cooler. "Brad!"

"What?" he laughs. "I'm not gonna lie to you, Celine. Your life plan is coming off *slightly* bitter and vengeful—"

I make that cough-laugh sound people do when they are both astonished and amused. "I *beg* your pardon?"

He ignores me. "But it's warranted! It's not a capital crime to have bad feelings when bad things happen to you."

Well, I do realize that. It just *feels* like a crime to have any feelings at all—like I should be okay no matter what. My dad doesn't rattle me. I can prove it.

A voice that sounds very like Giselle's asks, *By letting him shape your whole life?*

"What am I supposed to do?" I demand. "Just . . . forget about him? Let him get away with what he did? How is that *fair*?"

A sad little line forms between Brad's eyebrows. "It's not."

Something inside me that was venomous and ready to bite stands down. Now I feel deflated and directionless.

"But you know what I care about?" Brad's eyes are huge and lovely behind his glasses, like a cow angling for gourmet daisies. "Whether or not you're *happy* with your bitter, vengeful choices. Are you? Happy?"

I open my mouth, then close it.

"Ah, ah! No thinking. Do you want to be an overachieving corporate lawyer who goes camping with Katharine Breakspeare on the weekends? Yes or no? Answer quickly."

"I mean . . . I want some of those things."

"You're talking about the Katharine Breakspeare part," he says, "aren't you?"

I roll my eyes. "Shut up." I think I've had enough public self-reflection for one day. I feel uncertain, now—in my decisions, in myself. And if I can't be sure of me, what exactly do I have to hold on to? But I can't dump all that on Brad. I can't dump it on anyone. "Do *you* want to be an overachieving hotshot lawyer who goes camping with Katharine Breakspeare?" I ask, trying for a smile, trying to tease.

"No," Brad says instantly, thoughtlessly. Then his throat flushes brick-red.

I blink. "You mean no to the camping part."

He shifts awkwardly. "Yeah?"

Is he lying to me? He is. He definitely is. But that means . . .
"You . . . don't want to be a lawyer?"

He doesn't reply. I see a muscle move in his jaw, clenching it shut.

"Brad?"

He winces. "I don't *not* want to be a lawyer."

What would Minnie do in a moment like this? Be sensitive. "But you don't *not* not want to be a lawyer?"

"No," he says, "I do. I do. It'll be fun." But I recognize the hopeful tone in his voice, like he's negotiating with himself—I recognize it because sometimes I use it, too.

"It'll be fun," I repeat carefully. "But not as fun as . . . ?"

He huffs out a breath like a frustrated horse.

"Come on. I showed you mine; now show me yours."

"God, Celine," he laughs, and flops back onto the bed, then sits up again. Takes his glasses off, then puts them on again. Rubs his jaw, then mutters, "Sometimes I think I'd like to write a book or two?"

A little chain reaction goes off in my brain and a memory unlocks. "Oh yeah. Oh yeah! You wanted to be an author."

He groans and squeezes his eyes shut. "When I was ten!"

"But not anymore?"

"It's . . . not that easy."

"Why not?"

Brad bites his lip. I really wish he'd stop doing that; it's deeply inconsiderate to me, a person who can see him and is tragically vulnerable to the sight of an excellent mouth.

"Because," he says, and stands up abruptly. "Just . . . look at this." He fetches his laptop from the desk and sits beside me again, cracking it open. His screensaver is John Boyega being criminally hot in *StarWars*. Then he opens a series of folders and I'm faced with a page full of Word files. The labels start small: Draft 1. Draft 4. Draft 9. Before long, letters are introduced. Roman numerals. Bradley has written a lot of drafts.

"I can't finish anything," he announces, then slaps the laptop shut and puts it on his bedside table.

I blink. "Oh my God."

"I know!" He is disgusted with himself. "I keep trying, but——"

"No, Brad, that's what I'm saying. How many times have you tried to write this book?"

He glares at me like I just trod on his already-broken toe. "About a thousand, thank you, Celine."

"And you're still going?"

"I realize it's pointless, but you know what they say about the definition of insanity."

"Are you allowed to say things like that?"

"Hang on, let me consult with the mentally ill council." Brad pauses. "Yes."

"You want to know what I think?"

"Unfortunately," he sighs, "I do."

"I think you've got this all wrong. You think it's a bad thing that you've written so much. I don't."

Brad seems deeply skeptical—but, because he is sweet down to the bone, he props his elbows on his knees, props his chin on his hands, and listens. "Yeah?"

"Yeah. You only do something this much if you love it. And if you love it, you should go for it. Plus, I have no idea what it takes to write a book"—actually, I think I'd die of boredom—"but

I'm pretty sure you have to be exactly this committed. You know, to finish it."

Brad's eyes bug out. "But, Celine. Here is the point you are missing. I. HAVEN'T. FINISHED IT!"

My laughter spills out without permission. "Yes, Bradley, and here is the point *you're* missing: ONE. DAY. YOU. WILL."

That brings him up short. He opens his mouth, closes it, opens it again. "You . . . you don't know that."

"*You* don't know that," I counter. "I'm positive. You're Brad Fucking Graeme. I'd bet on you any day."

His smile is the softest, sweetest thing, like a spilled bottle of relief. "God, Celine. You're so lovely."

I blink. "What."

"Do you know what you just said to me? Or were you, like, in an emotional fugue state and you're going to snap out of it and forget the entire thing?" He pats my knee reassuringly. "That's okay. I'll remember."

Now that he mentions it, everything I just said *was* hideously mushy. And sentimental. And possibly revealed certain things about my . . . my unreasonable fondness for certain aspects of his character. Okay, fine, my unreasonable fondness for literally everything about him.

"Um," I croak. "Never mind. Pretend I never said anything. You're too tall and you get on my nerves, how's that?"

Apparently, it's hilarious, because Brad bursts out laughing. "You are *so* repressed." He sounds like a warm little brook hidden partway through a hike on a summer's day, an unexpected delight. And I don't think I'm repressed at all because I look at him and my heart does a very deliberate jump and I know exactly how I feel.

But why choose to dwell on that when it won't go anywhere? What am I going to do, put my hands on his cheeks and kiss his annoying face? Of course I'm not. You have to be sensible about feelings like this, or they'll run away with you. Liking someone this much is a dangerous game because what do you do when they're gone?

I don't know what to do with myself, so I pull a pillow out from behind his back and whack him with it.

"Hey!" He laughs harder, tugs it out of my grip, and whacks me back.

"Ow!" I yelp.

His amusement is replaced, instantly, by concern. "Shit, are you—"

Which gives me enough time to grab another pillow.

"Ah! Stop." Brad wraps burning fingers around my wrist and says sternly, "Violence is not the answer."

"You just whacked me!"

"That," he says loftily, "was self-defense."

When I transfer the pillow to my other hand, he grabs that wrist too. I try to shake him off; it does not work. He looks quite smug. So I lunge at him, which does not go how I'd hoped, since he's still holding both my wrists.

He falls back on his elbows, and I end up leaning quite heavily over him. If I were choosing to be interested in Bradley, this would be the perfect situation. I could take the weight off my right knee and let more of myself rest on *him,* and our mouths would be very close, and he would be in the ideal position to notice that I smell beguilingly of my lime shower gel and coconut edge control. Then he'd put his tongue in my mouth and come away with an enduring passion for fruit salad.

I let myself imagine that scenario for a few dangerous seconds before remembering that I'm not allowed to be interested in Bradley. So I keep all my weight on my right knee. The mattress sinks a bit, and I wobble and bite my lip.

Then Brad falls all the way onto his back and pulls me down with him.

. . .

Jordan 🖤: what's going on man keep me updated

Jordan 🖤: Brad

Jordan 🖤: BRAD! TF yall doing over there????

Jordan 🖤: ••••

CHAPTER ELEVEN

BRAD

Is this a bad idea? It might be a bad idea. But I'm like 18 percent sure I just caught a vibe, which is actually very sure, for me, and while I'm certainly not *in love* with Celine—that would be ridiculous, Jordan is deranged—I am definitely a tiny bit obsessed with the idea of kissing her. I think about it all the time. Like when we're arguing in Philosophy or when we all go into town to get frappes. Pretty soon she's going to notice how much time I waste thinking about her mouth—unless I can get ahead of the issue by getting at the mouth in question.

That would fix things, right? Actually doing it, I mean? That would fix the kiss obsession. Or make it ten times worse. Only one way to find out.

I pull her to me, a soft weight that presses my spine firmly into the mattress. She says with a low-level glower, "What was that for?" Coming from Celine, this is basically a polite inquiry.

I give her my best smile. "This friendship thing is going really well, don't you think?" I am testing the waters. If she says *Sure is, handsome,* and licks my neck, I'll take that as a green light.

Celine props herself up on her elbows to look down at me—but she doesn't get up. "Am I squashing you?"

"No."

"Okay." Her gaze avoids mine and her round cheeks hollow a little bit, like she's nibbling the insides. This close, she is all gleaming darkness and shiny pink makeup and long eyelashes that flutter away from me. "Um. Yes. It is. Going. Well."

I beam. "That was great, Cel. Deeply emotional. Ten out of ten."

She rolls her eyes, but she still hasn't moved. I'm feeling very optimistic about this, if you ignore the way my stomach is churning with nerves and terrible potential futures are flashing against the back of my skull like a sped-up cinema reel. I throw a very thick, dark curtain in front of the screen and say, "I'm going to suggest something."

She is rightly suspicious. "What?"

"Do you. I mean. Would you . . . like . . . to . . ." Whew. This is harder than I thought. My heart is playing a drum solo right now. How did I get Isabella to make out with me? Oh yes, I remember now: I said, *"Bella, I really like you,"* and she handled the rest. But if I tell Celine I like her, she'll probably jump out of the window as a reflex. For some reason that makes my heart hurt.

And yet . . .

"Celine, I really like you."

She rolls off me and lands on the floor with a very loud *thud.* Well, crap. I scramble to the edge of the bed just as she pops up like a daisy.

"Everything all right up there?" Dad shouts.

"Dropped a book," I shout back.

"Sorry," Celine says breathlessly, rubbing her hip. "Didn't realize the . . . floor was . . . there." Then she smiles brightly.

My stomach plummets into the earth's core. "Oh God. You don't like *me*."

Her jaw drops. "What are you talking about, Bradley? Of course I like you!"

"Right." I nod rapidly, trying not to die of embarrassment. Sadbarrassment. "Of course! We're friends!"

"That's what you meant, right?" she asks. "As friends."

That is very sweet of her, to give me an out. Except she's still smiling—not one of her normal, accidental smiles where her eyes scrunch up into dark shiny gems, but a perfect, polite smile that seems nervous. Or anxious. Or . . . something else I don't want her to be.

"Well, no," I say slowly. This is ridiculous. I am ridiculous. There is an enormous possibility I am making things worse—

Which might be worth the tiniest possibility of making them better.

"No," I repeat, more confident now. (If I'm going to do things wrong, I might as well do them with style and conviction.) "When I pulled you on top of me and, you know, gazed dreamily into your eyes and said I liked you, I did not mean as friends. Obviously."

Her mouth opens. Her mouth closes. Between that and her slow, slightly dazed blinks, pop her in a bowl and she could be a goldfish.

"It's okay, though," I add quickly. "I'm not going to be weird about it, or anything. I'm . . . I'm glad we're friends." Friends is good. Friends is an infinite number of times better than before.

There is no reason for my internal organs to be blowing away in the winds of my desolation. *I am completely fine.*

"Well," Celine says. Her voice is so pretty. Like shiny metal. I am very okay right now. "Gosh," she says after a moment.

I manage to be patient and reasonable for another 0.3 seconds. "Not to pressure you, but I would love a few complete sentences right now."

She sits down on the bed very suddenly. Actually, it's possible she fell. "Are you sure?"

I almost fall at that. "Am I sure?"

"That you, er . . . like me," she whispers.

I count to eight. "Celine. WHY WOULD I NOT BE SURE?"

"Well, I don't know!" She throws up her hands. "This all just seems very out of the blue—"

"It is *not*—"

"We've only been friends again for forty-nine days," she says, then adds guiltily, "give or take."

I stare. "You've been *counting*?"

She lifts her chin, defensive. "Haven't you?"

"Well, of course *I've* been counting. That's my thing! I count things! And I *like* you, remember? What have you been counting for?"

She folds her arms and shrugs.

I cannot believe this. I *cannot* believe this. "YOU LIKE ME BACK."

"Shut up!" she whispers. "Your brother is probably lurking outside like a sneaky alligator."

I'm so busy losing my mind I don't even have time to enjoy the nonsense coming out of her mouth. "Why the hell did you decide to argue with me about this? You impossible human being! Do you realize we could've been making out this whole time?"

Her whole body perks up like a meerkat. "Well, do you want to?"

"Of course I want to! Why do you think I even said anything?"

"Your heart was burning with tender sentiment?" she suggests dryly.

God, she is so annoyingly fantastic. "I was *being assertive.*"

"I see." She considers this for a second. "My turn?"

This takes the wind out of my sails and I finally absorb the truth: the person I like simultaneously likes me back, and anyone who's ever liked anyone knows that that almost *never* happens. Also, the person is Celine, which is like adding rocket fuel to a firework. Or to me. There is rocket fuel in me. "Okay," I say, but what I mean is: *Yes, definitely your turn, do something please, right now.*

She bites her lip and grabs my wrist and pulls me forward. Closer. To her. I shuffle over with all the grace and dignity of a Labrador puppy. My right knee touches her left. She leans into me and she smells like a holiday. I can see the texture of her skin. I can count her eyelashes. I can—

"Brad," she says softly, smiling, for real this time. "You're supposed to close your eyes."

But she's so pretty. "You first."

"On three."

I'm laughing as we count. *One, two, three.* My world is dark and Celine-scented. I feel her breath against my mouth as she speaks.

"You're right," she says. "I do like you too."

Fuck yeah.

"We should talk about it," she continues, and this time I think I feel the slightest brush of her lips against mine. Sensation glitters in my stomach. She's going to murder me.

"You're volunteering to talk about something?" I rasp, trying to sound amused and unaffected and seriously missing the mark. "You really do like me."

"Smartarse," she mutters. Then she very gently presses her lips to mine—only for a second, the single softest second of my life. An electric shock runs from my head to my toes and I'm vibrating with it.

"More," I tell her, and put a hand on her cheek. The curve fits my palm perfectly.

I feel her smile. "Okay."

This time, I kiss her. Longer. Harder. Her mouth is warm and silky and her breaths come quick. My brain falls out of my head. She holds my wrist again, and I can feel my pulse against her fingers, and it is very fast.

I should've been doing this for the last five thousand—

"Dad!" Mason shouts. "Brad's having sex!"

Great: my brother has arrived, right on schedule, to ruin my life. I jerk away from Celine, stomp over to the slightly ajar door (that absolute pervert freak), and shove it wide open. Mason's already running downstairs.

I turn around. Celine's eyes are wide and unfocused, her chest is heaving, and for a second, I forget to be pissed because I'm very pleased with myself.

"Hey," I murmur.

She blinks hard, presses her lips together, and stands up. "Crap. We should . . . go downstairs."

"Probably." I'm going to creep into Mason's room tonight and smother him while he sleeps.

As we head out onto the landing, our elbows touch. Something zips up my stomach. Cel slides me a scandalized sideways look and rubs her arm like I just bit her.

My own arm tingles. "I *really* like you."

"Shhh." She widens her eyes meaningfully at me and leads the way downstairs. "I don't want your dad to hear!"

Aw. She's so easily embarrassed but trust me; Dad's going to love this. Celine is one of his favorite people. Still, I keep my mouth shut because she's spooked, and I know feelings aren't her thing. We just had a moment and now she needs space. (God, I'm so mature. Someone should make a note of this.)

We reach the kitchen in adult silence and find Dad chopping spring onions at the island while staring at us with raised eyebrows (which is very poor kitchen safety; eyes on the knife, Dad).

"Hi," I say.

His eyebrows somehow get higher.

"Obviously," I announce, "Mason is a liar."

Mason, who is eating a rice cake over the sink, says, "Mo am mot." Crumbs spray across the front of his red Notts Forest shirt.

I eye him in disgust. "How are we related?"

He flips black curls out of his narrowed eyes. "You're afopded."

Dad sighs heavily. "Mason, don't talk with your mouth full, stop tormenting your brother, and go upstairs."

Mason snorts and heads for the door.

"By the way," Dad calls after him, "you're not going to no party tonight."

Mason whirls around. *"What?"*

"Remember our discussion," Dad reminds him, "about what good men do and do not say about ladies?"

Aha! Yes! I remember this! He is so screwed.

"I wasn't talking about *Celine*!" Mason wails. "I was talking about Brad!"

"But you were talking about Celine," I say solemnly. "You were violating her bodily autonomy with misogynistic lies for your own ends, Mason. You were treating her as collateral damage in a war between brothers. Mum is going to be so disappointed in you when she gets home."

Mason sputters. Celine looks very much like she is biting her tongue bloody, trying not to laugh. Dad seems amused, but he rolls his eyes and says, "That's enough, thank you, Bradley. Mason, go upstairs."

Mason huffs and stomps away.

"Now," Dad says seriously, doing that I Am Being Parental thing he does with his face. "You two. What's going on?"

He's asking a direct question and meeting my eyes. I try to mentally solder my jaw together, but I can already feel myself cracking under the fatherly pressure. "On? What do you mean? Nothing is . . . going." What is this sentence missing? Oh yeah. ". . . On," I add.

Celine eyes me like I've been abducted and replaced with a Brad-shaped scarecrow. Then she says, "I should head home. I told Giselle I'd make dinner tonight. Bye, Trev." She flicks an almost shy glance at me. "Um. Bye, Brad." Then she scurries off.

I follow her into the hallway so I can lock the door. "Cel—"

"Sorry," she whispers, "but I really don't know how to talk to dads." Then she vanishes in a puff of smoke, leaving me like a traitor to face the music alone. Which is fine, because Dad's obviously gonna tell Mum about this and Mum will definitely tell Neneh.

When I get back to the kitchen, Dad's finished the onions and started on the scotch bonnet. I hop onto one of the stools at the marble island and watch his hands move, waiting for the conversation to start. When it doesn't—when he just keeps chopping with this grim expression, and I start to wonder if I'm seriously in trouble—I crack like an egg. "You do know Mason's full of it. Right? Dad. Come on. Right?"

Also, I have had sex before. Dad *knows* I've had sex before because Mason *stole my jeans* and stretched them out with his massive quads and then put them in the wash basket without checking the pockets and Mum found a condom in there and I could've let *him* take the fall but I very nobly admitted it was mine, so really, you'd *think* he'd have my back every once in a while, but he doesn't because he's an enormous douche.

Dad laughs and finally looks at me. "I should hope he is, Bradley Thomas."

"So what's wrong?" I reach over to take the bulb of garlic, grab a press from the drawer, and make myself useful.

Dad hums. "You and Celine, huh?"

We should talk about it, she said. But then she put her tongue in my mouth, so . . . I shift in my seat and peel the first clove. "Yeah?"

Dad sighs again. Puts his knife down. Gives me his full and serious attention. "Is that a good idea?"

My frown is so intense it hurts my head. "Why wouldn't it be?"

"This is your last year of school," Dad says. "Law is a very demanding course."

Law, he says, like it's a done deal, like I'm an Olympian who wants this so bad it hurts and he's the hardworking coach watching my back. Of course this would come up. Of course.

"Competition is high and . . . final exams, that's a lot of pressure," he continues. "Trust me. I remember it well, and I never had to deal with the extra . . . difficulties you have."

I put down the garlic and try to keep up. "Is this an *I'm worried about how nuts you are* speech?"

"Bradley." He scowls. "I've told you not to say that."

I ignore him. "Because I thought I was doing good. Am I not doing good?" I *feel* good. Or I did, before my dad started talking in riddles.

"You're fine," Dad says, then falters. "I mean. Are you fine?"

I shrug. "Yeah?"

"Okay." He nods. "Okay. Well, all I'm saying is, let's keep it that way."

Have I missed something? "What's that got to do with Celine?"

Dad hesitates before speaking in his *tread carefully* tone, like I'm a bomb about to go off. "I love Celine. But I know you've always had . . . strong feelings about her."

Now I'm annoyed, because I was ready to argue, but that is technically true. My feelings for Celine have been positive and negative, platonic and combative and . . . and this new thing where I want to hold her hand for the next millennium, but no matter what, they've always been strong. "Okay," I say, trying to force my jaw to unclench.

"I don't know if now is a good time for those feelings to get even stronger," Dad finishes. "Aside from anything else, do you need all that added pressure right now?"

"Oh," I say tightly while feelings pop up like volcanic geysers in me. Ten minutes ago, I was having a fantastic time making out with the hottest girl on the planet and now I'm being lectured about my delicate soul. (Well, my delicate brain chemistry, but whatever.) "I don't see why liking Celine is pressure, though."

Dad opens his mouth, then closes it. "I can't tell you what to do, Brad," he lies, before telling me what to do. "I'm just saying maybe you should think twice before adding torrid romance to your list of things to worry about."

"Okay, but I'm not *worried*."

"And if you and Celine apply to universities miles apart, or you're too busy studying to go out on dates, or whatever, you won't be worried then?" There's a deep furrow between his eyebrows and his hands are flat against the chopping board, chilies forgotten. "You were always stuck on something or other that happened with Bella—"

"Don't *compare* them!"

Dad raises a hand like he's granting a point. "Right. No. Sorry."

Bella and Celine are not the same. There's no reason to mention their names in the same sentence. Plus, Bella didn't know about my OCD and she had . . . different ideas about relationships than I did. It was complicated. Me and Celine, we're simple. I know her and I want her, and she definitely knows me.

But she wants to talk, whispers that annoying little voice in the back of my head, the one that picks up on things I'd rather not notice.

"I'm just saying," Dad finishes, grabbing his knife again, "that first BEP expedition took a lot out of you. I know you haven't managed to finish your uni applications yet. And final exams are going to be . . . Law school requires very high—"

The words "I don't *care* about law school" burst out of me, like when you open a bottle of pop and it all fizzes over. I thought they were staying inside, but then something shook and twisted a bit too fast, and now the counter's all sticky and half my bottle is empty. There's no undoing it.

Dad drops his knife and looks at me with an expression so astonished and concerned (concernished, perhaps) you'd think my head had fallen off. "Pardon me?" he asks.

Now I feel like a dick. He's just trying to give me advice, the way he always does, and how do I react? By throwing inconvenient truths at his face. "Nothing," I say, picking up my garlic. "Sorry."

"Brad, are you—"

"I'm fine."

"You know you can tell me anything. If you're not feeling . . . If you're having any—"

"I'm in a bad mood." I force a smile. "You kind of rained on my parade, old man."

His expression softens. "Son. You know I'm not trying to be negative. I just want the best for you."

"I know."

"But I can't tell you what to do," he repeats.

Parents love to say shit like that, as if their words, their looks, their *expectations,* aren't as heavy as a small planet. Usually, my dad's word is law whether he knows it or not.

But not this time.

Turns out, when it comes to Celine, Dad's right: he can't tell me what to do. No one can.

• • •

CELINE

Minnie: You did WHAT?

Celine: IT WAS AN ACCIDENT

Minnie: lol no it wasn't, you've been drooling over him for centuries

Minnie: just astonished YOU finally noticed???

I have no idea why I tell Michaela anything. She's a deeply annoying human being.

After hovering in front of the Graeme house for a bit, I'm speed-walking home (very irresponsible while texting, I know, but needs must). Then I hear my literal worst nightmare behind me: it's Brad. Calling my name. Right after we just kissed.

And, God, the way we kissed. It was completely mortifying. Like, I saw fireworks and forgot my own name and momentarily considered putting his hand on my boob, all of which is very dangerous indeed because—because no one is supposed to feel like that. Like everything.

Brad can't be everything.

"Celine!"

I very slowly turn and, yep: my ears do not deceive me. He is sprinting down the path, a coat thrown over his clothes. Oh my God. I stand frozen like a statue and panic.

As soon as he reaches me, breathless, he asks, "You learned to cook?"

The tip of his nose is red with cold. His eyes are as dark as midnight—not the cold winter kind, but the warm summer sort where you can't sleep because the sheets stick to your skin and anyway, there are adventures out there to be had.

And his mouth is . . . soft. I know this firsthand because—

Midconversation, Celine.

"No," I reply, hoping he didn't notice my very minor dazed pause. "Why?"

He arches an eyebrow. "Because you just said you had to cook dinner."

Shit. "You shouldn't be allowed to look at people like that when you're interrogating them."

He arches another eyebrow and continues being unnervingly handsome. "Like what?"

I falter. "Never mind."

He grins like he knows exactly what my problem is. (Considering the enthusiasm with which I put my tongue down his throat—considering I admitted I liked him—he understands completely.) "Well, I'm glad I caught you out here. I was going to follow you home and sneak into your room. I had an elaborate plan that involved trellis-climbing." He pauses. "Except I probably wouldn't have done that because I just remembered how much I weigh."

"Also," I say, images of Brad in my room dancing in my head, "we don't have a trellis."

"That too," he allows cheerfully. "My mind is a dramatic and often inaccurate place. Point is—you said we should talk." His amusement fades, and he watches me closely. My stomach lurches under his attention, half giddy and half terrified.

Because, without his mouth distracting me, I've woken up to the facts of our situation: it's December. Final year. In roughly ten months, Brad and I will be separated. Once we leave Rosewood, we'll be geographically farther apart than ever before. We won't see each other every day. We'll meet new people and develop new social bubbles that have no chance of overlapping. We will write new chapters in our lives and I'll be a side character in his, and that will be fine and natural and understandable.

But I've experienced that before and I'm not doing it again. It hurt so much when we fell out years ago because we'd been so close. Close enough to feel like one person, and then we were ripped in two and I had to keep it together with blood gushing from my side and half of myself missing.

Well, I'm fine now, because I'm just me. I've felt the pull of him, but I've resisted.

If we get any closer—if he kisses me some more, and tells me how much he likes me, and smiles as if me just liking him back has set the world to rights . . .

We'll be one person again. And I can't have that. I can't.

"Celine," he says softly. "Talk."

So I do. "Listen. Brad. Earlier was, you know, fine . . ." God, I'm such a liar. "But we can't do it again."

His tentative smile falls like a sudden and catastrophic loss of the sun. After an agonizingly long pause, he says, so softly it's a struggle to hear: "Why not?"

I swallow hard. "Because . . . because what then?"

"Well, Celine," he says, "if you let me kiss you some more, and I kept doing it and you kept liking it, I think the next thing is . . . we'd be dating."

My throat seizes with terror or joy. Who can tell the difference, really? "But we can't be dating," I squeak.

His amusement is a puff of white in the air. "I mean, we definitely could be."

He makes it sound so easy. *Everything* is easy for him. "But, what about uni?"

"Ugh," he mutters. "Swear to God, uni is already ruining my life, and it hasn't even happened."

"Long distance never works." It's true, and this is the normal, rational way to phrase it, as opposed to something pathetic like: *You'd leave me eventually. But you can't leave if you're not mine.*

"Why?" he demands. "Because people can't resist the urge to rub their genitals all over other people during Freshers Week? Rest assured. I am not going to do that."

"I never thought you would." He wouldn't need to. He'd just need to . . . sit next to someone at the back of a lecture every day for six weeks, and realize he wants to take them out, and feel trapped by the fact that he couldn't because he had me sitting somewhere miles away thinking he was mine. That's all he'd need to do. Just, stop wanting to be mine.

Which would be perfectly reasonable. Normal. Part of growing up. And I never ever want it to happen, so I try again, scrambling for an explanation he'll accept. "We are very young, Brad, and people change, and the next few years of our lives will be *transformative*. I mean, I doubt *I'll* be transforming any time soon, but . . . but you will, and holding on too tight to parts of a previous stage in your life is just not a sensible idea."

He makes a sound of disgust and kicks the frozen grass beneath us. "Why," he demands, "is everyone telling me how not sensible it is to have feelings? What are we, fucking Vulcans?"

"I'm not telling you not to have feelings. I'd never tell you what to do in your own head."

He looks up—maybe because of what I said, or maybe because of how I accidentally said it, like trying to control him would be a capital crime. Which it would, for so many reasons, but if there's one thing I can't stand, it's showing my own feelings, and he teases them out of me without even trying.

Yet another reason not to kiss him again, as if I needed more.

"Celine." He makes my name sound like a sigh. Like a very gentle waterfall. "You said earlier that I could do anything."

"Books," I remind him desperately. "I was talking about books. Writing. Jobs. Dreams."

"Is work the only thing people are supposed to dream about? I thought fantasies were meant to be fun."

There's a second of teetering uncertainty where the world wobbles or shimmers or shifts and I'm not quite sure if I'm protecting myself or committing serious sabotage. Then everything slams back into place and logic prevails: everything ends. I don't want to have him if he's going to be gone. So I won't take him at all.

There. Logic. Who can argue with that?

"I'm sorry," I tell him.

His jaw shifts. This is his stubborn face. "I still like you. I'm not gonna stop."

I don't believe you.

He falters. "Are you asking me to stop?"

Say yes. Tell him not to look at you like that. Tell him not to say your name so sweetly. Tell him not to bump your shoulders together when you get frappes or touch your knees together in Philosophy. Tell him——

"I can't tell you what to do," is all I say, because I am pathetic and awful.

He chews on his lower lip, brows drawn together, eyes pinned to mine. "Did we fuck everything up today?"

No, no, no. If we did, it means no more Brad at all, ever, and I can't cope with that. "We're still friends. Always, okay? Always. Say it." I should be embarrassed, forcing someone to say something like that, but I'm more concerned with getting the words out of his mouth. As if they're a magic spell that sets us in stone. Friends 4 eva. Maybe I'll make him a bracelet.

"Cel," he laughs, though it's more exhausted than amused. "Okay. Always. Okay?"

"Okay. Good."

"Aw. I like it when you're bossy." But there's caution behind his confidence.

I hesitate. "Are you flirting with me?"

"You never asked me to stop."

No. And I'm the worst friend in the world because I still don't.

CHAPTER TWELVE

BRAD

Celine told me I could do anything. She also told me we can't be together. Here, then, are my options:

1. Celine never lies. I *can* do anything. One day, I'll write something worth reading.
2. Celine is a liar. We *can* be together. We just haven't been friends again long enough for her to trust me yet.

Turns out both things can't be true. So I spend the last two weeks of term being Celine's friend, because I'll never stop again, and flirting with her, because she doesn't seem to hate it. I also Google *Can I write a book?* because for the first time I'm seriously considering the question and Google is the smartest person in my life. When the suggested search brings up *How do you write a book,* which is an even better question, I feel like I've been struck by genius lightning.

Unfortunately, the various tips I find online do not help me finish my epic sci-fi novel in one week, so yet again, here I sit on Failure Avenue. I wonder what else I've messed up lately.

"Brad." Celine's hand closes around my elbow. She jerks me to a stop 0.2 inches away from a gleaming pillar of glass. It's Christmas break, and we're back at the Sherwood, that fancy hotel where we first heard about the BEP, ready to meet *the* Katharine Breakspeare and receive our scores so far. Apparently, I zoned out as we made our way through the ornate lobby.

To my left, a buttoned-up Sherwood employee gives me a dirty look from the polished reception desk. I try not to breathe too hard on their pristine glass as I pull away.

"Thanks. Sorry."

Celine's expression is concerned. Her hand is still on my elbow and I'm really enjoying it, although it would be better if I wasn't feeling this contact through a thick shirt and a winter coat. Screw you, December.

"Are you okay?" she asks.

"Yeah. Just thinking." About my tragically doomed creative future. Nothing major.

"Okay." She starts to pull her hand away.

I put mine on top of it. "Actually, I'm still feeling unsteady on my feet. You should keep that there."

"Brad." Her lips twitch at one corner.

"Or we could hold hands. That would be nice. For my balance, I mean."

"Brad." Her lips twitch some more. Her eyes are dancing. I

bet if I felt her cheek, she would be hot. "You're not allowed to flirt with me while Katharine Breakspeare's in the building."

I'm tired and nervous, so my brain suggests all kinds of terrible reasons for that, but I try to ignore it and question the source. "Why not?"

"It's unprofessional," she says primly, and starts walking toward the sleek silver elevator.

"Unprofessional? We're seventeen! What, exactly, is our profession?" I hurry after her.

"Explorers," is her crisp reply. The elevator slides open immediately, and we step inside.

Me and Celine each have a ten-minute slot with Katharine. Cel's is pretty much now; mine's in half an hour. We're here together because I offered her a lift, and because, once Raj has his appointment in an hour or so, we're all going out for dessert. And I'm repeating these basic facts to myself because, if I don't, the big dark thoughts in the back of my brain might overwhelm me.

Oops. I wasn't supposed to think about the thoughts.

But they're here now: worst-case scenarios about the meeting today, rushing in like shadows through a crack in the door. I used to hate elevators when I was a kid because I didn't understand them, and anything I didn't understand was based on luck, and luck was a monster I barely kept under control. Maybe that's why my guard slipped as soon as we got in here. Or maybe I'm just overwhelmed because I spent a significant portion of last night thinking about all the ways my conversation with Katharine could go wrong and now—fantastic!—I'm thinking about them again.

"Brad?" Celine's eyes meet mine in the elevator's mirrored

wall. She's paused in the act of pushing green and black braids behind her ears.

"Yeah?" I ask, but I can't fully hear my own voice because my head is so loud. Those thoughts are saying failure, dead end, disappointment-as-always. I count the floor numbers written on the elevator panel, one two three four five six seven eight. In thirty minutes, Katharine Breakspeare will tell me I'm out of the BEP because I suck, tough luck, shit happens. My moments of happiness are numbered, one two three four five six seven eight—

"Are you okay?"

"Yeah," I say. Then, "No."

She turns toward me—

"Wait, just—give me a minute."

She bites her lip, nods, turns back.

I've been tapping my knuckles against the elevator wall, one two three four five six seven eight, and now they hurt. My fault for trying to ignore my thoughts instead of, you know, accepting them and grounding myself in the present or what-fucking-ever but—"Do you know how annoying it is that intrusive thoughts come almost every time you want things to go well?"

Her eyes meet mine in the mirror. "I'll go with 'super fucking annoying.' Is that about right?"

Somehow, I smile. "Pretty much."

She smiles back.

Okay. Okay. I blow out a breath and look all my bad thoughts in the eye because I must not fear. These are mental distortions. My life isn't doomed to be a string of failures, and counting can't alter the path of fate even if it really feels like it *should,* and these thoughts aren't really mine, but I'll accept them because they're nothing I can't handle. *Fear is the mind killer. Fear is the little death that brings total obliteration.*

"Sorry," I mutter.

I will face my fear.

Celine scowls. "What for?"

I will permit it to pass over me and through me.

"I'm usually really good at, you know." I shrug. "Taking care of my brain."

"I know that, Brad. You're doing it right now."

This feels like a ludicrous compliment. I actually blush. "It's just hard to notice, sometimes, what's a reasonable train of thought and what's, um, not."

"Okay," she says calmly.

The elevator glides to a stop and the doors start to open. Already. Crap. Celine glances at me, then hits the *close* symbol and pushes button number eight.

I blink at her. "What are you doing?"

"You don't have to talk to me," she says, her eyes on the mirror. "Take your time."

"Your appointment is in—"

"*Relax,* Brad."

I splutter, laughing. "*You're* telling me to relax?"

She rolls her eyes. "Do as you're told."

Where the fear has gone there will be nothing.

Only we will remain.

By the time we reach the top floor, I have a firm grip on my endless store of worst-case BEP scenarios and have dismissed the idea that this elevator will crash to the ground unless I step on every floor panel. It won't. That's not how engineering works.

We glide back down again while Celine adjusts her black dress in the mirror. I put an arm around her waist and bury my face in her hair, just because. Because I can. Because this feels good, and she's soft and solid, and I want to say—

"Thank you."

"Deeply unnecessary," she mutters.

I grin, squeeze her again, step back. "Your hair smells amazing."

She cuts her eyes at me. "Don't start."

"Start what?" I ask, all innocent. "I'm just telling the truth. Speaking of, you look pretty today."

"So do you," she murmurs, then freezes. "I meant . . . you look . . ."

I am 100 percent positive she's blushing. "Gorgeous?"

"No."

"Stunning?"

"No—" laughter in her voice.

"Like your next boyfriend?"

"I don't do boyfriends." Celine snorts, and the elevator dings.

I frown as I follow her out into a cavernous cream hallway. Now, this is one hell of a distraction. "What do you mean you don't do boyfriends?" I thought she just didn't do *me*. Because we'll change, or whatever, which we *won't*—but I am, believe it or not, trying to respect her decision, so I heroically don't bring that up. "You had a boyfriend before. Didn't you?"

Her expression is appalled and astonished. (Appallished.) "Are you talking about *Luke?*"

"He wasn't your boyfriend?" If that's true, why the hell did I have to spend months watching him pant after her? Were they not making out in every dark corner like feral rabbits? Did I not once see him *give Celine his scarf*? I most certainly did.

Ugh. The fact that I'm jealous of Luke Darker right now? I may never find my dignity again.

"No," Celine says firmly, "Luke wasn't my boyfriend." She starts walking faster, like she's trying to outrun this conversation, her footsteps muffled by thick blue-and-gold patterned carpet.

"So what was he?"

"A guy."

Luke Darker was just *a guy*. Somebody needs to stop the press.

Wait—there's something more important going on here. We pass a wall of paintings with gold plaques underneath, which I ignore. "Do you not plan to date anyone? Ever?"

Celine gives a too-casual shrug. "Never thought about it."

"Why?"

"Hasn't come up."

I'd bet my left ball it came up with Luke and it's definitely come up with me. She's avoiding feelings again. Hard.

I know she likes me—she *said* she likes me—so I thought the anti-relationship issue was just a lack of trust. We've only been friends again for five minutes, and last time we broke, we shattered, so for her to doubt my feelings, or even her own—that is understandable.

But is she telling me she doesn't trust *anyone*?

I want more than this for you.

How do you tell someone a thing like that without coming off monumentally rude?

While I'm trying to figure that out, we reach an ornate door.

There's a golden plaque above it that says THE BLUE CONFER-
ENCE ROOM. Celine exhales and smooths down her skirt. I bet,
for once, she's panicking even harder than I am, what with her
Lord and Savior Katharine Breakspeare being in the next room.

Yet she still makes the time to grab my hand again. "Brad.
You know you've got this, right?"

God, I want to kiss her so badly, but instead, I say, "Back at
you, Bangura."

The door opens.

"Thank you," a familiar voice says, all easy confidence. Katharine. "I'm so glad we had the time to make this work." She's the
one who opened the door, but instead of walking through, she
holds it and steps aside to let out a stream of people. Not Explorers; adults in suits and wool coats. Celine and I move back,
hands parting, and I nod politely at everyone who makes eye
contact. Never a bad time to make a good impression. I hope
she remembers not to glare.

The last man out looks vaguely familiar—he's tall, though
not as tall as me, with brown skin and a bald head and silver-
framed glasses that flash in the light. There's something about
his dark, dark eyes that gnaws at my memory, but I can't quite
grasp it, so I just nod and wait for him to pass.

He doesn't pass.

He jerks to a stop as if he slammed into a pane of glass. I
hear his inhalation. I see the color leave his cheeks. His eyes
widen and he chokes out, "Celine?"

Oh.

Shit.

It's Celine's dad.

I've only seen him a handful of times, years ago. There are no pictures of him in the Bangura house. I turn to look at Celine so fast I feel the creak in my neck—but her exterior is the exact opposite of my explosive panic.

She stands there in front of her father, shoulders back, gaze steady, expression polite but blank. And she says, so, *so* calmly:

"I'm sorry. Do I know you?"

Mr. Soro looks like he has just been stabbed. I am suddenly having the time of my life. This moment could only be improved if he had a sudden bout of catastrophic diarrhea and shit himself in front of Katharine Breakspeare and had to waddle all the way home.

"I . . . ," he stammers. "I . . ."

Amazing. He can't collect a single word. What a sad excuse for a human being.

I am suddenly, monumentally furious. This *slug* is the reason why Celine—Celine, who is so much, when he is so little—second-guesses so many things in her life? Unbelievable.

Mr. Soro clears his throat and finally gets himself together. "I . . . ah . . . sorry . . . I'll just— Good seeing you." He makes an awkward motion with his arm, then follows through, scuttling off like a roach.

I watch him all the way down the corridor with what is probably an expression of sheer disgust on my face. Then I notice Katharine Breakspeare observing the scene with interest and plaster on the best blank mask I can. No way Celine wants this drama playing out in front of her hero.

I can't imagine how she feels right now. What do I do? I have to do *something*.

"Right, then," Katharine says. "Celine Bangura?"

This is supposed to be the part where Cel quietly but visibly explodes with pleasure because Katharine knows her name. Instead, there's not even a flicker in her eyes. "Yes," she says.

The two of them head inside and shut the door.

• • •

CELINE

When I was little, Mum would wash my hair for me. I'd lie down in the bathwater to rinse, my ears submerged, and hear her voice as if from miles away.

Sometimes Giselle washed my hair.

Dad never did.

The conference room Katharine Breakspeare leads me into is ornate but tastefully cream and blue, with a huge oval table of dark wood at its center. I drift past each leather chair like a ghost and wonder which one he sat in. Wonder if he's wondering about me.

Would it matter if he was? Would it change anything? He would still be a man who couldn't look his daughter in the eye. He would still be a big blank slate to me. I thought I hated my father but right now all I feel is exhausted, like he ripped into a vein and drained half of the life I had.

If he were someone else's dad, I would find him so pathetic. I wouldn't even bother to think his name.

A little flame catches and crackles, flickers, grows in the darkness of my roiling gut.

". . . really well, Celine," Katharine is saying, and I realize we are sitting down at the head of the table. A meter of gleaming wood separates us. She has a tablet in her hand and a slight, encouraging curve to her wide mouth. There are gossamer creases around her eyes, magnified by black-framed glasses, and her infamous blowout is smoothed back into a simple ponytail. I wish I was eating up these little details; my lack of enthusiasm feels like a bereavement.

I smile and make a vague but positive/appreciative/encouraging sound. Whatever she just said is a mystery to me. The leather seat of this chair is too warm, radiating through my tights. There's a faint ringing in my ears, which can't be good.

Mum's voice murmurs in my mind, *"You're okay. You're all right. You are my daughter."* I sit up straighter. Bangura women don't break.

"Your leadership score is very high," Katharine says, scrolling through the tablet. "Your team building is—"

"Low?" I interrupt like some mannerless heathen. It's not like I expected to do well. I don't like people and they don't like me. I don't trust people; why should they trust me? I'm prickly and harsh and—

"Actually," Katharine says, "your team-building score is also high. According to the feedback notes, you frequently supported and encouraged your fellow Explorers."

Well, that can't be right. Maybe she has someone else's file. Unless . . . Is she talking about the tent thing? Seriously? I was *bored* and everyone else was *slow,* so I sped them up. It was not that exciting.

"You acted, on multiple occasions, to mitigate the effect of . . . stronger personalities in the group," Katharine continues, "so quieter members could have their say."

This is just technical speak for *You shut Allen up,* which I only did because he desperately needed to be silenced. Really, it was my pleasure.

"You took care of the communal spaces; you gave other people's ideas a chance even when you didn't necessarily agree. . . ." Katharine finally looks up from the mystical tablet. "Yes, team building is one of your strengths. Your lowest score was actually creative thinking."

Hmm. Maybe this is about those rope-based obstacle courses we did and how I got stuck near the top of a tree and didn't even think to jump right back down.

Or it could be about that poisonous plant-life project we did—

"As you know, the final expedition at Glen Finglas will be more heavily weighted in the average. My advice would be to attempt a little more flexibility of thought. Have you ever heard the phrase *question the premise?*"

I don't care, I don't care, I don't care, I'm too hot and my eyes hurt, and I want to go. I take a deep breath and maintain my smile. "Is it like rejecting the premise?" Before I quit for final year, I was a three-year debate team champion.

"Yes, but not exactly. It's more internal."

"Okay. Then, no, I don't think so."

"I very much enjoy the work of Becca Syme," Katharine says, locking her tablet and putting it on the table. "She proposes that we might solve our problems more creatively if we paused to question the underlying premise beneath our established ideas. Does that make sense to you?"

I take another breath and force my brain to understand English. "Yes. Yes, I think so." For example: my dad is a disgrace and I should make him feel ashamed. The premise: That blood makes him my father? That I can make him feel anything at all?

Time passes and so does our conversation. Katharine congratulates me on making it through and wishes me luck in Scotland; then I'm stumbling out the door and Brad is there. So is Sophie. When our eyes meet, she gives me a look of concern that grates me into cheese, then disappears with Katharine. Brad is holding my hand.

"Cel. Celine. Talk to me."

"No." My mouth is numb, but I'm ready for an argument.

Except Brad doesn't argue. He just twines our fingers together and leads me down the hall. "Okay. What was your score?"

My mind comes up panic white. "I don't know."

"It's okay!" His thumb rubs the back of my hand. "It's okay, it's okay, you don't need to know. Five out of five. You're Celine Bangura. What else could it be?"

"She said I'm not a creative thinker."

"Pfft." Brad rolls his eyes. "What does Katharine Breakspeare know, anyway? Hey, Cel, look at that." He nods, and I realize he's brought me out to a long hallway with a wall of impressionist portraits showing celebrity guests who've stayed here. "Is that Freddie Mercury?" he asks.

I squint up at the portrait. "Can't be."

"Why not?"

"No way Freddie Mercury stayed here."

"But the teeth," Brad says reasonably. "We should Google it. Where's your phone?" Just like that, he drip, drip, drips oil onto my squeaky tin man joints and I feel myself loosen up. A bit. A fraction. Enough. By the time we're all finished with our meetings and heading to the dessert café, I seem perfectly fine.

Thomas doesn't show up, but the rest of us pile into a booth, and Aurora coos over the menu's gluten-free options and Raj eats so much ice cream cake he's almost sick, and I realize I genuinely missed them, and the distant ringing in my ears nearly goes away, and Brad holds my hand under the table all night.

Aurora gives me several sly and significant looks, but I very maturely do not engage.

By the time we call it a day and separate, I think I'm fine. The ringing is still there but it's so faint I can almost forget it. Brad and I are still holding hands as we walk across Trinity Square toward the car park, and the streetlights everywhere make the rain-slick paving slabs gleam like silver. A group of guys barely older than us arrange shabby-looking instruments a few meters away and put out an open guitar case for tips. I don't know how they can play when it's this cold; my fingers would riot if Brad's weren't keeping me warm.

"I don't think scores matter at this stage, anyway," he's saying. "That first expedition—it's just practice. Glen Finglas is more heavily weighted. And we know our strengths and weaknesses now, so we can do even better. This is still anyone's game." He pauses, giving me space to respond. When I don't, he keeps talking, cheerful as always. "I'm most looking forward to the—" He breaks off, then continues. "To finishing this whole thing. The suspense is killing me, you know?"

Except that's not what he was going to say. I know him well enough to notice when he's correcting himself, and it doesn't take an expert in Brad's interests to figure out where he was going before he hit that little catch in his voice: he's looking forward to the ball. The Explorers' Ball where we all celebrate and meet potential employers, including, oh yeah, my dad. I can't believe I thought I wanted to see him, or rather, wanted him to see me. I can't believe I thought his presence could do anything but ruin everything. I can't believe I talked to Katharine Breakspeare and I didn't even care, or remember everything she said, or ask her about the Harkness Oil case, or—

I don't even want to *go* to the stupid ball anymore, I don't ever want to see my dad again, I don't—

"Celine," Brad says, sounding so *wretched,* like someone out of a gothic novel, and it takes me a second to realize he sounds that way because of me. "Don't cry," he tells me.

I agree. *Don't cry, Celine.* Seriously, please. It's disgusting. But tears are already spilling, scalding hot, down my cheeks and off my chin at an alarming rate. Are teardrops supposed to be this huge? They're probably steaming in the winter air. They're probably pooling at the base of my throat like a pond. You could probably drown someone in the vicious, wavelike sobs that shudder through my chest. I press my hands to my face because I've never been so embarrassed in my life—I am *crying,* in *public*—but I can't stop I can't stop I can't—

"Come here," Brad says, "come on," and puts an arm around my waist. I can't see where we're going, but after a few steps he pushes down on my shoulder and I sit. There's an icy stone bench beneath me. Then Brad wraps his arms around me and I'm not cold anymore. I'm warm, but there's still this core of ice in me with a searing, volcanic fissure right down the middle, and all kinds of terrible things are spilling out of that crack.

I take my hands away from my face and bury it in Brad's shoulder instead. He smells like soap and curling up in bed. My fingers twist into the fabric of his coat and pull hard, too hard, but I can't make myself be careful.

"It's not *fair*." The words rip out of me in a sob.

"I know," he says.

He doesn't. He can't. But I don't envy him for it, the way I used to. Instead, I am so, so glad, because I don't want this for anyone.

"I shouldn't *feel* like this. No one should be able to make me *feel* like this."

"I'm sorry."

"I *hate* this."

"I'm sorry."

The buskers start playing a jaunty cover of "Hotline Bling."

"For fuck's sake," Brad mutters, "read the room."

Somehow, I giggle. Very wetly. With snot. "Read the square," I suggest.

His shoulder moves under my cheek as he huffs, a smile in his voice. "Nice. You're being pedantic. I was worried about you for a second."

I laugh and cry and snort and generally make a mess of myself. I can't believe I'm sobbing on his shoulder in the middle of Nottingham. "Shoot me now." I lift my head, clumsily wipe my cheeks with both hands, avoiding his gaze—

"Hey. Stop." Brad puts a gentle hand on my jaw, pushes my chin up until our eyes meet. His are warm and soft and focused as he produces a tissue from God-knows-where and dabs carefully around my face.

I sniff loudly and sit there being cleaned up like a child. "This is the worst."

"You're welcome." He gives me another tissue. "Blow."

I do as I am told.

"Put that in here." He has yet another, clean tissue—clearly he stays prepared, and why am I surprised?—spread open in his hand. I pop mine on top of it, and he wraps the whole thing up in a little parcel and puts it in his pocket. Then he pulls hand sanitizer out from his other pocket and squirts a healthy amount into my palm, and two colossal realizations hit me at once, which is deeply unfair, because lightning's not supposed to strike twice.

1. I love Bradley Graeme. As in, would give him a kidney, would wash his socks, would turn into a supervillain if he died. I love him so much I almost want to say it out loud, a dangerous and horrifying prospect I am not remotely equipped to deal with right now. Luckily, I have something else to distract me.
2. Giselle was right.

"What if everything about me is just a reaction to him?" I whisper. The band has moved on to "Despacito." I am convinced they're doing this on purpose.

Brad puts a hand on my knee and squeezes. "Are you listening to me?"

I blink. "Yes?"

"Your dad is just something that happened to you," he says. "Like that time you were sick and you ate a tub of Phish Food and all your vomit tasted like chocolate ice cream, so you don't eat it anymore."

I grimace. "Brad. Ew."

"What? It's an example. Your entire personality is not

because of Phish Food," Brad says seriously, "and it's not because of your dad, either."

He makes it sound so simple, but believing it is much harder. "That's just ice cream. This is——" My whole life plan. "My Steps to Success board says——"

"Change it."

"But that's not the *point*! The point is, how many things have I done or wanted to do just to . . . to show someone who is never going to care and never going to change? How pathetic does that make me?" It feels like everything is slightly twisted, like my vision doesn't align with the angle of the world around me. I thought I was someone strong. I might be the opposite.

"You know what you said to me before?" Brad asks, his voice low, his eyes pinned to mine. "You said it's not fair. Because you, Celine, are the kind of person who cares about fairness. You're the kind of person who wants justice, and that's not him—that's the opposite of him. It's all you. So you've been doing the most to balance the scales. So what? That doesn't make you pathetic. It makes you *yourself*. You just needed to figure out on your own that . . . that fairness is about you being happy, not him being punished."

A stubborn part of me wants to insist that he's wrong, that I'm still fucked up and this is the end of the world, but the thing is, he's making sense. And I like sense. I can follow his logic step-by-step and I think he's right.

I want things to be just. I want things to be good. I want harm to be made up for—the same things Katharine Breakspeare fights for when she takes on these human rights cases. That's what I care about. That's who I am. And maybe I've let that shape my choices in a way that does me no good, but choices can change. I have control over that. I have control over myself.

My dad doesn't.

Except that's not true, because I feel the weight of everything he's done—everything he hasn't done—on my back. And I don't know if it's ever going away.

But you can try to push it off, surely?

I swallow the last lump of tears. "You were right, before. I do avoid my feelings. But I'm going to . . . try. To do better." To let them drive my choices, instead of letting my dad rule over me. "And I . . . *feel* like I don't want to see him at the ball."

Brad nods slowly.

"But I can't just . . . not go. Can I? Wouldn't that be giving him too much power?"

Brad's response is careful. "I don't want him to ruin this for you. Either by upsetting you when you're there, or by taking it away from you altogether. I think maybe . . . you should talk to your mum."

My stomach thuds down into the concrete bench. "Right." Mum doesn't know anything about this because I've very specifically kept it from her, and suddenly that feels less like protection and more like the betrayal my sister said it was. We don't sneak around behind Mum's back. She's never done anything to deserve it. But I did it anyway, and now I'm meant to reveal all and, what, ask for her help? I got myself into this mess.

God, I can't think about this anymore. My head hurts, and the only good thing I can see is Brad. The only good thing I *feel* is Brad. The band is playing "Heat Wave," and that's what's rolling through me, sickly and nervous and hungry. "I'm going to ask you something."

He goes so still, the air around him vibrates in comparison. "Yeah?"

There's a lump of anxiety in my throat that's swelling by the second, but I manage to let it pass. "Do you— Can we, like . . . kiss? Again. Maybe?" I bite my lip. That was a Herculean task.

Brad stares at me. His eyes seem darker, pure black—like his pupils have grown to meet the midnight ring around his iris. His lips roll in, then out, full and soft and honestly impossible to resist, which is probably why I'm in this mess. Except, no. I'm in this mess because he's the kind of guy who says things like, "Why?"

Fear crackles inside me like a bonfire. *Because I love you.* "Why not?"

"Celine."

"Because you're hot, obviously."

He grins and flicks me between the eyes.

"Ow!"

"Stop objectifying me and tell me the truth."

Yeah, right. I know I just decided to face my feelings, but *accepting* that I love him is very different from admitting it aloud. Who says *I love you* after a couple months of rekindled friendship? Not me, thank you very much. I'm seventeen. My mum still does my laundry. I'm about to change my entire life plan because the first one was an overemotional mistake, so what exactly is my love worth? What's it going to do?

"Cel?" he whispers.

You know how many people stay with the person they adored when they were seventeen? Not a lot. But do you know how many friendships survive school and thrive for years?

Way more.

I finally decide. "I don't want to lose you," I say. It's the only truth I'm ready to tell.

"Okay, Celine," he says softly. "It's okay." His lips curve in a one-sided smile. My stomach lurches to the same side. "You don't trust me, do you?"

"I—" Really want to say yes. But my mouth tastes like a copper cage and I can't get out any more words. Disappointment sits heavy in my stomach. I'm supposed to be better than this.

Brad deserves better than this.

His throat bobs, and I glimpse something painful in his expression before it vanishes like it was never there. Maybe it wasn't. Maybe I'm projecting. Maybe I'm the only one who feels like my insides have just been ripped out.

He smiles his usual, beautiful smile and says, "You still want to kiss me, though."

I force myself to laugh, and once I've started, it's surprisingly easy. Everything's easy with him. My voice is hoarse, but I still push it out, still make the joke. "Don't judge. I have a theory that seventy percent of the global population wants to kiss you, and that's a conservative estimate."

"But you're the only one who gets to do it. Lucky you." His hand slides into my hair. His thumb traces the curve of my jaw. "Okay. So kiss me."

Something nervous squeezes in my stomach. My heart winces. "But—"

"Just kiss me. That's all. What's a little tongue between friends?"

Friends. Just like I wanted. Right? "You're ridiculous."

"You're beautiful." His mouth meets mine. This kiss is tender, careful, so sweet it makes the crack in my chest ache. Usually, when my eyes are closed, all I see is black, but when Brad's touching me, everything is gold and glowing. Safety blooms, like the gentle rise of music in the air as the band plays "Comfortable."

He pulls away slightly and murmurs against my mouth, "See, they're rooting for us."

I push down the last of my strange sadness, grab the back of his head, and put his lips on mine again. There's no way I'm even close to done with him.

But I make a mental note to tip those musicians.

CHAPTER THIRTEEN

BRAD

As soon as I drop Celine off, all the sparkle fizzes out of me and leaves disappointment behind, because what the hell was that? Did I basically just tell her we can be, like, friends who make out sometimes? Am I really so much of an absolute *sucker* I just gave a piece of myself to my literal dream girl without any of the commitment I want in return?

Well, yes, evidently. I pushed too hard at the worst possible moment, then backtracked all the way into her mouth.

"Stop objectifying me and tell me the truth."

Why did I ask her that? It's obvious Celine doesn't trust anyone as far as she can throw them—and I thought she'd be ready to pledge eternal devotion a couple of hours after bumping into the devil incarnate? She was *crying,* for God's sake. I am the literal worst.

I drum my fingertips against the steering wheel as slashes of streetlight whip past. My brain points out that we could be speeding straight off a bridge right now so we should probably check the speedometer and all of the mirrors eight times, or preferably stop driving altogether, but I remind my brain that there are no bridges on my route home because I do not, funnily enough, live in Venice. Just as I'm pulling into the driveaway behind my mum's Kia, my phone lights up on the passenger seat and my ringtone fills the car. I ignore it. Parking is very important to me.

So's Celine, and you fucked that right up.

Yes, thank you, brain. I appreciate the reminder.

Here's the problem: if I believed she had zero feelings for me, maybe I could get a grip, but I don't believe that. She *told* me she likes me, and, God, the way she *looks* at me . . . I know I should leave this alone, but I can't. I—care about her too much.

"You don't trust me, do you?"

What if she did?

Several brooding thoughts and a few pristine angles later, I switch off the engine and call Jordan back.

"Hey, man," he says, "what's good?"

Literally nothing. Except the way my mouth is still tingling with the memory of Celine's, but even that's bittersweet. "Just got home. You?"

"Whooooa. What is that?"

I frown at my house. Lights are on. Everyone's home. "What's what?"

"That voice, bruh. Who killed your cat?"

"I don't have a cat." They play with dead animals, and I really don't need that energy in my life.

"Meeting didn't go too well, huh?"

Actually, I didn't mention this to Cel, but my meeting did

go well. It went very well. My score for the practice expedition was 4.79. If I work as hard in Glen Finglas, and take my weakest trait into account—commitment, apparently, probably because I couldn't stop messing about with Raj or staring at Celine—I could be one of the top three Explorers. I could win. "I think . . . I have a real chance at the scholarship," I admit, the words rushing out on a sigh.

"Uh. Did I miss something? Is that . . . bad?"

"No. No, it's good," except no it's not because oh my God, I don't even care right now. I don't feel the slightest spark of excitement, and it's not only because I'm upset about Celine. When I check in with my feelings, I find a mountain of dread at the idea that I'm one step closer to making this law degree happen because—

I know what it feels like to want something so badly, it eats at you. I know how greedy I really am, how much I *need*. And now I know how it feels to go without.

I tap the handbrake, just to make sure it's on, and say, "I don't want to study law. It would be fine. But that's not enough." As soon as the words are released, it's like a too-tight belt around my waist loosens by a single notch. I breathe a little deeper and stare at my house. I can see the back of Dad's head through the living room window. The belt cinches tight again.

"Damn," Jordan says. "Okay."

We sit in silence for a moment.

"What do you want to do instead?"

"Um." I've never admitted this to anyone else—but no, I told Celine, and she didn't laugh or produce any of the other cruel and unlikely reactions my brain was convinced I would get. She just . . . supported me. She told me I could do anything.

So before I can second-guess it, I tell Jordan, "I've been trying to write a book."

"With the amount you read, that makes perfect sense."

Hold on. "I spill my tortured forbidden guts and all you can say is *it makes sense?*"

Jordan bursts out laughing. "*Writing a book* is your most tortured and forbidden secret? I love you, man. Don't ever change."

"It's ridiculous. Do you know how many copies the average book sells a year? It's in the low hundreds, Jordan. *Depressingly low.*" I'm trying to avoid specificity for the sake of my nerves, but the number flashes in my brain anyway, so—

"Buddy. We talked about this. Stop memorizing sad statistics."

I ignore him. "Do you know how many authors actually make a living writing? Thirteen point seven percent. And I'm supposed to believe I'll be part of that thirteen point seven percent when I can't even finish a book?"

"Well, yeah," Jordan says, like it's obvious. "You're Brad Graeme."

"*Why* do people keep *saying* that?"

"Because it's true. But I'm sensing a little aggression here, so let's move on."

A laugh bubbles out of me, leeching frustration with it, and I rub a hand over my face. "Sorry."

"That's okay. Show me the book, and I'll forgive you."

I shudder. "No. It's terrible."

"Somehow, I don't believe you."

This time, my laughter is bitter. "Mate. You know I always back myself. I'm not being modest here." This is not, for once, an attack of self-consciousness. "I know what a good book is.

I've read about seventy-five million of them. And my book? Is not a good book. It's not even a finished book, which seems like the absolute bare minimum."

"Okay, yeah, fair enough." Jordan snorts. "But it'll be good eventually, right?"

I exercise my right to remain silent.

Jordan keeps going like he's persuading a toddler out of a tantrum. Which is starting to feel annoyingly accurate. "And at least now you know what you should be studying, right?"

"Wrong."

"Come on, man. You want to write? Study English. Was that so hard?"

"My dad——" I want to say he'll flip, except that's not true. No, he'll just be devastated and disappointed and lots of other D words I don't like, and then there'll be all this added pressure because if I don't succeed, if I don't finish the book and make it a bestseller and then somehow trap that particular lightning in a bottle all over again for the rest of my life, I'll only be proving his disappointment right.

But what about my disappointment if I never even try?

"Your dad," Jordan says firmly, "is living his own life. You should live yours. You haven't finished uni applications yet and the deadline is next month. Apply to study English."

"I——" Want to. Badly. Even though I'm scared, even though I could fail, there's a black hole of *want to want to want to* sucking me in.

I didn't think I'd be that good at camping and hiking and other disgusting outdoor crap either, but I got a 4.79. Maybe Celine was right. Maybe I can do anything.

Still. "I wouldn't get in. I dropped English this year."

"But you got an A plus last year."

"Star," I correct automatically.

"A star, whatever. You got one."

"But—"

"But what?" Jordan demands, exasperated.

I search for another issue and come up blank. "I don't know. My brain is an unholy shitstorm of worst-case scenarios."

"I know. But that's . . . what's it called?"

"Intrusive thoughts," I murmur. I'm still staring at the living room window. Mum is in there, too, and so is Mason, and they're bouncing around in front of the TV and it looks like they're having fun. (This is especially monumental because Mason developed an allergy to fun when he turned thirteen.)

"Exactly," Jordan says. "They're not yours. So they're not the boss of you. Right?"

I told him that once. Now he's using it against me like a demon. "Ugh. God."

"Right." He sounds unbearably smug. "And, hey, I bet an English degree would make your book a lot less shit."

That's the final nail in the coffin of my law career. Because I've been thinking of this all wrong, haven't I? Thinking I need to be good enough to study. But maybe studying is what's supposed to make me good enough. I wouldn't try to join Dad in court without passing the bar.

Maybe there's nothing wrong with your first book being terrible when you don't really know what you're doing.

Or maybe it's terrible because you're terrible and no amount of education or practice will change that.

I take a deep breath, put up a shiny shield around my budding new hope, and watch the bullshit bounce right off of it.

"Jordan," I say, "I think you might be a genius."

"What do you mean *think*?"

We talk for another ten or fifteen minutes, long enough for the tension of the day to uncoil itself from around my spine. By the time I get out of the car and unlock the front door, I almost feel optimistic. I've made a decision. I'm happy with it, even though I'm nervous. Nothing can stop me now.

Except I've got to find a way to tell my parents.

I remember the last time I mentioned to my dad that maybe I didn't care about law. Remember the way his face fell, the way he was *concerned,* like I must've lost my mind, and dread thuds in my stomach—but I'm getting ahead of myself. There's really no guarantee an English course would accept me in the first place. So maybe . . . I should take this one step at a time? Apply first, then worry about the rest?

I don't know . . .

The house is warm and noisy. Mum pops out of the living room as I put my shoes away, all wrapped up in one of her woolly blue cardigans because she feels the cold every winter, even with the heat on. "Hey, baby!" She's shoved her long, dark curls up into an enormous bun, but it's slipping down as we speak. "We're playing some game on your brother's Switch. Come and join us."

I swallow my apprehension. "Okay."

"How was the meeting? How were your friends?"

"Friends are good. Me and Celine had chocolate orange cookie dough." And then I put my tongue in her mouth and broke my own heart, but I keep that part to myself as we walk into the living room. "The meeting went well."

Our Christmas tree is huge and sparkly in the corner, the

main lights turned off, so all focus is on the TV screen. Dad and Mason are running on the spot in front of it, but Dad still manages to grin over his shoulder. "That's my boy! You got that scholarship in the bag."

"Maybe."

Mum laughs and puts an arm around my shoulders, kissing my cheek. "Cheer up, Eeyore. It doesn't matter if you get the scholarship or not. Student loans never killed anybody."

This is the part where I joke, "No, but law might," and it is so smooth and charming everyone's too busy laughing to freak out over my sudden and abrupt change of life plan. Except I clearly don't have the guts God gave an eel because instead, I smile and hug Mum back and decide I'll mention it later.

Later, as in months from now when (if) I get acceptance letters. Time fixes everything, right?

I'm halfway to the sofa when I freeze, that last thought bouncing around the walls of my brain like a squash ball. *Time fixes everything.*

"Brad?" Mum says. "You okay?"

"Yeah," I reply. I'm not. I'm having a holy-shit, jump-out-of-the-bath epiphany. If time fixes everything, it could fix me and Celine.

All I have to do is be patient, right? She thinks I'm gonna leave, so I won't. She thinks nobody stays, so I will. It's really that simple. I won't *tell* her I'm trustworthy, I'll prove it.

The storm cloud above my head drifts away in the face of this genius plan. I sink into the sofa, my mood officially transformed, and announce, "I'll play Mason next."

"I'm gonna *obliterate* you," my little brother pants.

I grin. "Bring it on."

FEBRUARY

CHAPTER FOURTEEN

CELINE

SUNDAY, 6:56 P.M.

Minnie: soooo I got into Edge Lake 🦢

Celine: WHAT???

Celine: I KNEW IT!!!

Minnie: 👋

Celine: A SWAN, MICHAELA. YOU ARE AN EDGE LAKE SWAN

Minnie: thank u babe 🥹

Celine: pizza party when I get back

Minnie: well, who am i to decline pizza

Minnie: but in the meantime

Minnie: are you gonna be okay spending the week alone w ur new boyf?

Celine: we won't be alone

Celine: + why wouldn't I be okay???

Minnie: idk your animal lust might bubble over and you could lose your v card in the woods

Celine: virginity is a social construct and I have opted out

Celine: wait.

Celine: HE'S NOT MY BOYFRIEND MICHAELA

Minnie: hahahaha ok celine

I roll my eyes and close our chat because we're on the bus to Glen Finglas for the final expedition in Scotland—and after the last few months of normal life, I need to get back in the BEP zone. I need to be at my Breakspeare Explorer best. I need to *not* have a heart attack, and if Michaela keeps accusing me of a relationship I can't have, it's highly likely cardiac arrest will follow.

The fact is, Brad and I are not dating. We have been hanging out a lot, and touching a lot, and it's true that I am unfortunately in love with him, but that doesn't make us *dating*. I decimated any chance of that. It's February, which means I have a mere seven months to get over this teeth-aching obsession with him, take my frankly ludicrous feelings of *love* down the much safer avenue of *loving friendship,* and get used to the fact that come October, we'll be too far apart for our secret, 100 percent platonic make-out sessions to continue.

Minnie fantasizing about things that will never happen really doesn't help.

Aurora's sitting next to me drawing a scary-good picture of a thistle in a leather-bound notebook with thick, creamy pages, so I open my camera app and turn my attention to her. "Hey, Rory."

She clocks my phone and holds her open scrapbook in front of her face. "Celiiiiine."

"What? You look cute!"

"No, I don't. The presence of any camera within a ten-meter radius makes my facial muscles freeze in a very awkward position. This is a fact," she says firmly. "It's been scientifically tested."

I roll my eyes. "Well, then duck down so I can get a shot of the Great British countryside passing us by."

"Of course," she says. "I live to serve you. My spine is foldable anyway, for your convenience—"

I snort and push her back against the seat. The idyllic view from our window involves a potholed main road, a traffic queue that consists mainly of red Ford Kas and gray Vauxhall Astras, and a fenced off, barren field in which a single skinny goat gnaws on what looks like a large pair of knickers.

I grimace and let Aurora sit up. "Never mind." And then, like an incredibly dim moth to an incredibly bright flame, I turn toward the seat across the aisle. Toward Brad.

"Hey," I say casually. "Smile."

He cuts off his conversation with Raj, looks at me, and lights up like a bulb. Soft lips, strong teeth, eyes dark like a secret. Something swoops in my stomach, which is a completely normal occurrence; sometimes my stomach swoops around Minnie too. Usually with dread, after she tells me about a joint Halloween costume or a new makeup technique she wants to practice on me, but still. Swooping happens.

"What are you doing?" Brad asks, all innocent, while twinkling at my phone like a professional sparkler.

"I'm going to make a BEP TikTok."

"Oh yeah," Raj says, leaning forward. "You're internet famous."

"Not really," I mutter, but Brad's talking over me. "Yeah, she has thirty-two thousand followers. She made this video about trees recently that went viral." He turns away from the camera. I can see the precise, diamond parts in the vivid dark of his hair, and the sharp angle of his jaw shifting as he talks, talks, talks about me. "It was, about, like, how all the trees in the world are baby trees. There used to be bigger trees with trunks like volcanoes. Like mountains! But they all died and the ones we think are big are actually just saplings growing back. . . ." He trails off, shifting in his seat, rummaging through the pockets of his jeans. "Hang on, I'm not explaining it right. I'll show you."

I am gobsmacked.

Then Aurora leans over my shoulder and murmurs, "Three minutes of Brad footage. That'll make an excellent TikTok."

I blink, scowl, and lock my phone. "Aren't you supposed to be drawing?"

By the time we arrive at Glen Finglas, it's getting dark. We pile off the minibus in a jumble of excitement and nerves, and as we're herded into the campsite, it becomes more and more obvious who's gone from the group—and who's been added. There's a new supervisor, an older East Asian woman with graying hair and an expression of boredom to rival Holly's. I have no idea why they've brought someone new in because when I count heads, I find there's only nine of us Explorers left.

Nine.

We each have a one in three chance at the scholarship, except those chances aren't equal——they depend partly on our practice score. And I don't know what mine is.

Not for the first time, I curse my father with the force of a thousand suns. Hey, I'm supposed to be feeling my feelings, and raging frustration is most definitely a feeling.

A gloved hand bumps against mine. In the low light, Brad is all eyes and shadowed cheekbones that point me directly to his mouth. The tip of his tongue slips out to wet his lower lip. I remember this morning, when he dragged me around the back of the minibus and ran his tongue very slowly over *my* lower lip, and something in my stomach clenches like a fist.

Brad taps a finger between my eyebrows. "That's better."

I feel slightly dazed. "What?"

He nudges me. "Come on."

Sunny Days Campsite is a long, thin stretch of manicured land sandwiched between an eldritch-looking forest and a dark, gently flowing stream. Holly and Zion herd us like cats past rich old people in their campervans toward the plots reserved for us. I spy a dad sitting with two kids outside a tent, pointing up at the moon already visible in the purple-stained sky. One tiny corner of my heart twists.

I've been thinking since—December.

Since I saw my dad.

I've been thinking that I need someone to talk to, and since I refuse to dump any more of my feelings on Minnie or Brad or Mum or Giselle, maybe that someone should be a professional? To help take care of my feelings. Like going to the dentist. Like Brad said.

I don't know. It's just an idea.

The air is cold and damp and about as miserable as you'd expect Scottish air to be in late winter. We blow on our icy fingers and gossip as we trudge over.

"Where's Thomas?" Aurora asks.

"He texted me," Raj says. Then he whips out his phone, adjusts imaginary spectacles, and takes a stab at Thomas's private school accent: "'Not got the time, to be quite honest,'" he recites solemnly. "'Exams are coming sooner than you think and freezing one's balls off in the woods is not *conducive* to success.'"

"He never said *conducive*." Sophie snorts from my left.

"Oh yes," Raj assures her, "he did."

"Where's Allen?" I ask.

It's Aurora who answers quietly. "I heard he was caught last expedition having sex with someone in the laundry room. Apparently, they used a Mars bar wrapper and a rubber band as protection."

There is an appalled silence before I say firmly, "Well, that can't possibly be true. Who on earth would have sex with Allen?"

For some reason, Brad finds this hilarious.

"Right, Breakspeare Explorers," Holly announces, her determined monotone carving through the chatter. "Here we are. First: allow me to introduce an additional supervisor, Rebecca. Since this expedition covers such a large area, she'll be joining me and Zion as your emergency contacts. Get her number from one of us before the end of the day, understood?"

We all mumble obediently. Brad says, "Hi, Ms. Rebecca!" because of course he does.

Our new supervisor blinks, then cracks a cheek-creasing smile. She has cute little gap teeth that do not match her stark silvery hair and frown-creased forehead. "Hello, young man," she says, charmed.

Holly is clearly disgusted with Rebecca's lack of resistance. She moves swiftly and severely on. "This campsite will be your home for one night only so Don't. Get. Comfortable. You have the rest of the day to put up your tents in groups of two or three and get settled in."

Sophie stamps one booted foot against the concrete-hard ground and mutters, "Christ alive, Hol, not asking for much."

From the front of the group, Zion shoots us a stern look. (Sophie's voice does carry.) I straighten my spine and adopt a serious expression to show I'm a responsible Explorer who respects our supervisors and is ready for anything.

Bradley catches my eye and mouths, "What's up with your face?"

"The camp's water pumps are over here," Holly tells us, stabbing her arm out like a very tan signpost who does a lot of Pilates. "Dispose of rubbish in the appropriate bins over *here*. Toilets and showers are *here*."

That final *here* looks perilously close to the actual forest. I squint over at the trees and make out a stone path with a few red signs that seem to say BATHROOM. Um. Whose idea was it to bury the toilets in the woods???

"What if I need to pee in the middle of the night?!" Aurora whispers.

"Squat, babe," is Sophie's advice.

"Are you all right, mate?" I hear Raj murmur. When I look over, Brad seems to be seriously contemplating his life choices.

"Fine," he whispers back. "Just coming to terms with the whole *public shower* thing."

"My mum packed some sanitizing wipes, if you want them."

Brad is clearly offended by the suggestion that he has not come armed to the teeth with his own cleaning products. "Um. Thank you. But. I have my own."

"Tomorrow morning," Holly continues, "you'll need to pack up your tents, take your maps, and begin day one of the expedition through Glen Finglas. We expect to see you for dinner at the Duke's Pass campsite by four o'clock, ready to rest up before the next day's hike. Your route and your time management are your responsibility. The manner in which you travel is your responsibility."

Our group exchanges furtive glances; we've already decided to move as a team. Strength in numbers. Plus, I'd be bored to tears if I spent the next three days wandering through the woods on my own.

Anyway, Brad and I have to stick together. Our parents told us to, so we're only doing the responsible thing.

"There are multiple Golden Compasses hidden on various routes, with clues marked on your maps. We'll be considering your speed, efficiency, and hunting skills alongside the usual

Explorer qualities, as laid out in your handbooks. You will be given your GoPro cameras in the morning to record your expedition experience. This footage, along with your interviews at the campsite every evening, will be used to devise your scores."

Another significant look, this time slightly (okay, massively) stressed, or maybe that's just me. We can turn the cameras on and off whenever we want—for example, if we have to poop in a bush, which is a possibility no one's mentioned but I bet it's happened to someone before—but just the thought of being filmed during every single moment of this woodland fiasco is kind of high pressure. Film doesn't change or fade. Film is precise and unforgiving. I have to be the perfect BEP alum these next few days. I want a scholarship.

But do I want to show up at the ball and claim it, if it means seeing my father? In the months since I laid eyes on him, I still haven't decided, and it's eating me alive.

"Good night, Explorers," Holly says, all doom and gloom. "And good luck."

There's an angsty, wind-howling pause.

Then Zion announces, "I brought hot chocolate, by the way. Shall we set up the camping stoves?"

• • •

BRAD

The first day of our hike dawns so bright and so frosty, I am in serious danger of snow blindness. It turns out Scotland is like a fear factor version of England, in that almost everything's the same but 10,000 times more extreme. The sky? Bluer. The grass? Greener. Unfortunately, the cold is also colder, and the morning dew is wetter. I learned that last part around 6:00 a.m., when I was woken up by the *drip-drip-drip* of icy water on my nose.

That's right. Our tent *let in water.* I mean, Raj says it was condensation and called it "perfectly natural" but the point is . . . outside water *touched my face.* I may never sleep again. I'm still scrubbing at my nose in absentminded disgust when Celine appears, looking ridiculously gorgeous for a girl who slept on the ground last night like the rest of us. Her cheeks are shiny and rounded by her way-too-chirpy smile. She makes her plain black rain jacket look Instagram-worthy, and the straps of her Breakspeare-issued rucksack are doing magnificent things to her boobs. If I don't die of horror during this expedition, I might die of lust instead.

"Hey," she says to Raj, then catches my wrist and tugs my hand off my face. I tangle our fingers together. She gives me a look and pulls gently away because we are not a couple. We are next-to-nothing. I can only touch her in private, and that might never change.

Every time I remember those facts, a section of my stomach shrivels up and curls in on itself. At this rate I won't have anywhere to put my food and I'll be permanently nauseous.

"Your nose is red," she murmurs.

I roll my lips inward, curl my hand into a fist, and remind myself of a few things.

You offered her this. You mostly enjoy this. And it's not forever.

"Are you okay?" Celine nudges me.

"Yeah." I'm getting myself together. Remembering the plan, because that's a thing I do now: I have plans to reach my goals, and I execute them. I learned that from Celine. Right now, my plans go something like this:

Goal A: Become a writer.

1. Apply to uni in Leeds and Bristol, where I'll study English. ✓
2. Receive acceptance letters. **?**
3. Tell parents. **X**

I'm still working on that last one.

And then there's Goal B: Date Celine. Unfortunately, this plan's not quite as straightforward, but it goes something like this:

1. Kiss Celine a lot. ✓
2. Show her she can trust me. **?**
3. Confess my true feelings and ask her for more (third time's the charm). **X**

Things get complicated after that because the rest is up to Cel. Either she'll say YES PLEASE! and I will live the rest of my life in a frankly indecent state of joy (that's my preferred outcome), or she'll say no. She'll say, *It's not about trust.* She'll say, *I'm just not that into you.* And I'll have to get over it, some-how, and fall out of—you know, stop caring about her like that, somehow, and just spend the rest of my life slowly and quietly dying of longing in the corner. Which will make me a real drag at parties.

"Have you two packed up your tent yet?" Celine asks, louder this time.

Raj looks at her, then looks at our still very much upright tent. "What do you think?"

"You do realize we're the last ones still here? Sophie's gonna lose it."

"Did someone say my name?" Sophie calls, trudging across the grass toward us with maps tucked under her arms and Aurora hurrying behind. "Guys, is that your tent still up? Come on. Have a word."

"Brad was having a crisis," Raj says, and my cheeks heat because I think he's talking about my very minor and totally reasonable water-based freak-out. Then he says, "Couldn't decide what to wear," and my cheeks get even hotter. I didn't think he'd noticed that. I'm just trying to look . . . you know, dateable! In walking boots! It's harder than you think.

Celine looks me up and down, her long braids falling forward as she absorbs my forest-green tracksuit and white thermal shirt. It's casual and practical because, duh, but coordinating colors seem more effortlessly put-together and green looks amazing on me. I am an autumn. Celine clearly agrees because she has the same look on her face that she gets when I put aside whatever book I'm reading and tackle her onto my bed. This look involves slightly vacant eyes and a small bite of the lower lip, and I like it very much.

I arch an eyebrow. "What are you thinking about?"

"Nothing," she murmurs under the sound of Sophie and Raj bickering.

"Liar."

"Take your tent down before Soph has conniptions," Celine says. "And don't forget to bend from the waist. I read somewhere that crouching is bad for your knees."

My snort is skeptical. "I am feeling very objectified right now."

She grins. "I have no idea what you mean."

● ● ●

CELINE

The aim of this expedition is to find as many Golden Compasses as possible while reaching your destination within the allotted time frame. So here's our galaxy brain idea: we'll work as a team to find the most compasses in the least amount of time.

Theoretically, I mean.

Of course, compasses aren't the only thing that contribute to our scores this expedition. We have to show all the usual Breakspeare qualities while we're camping under Zion's, Rebecca's, and Holly's watchful eyes and have to illustrate them during our end-of-day interviews, and everything we say has to be backed up by the footage taken from the little cameras attached to our coats. Maybe that's why the first two hours of our trek through the woods are quiet and awkward; we all feel super self-conscious.

Or maybe it's because everyone is too busy panting at the grueling pace Sophie's set. Honestly, that girl must have an engine where her lungs should be: she's striding ahead like it's nothing, even with her rucksack full to the brim with supplies.

We're supposed to carry a third of our bodyweight while we trek, but I am a delicate flower, so Brad took most of mine, thank God. I slide a look at him out of the corner of my eye, partly to make sure he hasn't collapsed under the strain and partly because he's too gorgeous not to look at. This thing we're doing, where we spend all our time together and sneak off to make out and talk about the future while carefully avoiding the distance that future will put between us—I thought it would make things easier.

Nothing about this is easy.

I know the texture of his skin. I know the way his breathing changes when I twist my fingers into his clothes and pull him closer. I also know the way he sighs when he's thinking bad thoughts, I know he's aware of exactly how handsome he is and enjoys it very much, I know he turns into a five-year-old when he's around his little brother. And I love it. All of it.

I should put a stop to this, but every time I try, I learn the hard way that it's impossible.

I am trapped by my own choices. *Just take him or leave him.* Except I'm pretty sure I lost my chance to take him like that in December, and I can never leave Brad again, so this halfway house is all we have left. My vision blurs for the barest second, turning the image of him wispy around the edges like he's a ghost. Then I blink and everything's clean and crisp and clear, the way it's supposed to be.

"Hey." Aurora's voice snaps me out of my thoughts. I realize I've been staring blankly at Brad's head for way too long and pin my gaze to the forest floor instead. It's all mulchy, frosty moss and twigs almost as thick as my wrist. Glen Finglas, it turns out, is vast and twisty, with ancient trees that stand miles above me like sentinels.

I suck in a breath of cold, green-tasting air and face Aurora. "Yeah?"

"Is Brad . . . okay?" she asks, her voice a whisper.

There's something in her tone, in the careful light of her wide, blue eyes, that makes my expression shutter and my voice harden. "He's fine. Why?"

Some people know Brad has OCD. Some people don't. It

really doesn't matter because it's no one else's business. The problem is when people notice there's something different about him, don't have a name for it, and make it a *thing*. Aurora is my friend, and I like her a lot, but if she turns out to be one of those people, I will rip out all her hair and knit a scarf with it.

She raises her hands like maybe she read the hair-scarf intent in my eyes and murmurs, "I just noticed he, um, is bothered by certain things, that's all. And he's staring at that log pretty hard and I was worried he might be—"

"What?" I whip around to check. Brad is indeed staring at a log pretty hard, although *log* might be the wrong word: we're approaching a moss-carpeted clearing, and at the center of that clearing is a vast, felled tree trunk, all smoothed out by time and weather but ragged like a wound at both ends. It's hollow, and inside there's a wealth of all the things that fuck Brad's mood right up, like clusters of mushrooms and creepy little bugs and . . . "Thanks. And, er, sorry," I say to Aurora, then rush over to stand by his side.

The thing about Brad is, he always looks so pleasant and so pretty, it's hard to tell when he's having a moment. Right now, his dark eyes are narrowed but his mouth is soft and slightly parted. His jaw is sharp as ever, but not tense. His hands are in his pockets so I can't tell if he's clenching his fists, if he's tapping his fingers . . .

Just ask. Duh.

"Brad?"

"Cel," he murmurs, his focus fixated on the trunk.

"Are you okay?"

His lips tip into a tiny, absent smile. "You mean, am I having a series of dark and inescapable thoughts about fungus and spores and effervescent rabies germs floating up from fox urine and into my body?"

"Um . . ."

"Because no, not really."

My response is far from helpful. ". . . Kind of . . . sounds like you might be?"

"Well, maybe," he allows, "but only a very normal amount."

Oh dear. "Is this one of those times when I should give you a minute, or is this, like, a time when I should do something else?" No response. "You'd tell me, right, if I should do something else? Brad!"

He finally tears his eyes away from the tree. His smile widens into something slow and familiar that burns away the cold around us like hot coffee. "Are you worried about me, love?"

My heart doesn't jump at that word, or if it does, it's a jump of shock. Of minor surprise. Certainly nothing else because it's normal to call people *love*. The postman calls me *love*, for heaven's sake. Anyway, knowing Brad, he's just trying to distract me.

I bite my lip and squeeze his elbow, studying his face like I can read his thoughts written there. And maybe I can, at least a little bit, because I realize with an exhale that he's doing fine. The concern whirling in my gut eases. "Why would I be worried about you?" I ask, eyebrows raised.

"Because we're *such* good friends." There's a tease in his voice that makes me smile against my will.

"True," I allow, trying and failing to fight that grin.

"Wonderfully close," he continues.

Still not as close as I'd like.

"Some people might call us intimates," Brad adds.

"No one would call us that this side of the year 1940."

His voice is singsongy and infuriating and wonderful. "If you say so, Celine."

"What are you two loitering over there for?" Sophie demands a few meters away.

Brad shoots me one last grin before he looks at her over my shoulder. "I think we need to go south here."

"But south is the way we came!"

"Just a little bit. Off the trail. Come here, look at your map." Then Brad pulls out his own and shows us all one of the Golden Compass clues, and where we are on the grid right now, and reminds us this trunk must be the shapeless, blobby landmark in sector E6, so if we go *south* . . .

And that's how Brad, and his vivid focus, and all the tiny details he can't stop himself from noticing, get us our first Golden Compass.

CHAPTER FIFTEEN

BRAD

We get to the next campsite in time—in fact, half an hour early—with five Golden Compasses. I found three of them, which doesn't technically matter since we're working as a team—but our cameras will have caught that, right? And anything that gets me closer to the scholarship, I'll take. Now that I know I'll be studying English, I've started to have all kinds of hopes, started to imagine myself wearing burgundy brogues and, like, coffee-colored houndstooth trousers and a navy turtleneck to lectures, where I discuss the nature of the creative mind with super-smart professors, and then I go home and write 10,000 words of pure gold.

And I know uni won't be like that; I know I'll actually have to work and I'll probably fail a bit and my first book will still be near impossible, but the point is, I *want* to go. And I'm remembering that if I get the scholarship, I can spend my full loan on better housing to avoid having a roommate. (Because, seriously, can you imagine having a roommate? What if he's like Mason? I'd rather choke.)

So when we break out of the woods and into the Duke's Pass campsite, I'm already planning the stuff I'm gonna say in this evening's interview to wow our supervisors. I will modestly but accurately portray what an asset I've been to the team, et cetera. Judging by the super-serious expression on Celine's face, she's planning the same thing.

"Hey," I say, bumping our shoulders. "What are you gonna say in the interview?"

She blinks hard, eyelashes fluttering like sooty wings. "What?" Her lips are slightly parted, and I'd like to kiss them, but I'd also like to know what exactly she was thinking just then, if it wasn't about Holly, Rebecca, and Zion. That furrow between her eyebrows is only acceptable if she's scheming. Otherwise, it means she's worried, and I don't want Celine worried.

"What's up?" I ask.

"Nothing," she says, the word landing too deliberately to be true.

"Cel . . ."

"Nothing, really." Her fingertips brush against my wrist, finding the gap between my gloves and my coat with heat-seeking precision.

My stomach flips around like a carnival roller coaster. "Not fair."

"You're so easy."

"Are you slut-shaming me?"

She grins. Slides her fingers into mine, leans into me, and just like that we're officially holding hands in public. Like a *couple*. Like she doesn't care. "Maaaybe. What are you gonna do about it?"

So much.

"Hey, look!" Raj calls. "They have a park!" He rushes ahead of us toward the little wooden play area, and Celine slips from my grasp—supposedly to follow Raj, but I feel a bit deflated. Sometimes I think she wants what I want, feels what I feel. Other times, it's like watching her close her eyes and turn away.

Patience, I remind myself. *Patience.* It's just that waiting is starting to feel a bit like lying. And I don't lie to Celine.

"Guys," Sophie is saying, "we're supposed to be responsible and super-mature explorers here."

"Who wants to play on the swings?" Raj asks.

Aurora squeals and runs to join him.

"Oh, for God's sake." Sophie gives me a look. "Do something."

Celine seems to find this hilarious.

I sigh and look around until my eyes land on the park's little green-and-gold sign. "It's only for children up to twelve years," I call.

"I could pass for twelve!"

"Raj. You have a mustache."

"Says you"—Celine grins over her shoulder—"Mr. Five O'clock Shadow."

"Get him, Celine!" Raj is gleeful.

I arch an unimpressed eyebrow at her. "Are you undermining my authority?"

"And what authority is that?" she asks with syrupy sweetness.

Sophie groans. "Jesus H. Christ. It's like drowning in a bath of hormones." Then she stomps into the park, picks Aurora up, and bodily carries her away from the swings.

Celine bites her lip and follows.

And I make a decision. Since I'm not going to sleep in my grotesque condensation-dripping tent tonight, maybe there's something else I can do with that time instead.

. . .

CELINE

Aurora, Sophie, and I are packed like sausages in our tent, huddling for warmth and discussing campsite snoring etiquette.

"It's not his fault," Aurora says mournfully. "He could have some kind of condition." It's pitch dark, countryside dark, but I can imagine her expression of wide-eyed sympathy. Then our mystery neighbor's earthquake-level snore reverberates through the campsite, loud enough you'd think the perpetrator was in here with us, and I imagine a little smile sneaking onto her face.

"Fair enough," Sophie allows, "but I didn't notice anyone on this campsite sleeping alone. So whoever's next to him better roll him onto his side sharpish."

"They must be used to it," I muse. "Maybe they're asleep right now."

"With that racket?!"

"Maybe they find it soothing after decades of living and sleeping side by side in loving harmony. Maybe it's like a lullaby and they can't drop off without it." I don't realize that was a weird thing to say until both girls pause.

Sophie's the one who finally responds. "Celine. What are you on?"

"The sweet drug of true love," Aurora says.

"What?" I squawk. "What are you talking—" But before

I can get to the bottom of that disturbing comment, a noise comes from outside. And it's not a snore. It's my name, whispered in a voice I know too well.

My heart perks up like a well-trained dog.

"That better not be Brad," Sophie mutters.

Aurora dissolves into hysterics.

I tut at them and grab my phone, flipping on the torch and unzipping the tent with inhuman speed. "Are you okay?" I ask, just as the flap peels open to reveal a shadowy shape I recognize. The moon is full, and the clouds covering it shift away just as he smiles at me. Bradley Graeme by moonlight is a mind-wiping, pulse-pounding sight most people would pay to see for aesthetic reasons alone. But when I look at him—when I compare the light in his eyes to the scattered stars in the sky and find his brighter, when I wish I could touch every inch of him the way this silver glow does—it's not just aesthetic. At all.

Lately, when I'm falling asleep, I have this weird half-awake fantasy of Brad giving me a tiny piece of himself and letting me put it in my pocket and keep it. I should really Google dream symbolism and figure out what that means—I could make a TikTok about it—except I'm afraid of the answer.

I don't know how long I can keep doing this.

"Hey." Brad pokes the tip of my nose with unnerving accuracy. "Pay attention. Want to go to the park?"

I flush hot and look down at myself. "Er, I'm wearing my pajamas."

"Want to change?"

"We have a curfew."

"Want to break it?"

I remember I am still going, inch by torturous inch, through the arduous trial of acknowledging and expressing my true feelings. "Yes."

He beams. "Good. I'll wait here. Wear your gloves."

I roll my eyes, zip up the tent, and ignore Aurora and Sophie's sniggering while I hurriedly throw on a tracksuit. And a coat. And a scarf. And gloves, because wearing all that without them would be weird, not because he told me to. When I crawl out of the tent and zip it up behind me, the campsite is still and quiet, except for the haunting hoot of a nearby owl, the ominous howl of wind blowing through the forest to the north, and the resonant snore of That One Guy.

Brad is waiting with his hands in his pockets, but as soon as I stand up, he hooks our arms together like he's escorting me around a ballroom and we head slowly, cautiously, toward the park. "How is it this dark?" he asks.

"Well, at night, the sun goes away—"

He elbows my ribs. "The sun does not *go away*."

"You're such a pedant."

"We would fly out into space and die."

I tut. "You don't know that."

"Celine," he says seriously, "if you tell me you've been swayed by a conspiracy theory against the existence of gravity, I will be forced to reconsider our—"

I think he's going to say *relationship*—which would be a problem, obviously, because we're not in a relationship. And that's a good thing, a safe and sensible thing, so I'm relieved when he says, "reconsider our friendship." I am. I am.

If I fall quiet, it's because I have to concentrate. The park is on the other side of the campsite and when clouds blow in front of the moon, which they do every few seconds, we might as well be stumbling around with clay pasted over our eyes.

"What's wrong?" Brad asks.

"I'm trying not to smack into the side of someone's caravan."

"I mean lately. With you. You seemed off today."

There he goes again, noticing things. "It's nothing."

The moon reappears, and we're here at the park, which is a convenient distraction. Brad slooowwwly eases the gate open but it still squeaks. We both freeze.

Neither Holly, Rebecca, nor Zion pop out of their tents and start waving red flags of Disqualification and Doom in our direction, so we slip into the park. I thought we'd head for the swings, but instead, Brad tugs me toward a little castle on wooden stilts.

"Why are we even doing this?" I grumble. "Breaking curfew. I must've lost my mind."

"We did it before, remember?"

"Yes, and almost got caught, and clearly failed to learn our lesson."

"I guess you can't resist me." He winks, and, God, the truth rips right through my heart. We clamber into this tiny starlit fairy-tale castle, and I ache. The wood floor is hard and freezing cold under my bum, but Brad pulls me backward until I'm leaning against his chest and this is more than worth it. His thighs bracket mine. He breathes in deep and I feel his lungs expand, feel the heat of his breath rush past my neck as he wraps his arms around me and laces his fingers together over my stomach.

"Well, this is cozy," I say dryly, because it's either that or I faint with happiness.

"Shut up," he replies, and noses my hair out of the way to kiss a spot just beneath my left ear.

Okay, my options have been exhausted: fainting is all I have now.

"Tell me what's wrong," he murmurs.

I love you. "Nothing."

"You seem distracted."

"I'm always distracted. It's an unfortunate side effect of being intelligent. You wouldn't know."

He laughs and I feel warm and fuzzy inside. I even let myself enjoy it. Then he softly quiets down, and there's a long pause before he murmurs, sounding only a little sad: "I wish you'd trust me, Celine. I really, really do."

The thing is, I trust Brad an impossible amount. Like, if the world was ending—if the aliens came or an asteroid hit or a hungry god burst out of the earth and demanded retribution—and I couldn't save the day because I happened to be in a coma or, like, waiting for my pedicure to dry, I think Brad could save the world instead. I would trust him to do it without a second thought.

So tell him.

But I can't. Because what I really want is to spill *all* my feelings, to say *I trust you,* yeah, but also *I love you and I think I always will, even if one day you leave me behind.* And when it comes down to it, I'm still not brave enough for that. I'm still not brave enough to risk being left.

But maybe one day I could be? If I tried really hard? That's not impossible, right?

For now, I tell him *a* truth, if not *the* truth. "We finish the expedition in two more days. Then we have a day or so to rest, and then . . ."

He follows my drift, because when doesn't he? "Then it's time for the Explorers' Ball."

My heart is heavy like a stone at the thought. "I bet he'll be there."

Brad doesn't ask who.

"You were right," I admit. "I need to tell my mum."

"Yeah. Sorry."

I exhale all my frustration (don't worry, it regrows like mold) and let my head fall back against his shoulder. He kisses my cheek, almost absentmindedly, and in that moment, I want want *want* so bad I could eat the world.

"I get it," Brad says. "You know I still haven't talked to my parents about my writing yet."

Yes, just like I know how happy Trev is to have one of his children follow in his footsteps. Still, I fumble for Brad's hand in the dark and say, "Your dad loves you. He's always going to love you."

"I know. I'm just a coward. We all are, a little bit, sometimes. It's not as terrible as people make it out to be." He pauses. "Still pretty terrible, though."

"Hey!"

"Hey yourself. I'm slagging both of us off, so it's fine."

I consider this for a moment. "Fair enough. We don't have to stay cowards, though. That's not who I want to be."

There's a long pause before he says slowly, softly, "No. Me neither."

Brad falls silent again, and I start to worry he's gotten lost in his own head. "Hey." I squeeze his hand and search for a lighter topic. "When did you become a Golden Compass bloodhound, by the way?"

I feel his chest puff out behind me. "Don't hate me 'cause you ain't me."

"That scholarship is yours." I'm serious: he's good. In fact, annoyingly, he's better than me—but if there's anyone I'd accept being second best to, it's him.

"You didn't hear that girl Vanessa got back hours before anyone else?" He huffs. "And she got three compasses on her own. She's like the Terminator."

"She's like Sarah Connor."

"Ce-*line*. Yes. Have you ever seen the TV show?"

"Why would you even ask me that? Of course, I've seen the show."

From then on everything is easy and light, just like it should be, just like I need it. We spend too many hours in our castle under the stars, and when we finally stumble back to the tents, Brad kisses the life out of me.

"Try to sleep," I whisper against his mouth.

"Celine," he says, "did you know tents get *condensation*?"

My lips twitch. "Yes?"

"Disgusting," he mutters. "Outside and inside are two separate places." Then he kisses me some more. His mouth feathers across the corner of mine, eases my lips apart, tastes me softly. His hands cradle my face, thumbs sweeping hypnotic arcs over my cheeks. I know Brad is into me because he touches me anywhere I'll let him, but when he kisses me like this—like the rest of my body doesn't exactly matter or isn't what he wants—that's when I start to get unwise ideas like, maybe he loves me too.

I mean, I know he *likes* me. It could happen, right?

"Good night, Cel," he whispers, and sends me to bed.

Sophie's snoring (how the tables have turned) but Aurora's

still awake. She whispers to me like air from a party balloon. "I ship this so hard."

I struggle back into my sleeping bag and thank God she can't see me smiling. "That's not—We're not like that."

She ignores me. "I *knew* you were into him. I knew it the first day at the cabin in Sherwood Forest, when he stopped to talk to you—"

"What?" My eyes are so wide they could pop out of my head at any moment. "But I didn't—" Did I?

"And now you're in *love*—"

I bite the side of my tongue, force myself to say it calmly. "I am not in love."

Aurora snickers. "Okay, Celine. You just spent the whole day shooting heart eyes at him, then snuck off with him in the middle of the night. Nothing to see here!" She is gleeful.

"I'm . . . ignoring you now," I manage, trying to push humor into words that taste like chalk. Is she right? Am I that transparent? I must be—it's not like she's making things up. And yeah, I want to tell Brad how I feel eventually—but not by *accident*. It's supposed to be a choice, one I make in the future, when I'm stronger or braver or just . . . generally better than I am right now. What happens when we go back to school? When I'm in love with him right in front of everyone? What happens if he *notices* and he doesn't . . . he isn't . . .

I lie awake all night with a nest of snakes under my ribs.

CHAPTER SIXTEEN

BRAD

I want to tell Celine the truth today.

My brain graciously allows me two hours of sleep; then I get up early to use the bathroom before anyone else. Just like our last campsite, the loos and showers are awkwardly tucked into the edge of the forest, halfway up a jagged hill with winding, white-pebble paths that I assume are supposed to be helpful but are actually quite slippery. There's no fence to separate the path from the ragged drops of the hill face, either, which is *deeply* irresponsible in my opinion, and I spend half the walk up fighting with my brain to avoid counting steps. When I manage to reach the facilities, I find them predictably dingy and disgusting—and there's still another whole night of camping before my return to sweet, sweet civilization. Ugh.

But even this literal torture barely dampens my mood because I'm going to ask Celine to give me a chance, and after last night, I think she'll say yes.

We're being brave, right? Together. We decided. And the fact is, Celine's a person, not a plan. If I'm trying to gain her trust, I want her to know how I feel. If she's going to reject me, that's okay too. But I'm gonna make it clear that I'm here until she asks me to leave, and just the thought of admitting it has me bouncing around like a cartoon character.

I'm grinning so much that when I crawl back into our tent, Raj takes one look at me, groans, and turns over. "*Why* is your face doing that at this hour of the morning?"

"I'm gonna talk to Celine." Too late, I realize this means very little to Raj because he (1) doesn't know that we're secret make-out partners and (2) has no idea I lo— I'm pining after her and have been for roughly a century.

Still, he looks over his shoulder and cracks one eye open to stare at me. "Huh. Well. Good?"

"Yes," I say, my fingers drumming out a rapid beat against my thighs. "So good. I hope." God, what if it's not good? No, no, fear is the mind killer. Just do it, tell the truth. "*So* good."

"Nice one, pal."

I high-five his sleepily upheld hand, choose today's outfit (burgundy this time, she likes red), and basically run to her tent.

Sophie unzips the flap and squints at me, or possibly at the bright-white morning sun. Her hair is still wrapped up in a pink-and-blue scarf and she has a pillow crease on her cheek, which— How does she fit a pillow in her rucksack? Very impressive. Unfortunately, her expression suggests she's less than impressed with me. "Mate. Just marry her already."

Not a bad idea. Wait, no, I am a teenager. I can't get married; Mum would cry. "Hey, Soph! Celine in?" That was very loud. I think I'm nervous.

Slowly, Sophie raises delicate fingers to her temple. "Why. Are you so cheerful. At seven in the morning."

"It's my naturally sunny disposition."

"Well, take it down a notch, babe. You're giving me a migraine. And no, Celine's not here. She went to the bathroom."

"Oh." I should wait for her to come back. Exceeeeept I'm not going to do that because I have decided to confess my true lo—*feelings*—so I need to do it now before my nervous excitement turns to nervous catastrophe. Back up the danger hill I go. "Okay, thanks, Sophie, bye!"

I zip past Zion on my way to the white-pebbled path and he laughs after me, "That's the spirit!" I'll take that as a good omen.

I've got this. One hundred percent.

● ● ●

CELINE

Getting changed in the communal showers is not in my top ten favorite life experiences, or even my top thousand, but I'm not about to waltz back to my tent in a towel—at least, not in *this* weather. So I awkwardly balance on my shower shoes to avoid touching the wet and mildly gross tiled floor while I layer on my tracksuit, then stuff my pajamas into a bag and ram my little towel on top.

I wasn't even planning to shower on this expedition—I thought I'd just wash the necessities and keep it moving, mainly to avoid this exact situation, but I needed a shower for emotional purposes because my brain is scrambled. Unfortunately, the water was lukewarm, the pressure was weak, and the snakes under my ribs slither on. What would I rather do: tell Brad the truth before I'm ready or have him figure it out? I still haven't decided.

So obviously, when I open the bathroom door, he's standing right there.

"Celine!" He straightens up from the mammoth fir trunk he's been leaning on, a smile lighting up his face. He's wearing his glasses, the gold frames bright against his brown skin in the morning sun, and I want to put my fingertip in his shallow little dimple. I want to kiss him and taste all that happiness.

For God's sake, I'm supposed to be in turmoil right now. This boy is so contagious, the World Health Organization should be notified. "What are you doing here?" I ask, and my voice comes out breathless.

There's an odd little pause before he answers. "I came to walk you back so you wouldn't get eaten by wolves. Did you shower? Give me that." He takes my bag and eyes the towel sitting on top as we fall into step together. "I hope you're going to dry that properly, Celine. You can catch communicable diseases from towels. Damp fabric is a breeding ground for bacteria and wet skin is receptive to all kinds of . . ." He breaks off with a shudder. "Although, how you're supposed to dry anything properly in this damp— God, who even *invented* camping?"

"I don't think it was a matter of invention," I say.

He laughs and I see liquid gold rolling through the air. I adore him. Then his smile fades slightly and he says, "I thought maybe we could talk."

His voice is quiet. Cautious. The snakes in my middle lift their heads and flick out their tongues, tasting the breeze, unanimous in their conclusion: smells like doom.

There are only two types of talking: the type that is fine

and normal, which doesn't need announcing, and the type that's terrible, which requires an Official Moment. People say they want to talk before they break up with you, but Brad and I can't break up because we're not together. Still, my throat constricts. It turns out a lack of official title and public affection doesn't help much when you love someone regardless.

Fuck. Fuck, fuck, *fuck*. If Aurora noticed how I feel, Brad must have noticed too, and now he's going to tell me it's too much. I'm too much. I have been since we were little. We take a few more steps in silence before I manage to force out the word: "Okay." Thank God it sounds unaffected, slightly curious, rather than crumbling and afraid.

It's fine. You're fine. This is fine. Usually, this mantra pours concrete over the fresh green shoots of my feelings, but this time, it's not working. I love Brad Graeme. And I am not fine at all.

The white chips of stone beneath our feet crunch with every step. Trees as tall as ten of us stand solemnly to each side. We take one of the path's winding bends and I look down the jagged face of the hill toward our campsite. How far away are we? How many bends and silent, knowing trees will we pass before I can slip into my tent and cry in peace?

"Here's the thing," Brad says, then breaks off with a nervous exhalation that clouds in front of us. I look down to see his fingers tapping against his thighs, one two three four five six seven eight.

"God," he mutters, "just say it. Okay. Okay." He stops walking and turns to look at me.

But I can't let him leave me first. "I think we should stop."

He blinks. "What?"

"Stop. You know." I nod at the space between us and grit my

teeth, imagine them rattling with each panicked thud of my heart. "This."

Brad blinks some more, like his glasses have suddenly stopped working. His eyes are huge and dark and endless. "I don't . . ." He presses his lips together, then lets them part. I wonder if he knows what a torturer he is. "You mean . . . we should stop . . . seeing each other?" Now the blade of his jaw, his cheekbones, stand out as harsh as the cold. His dimple is nowhere to be found.

I force a laugh but it's more like a bark. "I mean, we were never *seeing* each other—"

"You know what I mean."

"What are you looking at me like that for?" Because instead of relief—I just made it easier for him, I just broke my own heart like the excellent friend I am—Brad looks . . . devastated. Gaze pained, mouth sad. I know that expression well.

Not on him, though. I don't want to see this on him. My nest of snakes seethes and writhes and I have the sickening feeling I've done something very wrong.

You're avoidant.

Brad's throat bobs as he swallows. His jaw shifts and his nostrils flare.

I wish you would trust me, Celine.

"Fine," he whispers.

When I was a kid, I jumped out of a tree and broke my ankle. It hurt so much I wanted to be sick, and all I could do was lie there in the dirt and sob and think, *Just let me go back in time and I won't jump again. I won't do it again.*

But you can't snatch back some choices as easily as you make them. Now I'm stuck in the dirt with this anxious, burning nausea I can't undo.

"Brad," I say, uncertain, lips numb—

"What?" His whole body is a stark straight line and it's arrowing away from me. He strides down the path. "What else do you want me to say?"

"It . . . it was only supposed to be temporary anyway," I blurt, hurrying after him.

"I know."

"It's not like we're breaking up. We're not breaking up. We weren't—"

"I *know*!" he shouts. Above us, a handful of wood pigeons burst into flight.

"Well, what are you being a dick for, then?"

"Oh, piss off, Celine!"

"*You* piss off!"

He whirls around to face me. "*You*—"

Someone clears their throat. We turn in unison to find an older white lady standing on the path in front of us, clutching a wash bag. "*Pardon,*" she says. "I, uh, may I . . . ?"

"Pardon, pardon," Brad mutters, gaze lowered. "Pardonnez-nous." We step aside. The lady scuttles past. As soon as she's gone, he heads off again.

"Where are you going?" I shout after him.

"Away!" he shouts back.

Don't don't don't don't don't I'm sorry. "You . . . you still have my bag!"

"What do you think I'm gonna do, Celine, EAT IT?" He disappears around the bend.

I growl and kick a tree. Of course, I'm only wearing slides, so all I do is hurt my toe. The tree stares down at me judgmentally while I hop around hissing in pain. *Well, what did you expect?* it seems to say. *You're soft and fleshy. I'm literally made of wood.*

"Shut up," I mutter, then realize I've officially hit rock bottom. "FUCK!"

The tree does not reply.

What is his problem? *He* wanted to "talk" to *me*.

Maybe he wasn't ending it.

Or maybe he was.

He clearly wasn't.

Well, he would've eventually. He's done it before. He would've reached into my stomach and yanked out my guts with big, greedy fists and he wouldn't even know he was doing it because he doesn't know I love him. I can't *believe* I love him. What the bloody hell am I playing at, *loving* him?

Except I can't quite bring myself to care about the danger of it all, not when Brad's expression is front and center in my mind, looking like someone just yanked out *his* guts. That someone being me.

Oh, God. It was me. My hands shake. My tongue feels sharp in my mouth.

I take a deep breath and squeeze my prickly eyes shut. The sky is too bright a gray today, even with all these old, thick branches obscuring my view. The forest smells like fresh, green frost and slowly rotting bark. I press my palms to my thighs and bend forward and refuse to cry.

I lied to Brad's face just to save my own feelings. I didn't even let him speak because—

Because I'm scared of everything, I'm scared of loving him, I'm scared of being hurt—

And so I hurt him instead. Is that the kind of love I have to give?

My chest burns. I messed up. I'm messed up. I took my worst fear and did it to him.

Take it back.

I run.

• • •

BRAD

After approximately ten seconds of self-righteous storming I realize I'm being a dick.

Whatever happened to friendship first? Celine never promised to want me back. In fact, she's always said the exact opposite, but here I am throwing a hissy fit because my stupid heart is broken. Ugh, I'm *that guy,* aren't I?

Still, this hurts. It hurts like there's a hole in me. I drag my glasses off my face and swipe angrily at my cheeks. Tears feel even hotter when it's freezing. For God's sake, who falls in love with their best friend? Doesn't everyone know that's a bad idea? Especially when said best friend is still working through 27,000 issues and has goals that have nothing to do with you and—

Well, I guess everyone was right: I love Celine. I love her so much, I could throw up right now. Thank God I didn't tell her. I would've told her, and then what? Did I really think I could just, what, teach her to want a relationship by sticking my tongue down her throat? How *arrogant* is that? Later, when I'm not literally splintering in two, I'm positive my brain will present me with a sixty-five-page annotated essay on what a douche bag I am. She didn't want to change the rules; I did.

I put down her bag and grasp my forearms, let my fingers dig into my flesh, but it doesn't stop all the pieces of me drifting apart. Shit. There's a rapid crunch sound coming up behind me, like fast footsteps against the stone, and my stomach drops. I can't talk to anyone right now.

"Brad?"

I *certainly* can't talk to Celine. She looks so pretty fresh out of the shower with no makeup on, those fine folds in her eyelids like silk, the texture of her skin——

Bradley Thomas Graeme, I am begging *you to get a grip right now.*

I start to rush down the path, which is hardly my finest moment, but one thing I'm rarely accused of is maturity. Celine must round the corner fast enough to see me, though, because she calls my name again, and this time it sounds so . . . ragged, like I just ripped part of her open, like I'm hurting her exactly the way she just hurt me.

And it turns out I can't ignore her after all.

I spin around. Fast. Too fast. Frost slides under my heel, chips of stone spray out in an ominous arc, and then the world lurches to the left. I see an angled slice of Celine's wide eyes before the air is sucked out of my stomach and gravity wins. My right side cracks hard against frozen ground, then *bounces* somehow and keeps on going.

Yep. I fall right down the goddamn hill.

Somewhere in the back of my mind, my OCD whispers, *Told you so.*

CHAPTER SEVENTEEN

BRAD

You know those artsy war films where they let dirt splatter across the camera and roll around a lot, so the shots make you feel dizzy? Turns out falling down a hill is a lot like that, but faster and way more painful. I land at the very bottom, kind of like a ragdoll in that my body flops around with no input from me, but also not like a rag doll at all because I have bones and they are NOT HAPPY.

"Brad!" Celine sounds very upset, so I give myself a solid two seconds to splinter into a thousand pieces of physical agony, then try lifting my head. Lucky me, it works. It also triggers a splitting headache that turns my vision white, but I'm not going to think about that because the moment I do—

Oh my God. We're going to die. We've gone blind. We're already dead. Is everything still working? ARE WE GHOSTS?

Ah. Right on cue.

A few blinks, and I can see again, even if it's painful. Oh, crap, where are my glasses? They were so cute. And so expensive. Mum's gonna kill me.

Shit. I fell down a hill. *Mum's gonna kill me.*

Wait. Focus. What were we doing again? Oh yes. I look up very, very slowly, and squint at the blurry shape of Celine, who is carefully edging her way down the same treacherous hill that attempted to take my life. "STOP," I tell her, but something's clearly wrong with me because my voice is faint and raspy and my body hurts like someone stabbed me in the ribs. I feel sick. This is the worst pain I've ever felt. I make a mental note of the sensation in case I need to use it in a book; my hero is definitely the type to get stabbed every so often.

Meanwhile, Celine shouts "NO," back at me and continues to court death like an idiot. Now I have to observe every single step she takes or else she might fall and die while I'm not looking. I hope she's happy.

I remember with a lurch that *I'm* not happy because she doesn't want what I want, and now I hurt on the inside and on the outside. What a thrilling adventure life is, and by "thrilling adventure," I mean it's shit.

"Brad?" This time it's not Celine who calls my name, but someone who sounds alarmingly like Holly, if Holly was less than utterly monotonous for once. I can't tell for sure who it is because they're on my right side, and Celine is on my left, and I can't look away from Celine. She could fall if I'm not looking. So I will look.

"Brad, can you hear me?" not-Holly demands.

I mumble, "Yeah?"

"Can you turn your head?"

"Yeah."

There's a pause. "Well, do it, then," probably-Holly says. Her voice is more familiar when she's annoyed.

"No," I say. "I'm busy."

More footsteps, and I sense another body beside me. "What happened?" Rebecca asks.

"He fell!" Celine calls.

"Can he move his head? Brad, can you move your head for me?"

"In a minute."

"Can you sit up?"

Well, duh. Except when I do, it's less sitting and more dragging. My body suddenly weighs a ton compared to my arms, which feel limp and noodley. My lungs hurt. Or . . . something hurts? I can't tell what hurts, maybe everything. Am I'm dying? What if I've cracked my ribs and stabbed myself in the lung and I'm literally drowning in my own blood right now and after I die my parents are gonna receive my uni acceptance letters in the summer and forever remember me as a sneaky *liar*—

Whatever I've done to myself, the pain is an excellent mindfulness tool, because I notice the too-rapid pace of my breathing by how much it hurts. *I must not fear,* I remind myself. Fear is the little death that . . . that brings . . . I can't remember the rest. My head is too busy spinning.

"Brad," Celine says, her voice shaking. She's finally done clambering down that cliff. She's next to me.

"Hey," I say, because talking seems like an excellent distraction from my brain's current attempts to eat itself. "Are you sure you want to break up? I really don't think we should."

"Oh, Brad." Crap. She's crying.

Someone punches me in the ribs with a brick fist. *"Ow,"* I snap. My side burns. And aches. And burns.

"Call an ambulance," Zion says.

"What? No." *Now* I turn my head. Like I thought, Holly and Rebecca are there, with Zion just arriving (yet already making terrible suggestions?) and a load of campers milling behind them at a distance. I can see Raj raking his hands through his hair *way* too hard. He's lucky he has so much of it, or he'd be at risk of going bald. Sometimes I worry about going bald, but Dad still has hair so I'm probably safe. Of course, his hairline *is* slightly questionable, not that anyone notices since he keeps it so short. Maybe that's what I'll do. But I think Celine likes my hair long. I turn to her. "Do you like my hair?"

She bites her lip as she answers. "I'm sorry I'm sorry I'm sorry I'm—"

"Hey," I say, raising a hand to her mouth. "You'll hurt yourself."

"Ambulance service, please," Zion says, reminding me that he's doing something silly.

He is unusually grim-faced as he talks into the phone but that's okay because I'm going to stop him. "No. Noooo. Have to finish the expedition." I need the scholarship. If I share a bathroom with a Mason-alike, I'll probably end up killing him. But for some reason I can't figure out how to explain all that, so instead I choke out, "I'm . . . going to be a writer."

"Brad," Holly says, "shut up."

The ambulance arrives I-don't-know-how-long later. At this point I'm feeling much better (physically) and this is all beyond embarrassing. A nice paramedic prods me in various places before declaring me Still Alive. Celine wrings her hands over me like a war widow and it's starting to piss me off because every so often my brain tries to say, *See, she cares about you!* but then I remember she cares about me *up to a point*. That, while I thought we were closer than ever, she was . . . done with me? I don't even know, but it hurts worse than the ache in my ribs.

Then someone helps me hobble over to the ambulance and it turns out, nope, I was wrong—everything definitely still hurts.

"I should go with him," Celine's saying, not like she's asking but like it's common sense, really, so Holly and Rebecca better step aside before she makes them.

Except for once, her never-ending confidence doesn't work, because Zion says, "Only one person can go in the ambulance with him—"

"Yes," Celine grits out. "Me."

"And it's going to be me," Zion says, "because I'm the responsible adult here."

Celine laughs in his face. "Listen. I'm going with him one way or another. I don't know what else to tell you."

And I don't know what she's playing at, but at this rate she's going to lose all her BEP matrix points and—

Wait.

"Can you manage, mate?" the paramedic asks as she helps me into the ambulance.

I don't answer. I'm too busy thinking—Celine wants to leave? With me? Right now? She must have forgotten. "Celine," I call, loud enough to hurt my own head. I can't see her; she's behind me and I'm not looking around because moving my eyes is not a lot of fun right now, but there's a pause in her argument with our supervisors. "Don't come with me," I say. She can't quit now. She's almost halfway through this expedition. She has to get the scholarship. If I can't get it, she has to. I think I tell her that. "Celine," I repeat when she doesn't respond, "don't—"

"Okay," she says, her voice rough. "Fine. Okay."

• • •

The last time I stayed at a hospital—the only time, actually—they took my tonsils out. This time, they put bandages all over me, give me medicine, and say I'm under observation. An old nurse with a Glaswegian accent I barely understand tells me I'm a verra lucky boy because I have no broken bones. *I* would consider cracked ribs broken, but okay, I guess? It's hard to care too much about details when you are wallowing in a pit of despair—which is also very hard to do when you've been put on a sunshine-yellow-painted pediatric ward because you are still seventeen, but I manage anyway.

"Feel up to eating yet?" Zion asks. He's been asking every ten minutes for the last several hours.

"No," I mutter. I am too sad to eat. Also, I feel really nauseous. But it's mostly the sadness.

"There's jelly," he cajoles.

"No." I look him in the eye. "Thank you."

He sighs. His dreadlocks sway mournfully.

First, Celine doesn't want me, and now I won't get a scholarship. The first part feels like my heart's been ripped out and the second fills the hole left behind with burning but impotent rage. *Why* did I have to fall down the bloody hill? Running away from Celine, no less. I'm furious with myself. In fact, I'm so busy glaring at my crisp white hospital sheets, it takes me several seconds to notice my actual mother waltz into the ward. By the time I recognize her presence, Dad's already followed her in. Then comes, horror of horrors, Mason. Just like that, three-quarters of my immediate family stride past the rest of the beds on the ward and surround mine in a cocoon of overloud questions and not entirely unwelcome concern. Someone draws the curtains all around us, and it begins.

"My baby!" Mum wails. "What *happened*?"

"Look at you!" Dad says, horrified. "Is someone seeing to my son?" He looks around like a nurse might crawl out from under the bed. "Hello?" He's wearing a suit underneath his wool coat. Mum is wearing—oh God—scrubs underneath hers.

"Did you come from work?" I demand.

"Of course we did!" Mum says, outraged. "No child of mine will suffer alone in some foreign country!"

"Mum," Mason sighs, "it's *Scotland*."

I notice, even with my blurrier-than-usual vision, that he's wearing his Forest Academy uniform. "Did you leave *practice* for me?"

"*Obviously* not." Mason snorts, just as Dad says, "No, he skipped it. By the way, your sister wanted us to FaceTime you when we arrived, but—"

"I told her it probably wasn't a good idea," Mum finishes. "You have a concussion." She pauses, then repeats as if riding a fresh wave of horror: "A *concussion*!"

Zion chooses this moment to stand up and intercede. "Mr. and Mrs. Graeme, hello, we spoke on the phone."

"Ah!" Dad has found someone to question. "What's happened here, then? How did he fall? Bradley is not reckless. He is typically very careful. So I'm not entirely sure——"

I zone out. It's incredibly easy. I have a lot to think about, like worrying a loose tooth.

When I start paying attention again, Zion has escaped and Mason is eating my jelly. "Hey," I say. "That's mine."

"Come and take it, then."

I would, but there's a tiny kernel of worry in the back of my mind regarding the possibility of minute but potentially deadly spinal damage that the doctors missed but that I could make worse if I move too much and I don't want to give that worry any ammunition. I have erected an emergency shield in my head for all my unwanted thoughts to bounce off of, but that sort of thing can't last forever, and I don't have the energy to be mindful or take care of myself or whatever you want to call it. I am exhausted.

"Stop tormenting your brother," Mum says, and Mason huffs.

"How are you feeling, kiddo?" Dad asks. There are deep grooves bracketing his mouth, and it's entirely possible his hair got even grayer since I last saw him. My fault. Mum's expression is tight, too, her eyes shadowed behind her glasses for all she's trying to smile. I know they're worried about me, but the honest answer is that I feel vile in every sense of the word and I bet I will for a long, long time.

So what's the point of mincing words? You know what trying to keep people comfortable gets you? Heartbreak. "I feel terrible. I didn't finish the expedition, I won't get the scholarship, and——" I can't say anything about Celine. I won't. I swallow it down like jagged glass. "My ribs hurt, and my head hurts and

I skinned my hip really bad and it feels gross and I'm——" About to say something I maybe shouldn't but desperately want to because why the hell not? "I'm not going to study law."

There is a long pause. Then Dad says, "Come again?"

I suck in a shallow breath and look up from the sheets. At his face. At Mum's confusion. Back to Dad. "I'm not studying law. In October. I did something."

There's another pause. Then my brother snickers. "Oh my God. What did you do?"

I lift my chin and say firmly, "I applied to study something else."

Dad appears to be frozen. Mum asks carefully, "Applied to study what, sweetheart?"

"Um. English."

Dad is still frozen. I am slightly (massively) concerned.

Mason is laughing so hard he's clutching his stomach like a cartoon, my jelly abandoned. "What? *Why?*"

"You . . . you don't even study English at school now," Mum says.

"I know but my grades are good, and my personal statement is incredible." That's what Celine called it. *Incredible.*

Ouch. No thinking about Celine.

"What?" That's Dad, finally, his voice thready with disbelief. "But . . . when . . . you told me you had— Why would you do this?" He leans forward, puts a hand on my forehead as if to check my temperature. "Are you okay?" He's scanning my body like he might discover a badge that says TEMPORARILY ADDLED, DON'T LISTEN TO A WORD THIS PERSON SAYS. Maybe he finds it because he starts to laugh nervously. "Of course. You've bumped your head, son. That's o——"

"I'm not delusional, Dad." I try to roll my eyes and discover the hard way that that is *not* a good idea. "Ow."

"CAN WE GET SOME MORE PAINKILLERS FOR MY SON, PLEASE?" Dad gets louder when he is panicking.

A nurse with a pink hijab and a steely gaze sticks her head between the curtains and practically pins him to a wall. "Sir. There are children sleeping."

Dad clears his throat. "Right. Sorry."

The nurse softens. "I'll see what we can do." She disappears.

"Why would you want to study . . . anything else?" Dad demands as soon as she's gone. "Is this . . . Are you feeling too much pressure? I was worried you might. You shouldn't. You can do anything, Brad, anything at all—"

I know I can because that's how he raised me. "Like English?" I suggest.

Dad is baffled. "You love law! You were so excited—"

"No, he wasn't, Dad," Mason says, boredom dripping from each word. "*You* were excited. Brad didn't care."

I blink at my little brother, astonished.

He tuts and shifts in his chair self-consciously. "What? You're not subtle."

I have no idea what to say except . . . "Thanks?"

Mason is appalled. "I'm not, like, *helping* you. Just glad I won't be the only family disappointment."

Both my parents start at that, like they've been electrocuted. "I beg your pardon?" Mum demands. "Mason Ashley Graeme, you are not a disappointment. I don't ever want to hear that out of your mouth again."

"Yeah, okay." Mason snorts. "Admit it. You want us to be like Emily. You want us to be like you. But I'm not a genius—"

"Mase," I say. "You're a *football* genius. That's just as good. You know that, right?"

He falters, splotches of red climbing up his neck. "Well. Whatever." His scowl returns but it's not nearly as hard-core. Mason turns toward our parents. "The point is, I don't like school, and Brad *is* a genius, but he doesn't even care. So get over it, both of you."

Dad holds up his hands, his frown pure confusion. "Boys. What is this all about? You know we don't care what you do in life. We just want you to be happy."

"Then why do you make me study when I'm going to be a footballer?" Mason demands.

"Because if your legs fall off, you're going to need a proper education, Mason!" Mum says, exasperated. "Why do you think? We only want the best for you!"

"And why were you so upset," I ask Dad, "when I mentioned before that I didn't want to study law?"

Dad's mouth drops open and stays that way for long seconds before he answers. "I . . . I . . . You took me by surprise. I don't understand. I thought . . ." He looks so sad for a moment I sort of feel bad. But then he pulls himself together and shakes his head. "It doesn't matter what I thought. I'm sorry, to both of you, if we've ever made you feel like you can't . . . live the lives you want." He looks at me. "I thought you were passionate about law, Brad. I thought you just needed support. I didn't realize it wasn't actually something you wanted."

In fairness, I never told him either. All the tension coiled in my gut unwinds, leaving behind relief and a little pit of guilt. "I'm sorry," I say, because I really am. He's my dad. And I assumed he'd, what, lock me in the house and insist I could only follow the path he chose? All my worry, all my sneaking around, feels so out of proportion now. "I didn't want to let you down." It took a while for *me* to believe I could pursue writing. Other people believing in me felt like too big an ask.

You asked it of Celine.

Stop thinking about her.

"English, eh?" Dad says after a moment. His voice is uncertain, but he seems determined, and Mum smiles at us both encouragingly. "What's that for, then?"

I swallow down my embarrassment and admit, "I want to, er . . . write books?"

Mason bursts out laughing. I barely mind.

• • •

CELINE

After they send Brad off in the ambulance, I text him a thousand variations of I'M SORRY I DIDN'T MEAN IT ARE YOU OKAY CAN WE TALK. Then I find his phone vibrating in the tall grass at the base of the hill where he fell and come to my senses.

He's hurt. He's gone. And I fucked everything up, even before all that.

He didn't want me to go with him.

Since I have nothing better to do, I force myself to complete the day's expedition. The thought of a scholarship should motivate me but every time I think about it, I imagine coming face to face with my father at the Explorers' Ball on Saturday and instead of feeling triumphant, I feel small. Brad would've had my back. I doubt he will anymore.

My BEP performance lacks any sparkle or sophistication whatsoever. I don't find Golden Compasses. I don't giggle with Sophie and Aurora in our tent. Everyone creeps around me like my dog just died. I'm glad because it's annoying, and if I wasn't annoyed, I might be crying instead.

We finish the Glen Finglas expedition on Wednesday night and pile into the coach on Thursday morning, and I know I'm being a completely miserable drama queen, but I sit alone at the back so as not to infect everyone else's happiness with my grim and gray mood. This gives me a lot of time to gaze out the window and ruminate on my sins.

I have to fix this. I have to fix everything, and as much as my pride and my nerves cringe away from it, I'm done coddling both. Either I face my feelings, or I don't. Either I try, really *try*, to move on from everything my dad put us through, or I spend the rest of my life living in his shadow. I know what I want to do. And I'm Celine bloody Bangura, so I have no excuse not to do it.

That's what I tell myself, again and again, as I step off the bus in front of the Sherwood. Mum is waiting by her parked Corsa down the street, bundled up in her bright blue coat, arms folded against the cold. She spots me and waves, her whole face lighting up with this wide, welcoming smile, and my chest heaves.

Beside me, Aurora whispers, "Celine, are you okay?"

"I'm fine," I gasp.

"Are you *crying*?"

"Don't be ridiculous. I'll text you later." Then I rush off before anyone else notices the literal ocean spilling down my cheeks.

Mum's not wearing her glasses, so she doesn't notice my expression until I'm a foot away and throwing myself into her arms. "Celine?" she asks, her confusion muffled by my hair, a comforting vibration through my entire tense body. "Baby? What's wrong?"

"Nothing," I sob.

"Oh, sweetheart. Come here, give me your bag. Get in the car." Mum directs my basic functions like I'm five again and stuffs me into the passenger seat. Then she's in the driver's seat, picking up her glasses from the dashboard and peering at me like the clue to my inner turmoil might be tattooed on my face. Spoiler alert: it is not.

"Is this about Bradley?" Mum asks.

I would honestly rather die than say yes, because that would involve admitting to my mother that I have a romantic connection with another human person, and since I haven't even managed to admit that to the person in question, I'm clearly not there yet.

Brad's phone sits heavy in my pocket, vibrating with a text that's probably from Jordan.

"He's doing well," Mum says. "Back at home resting. Just some cracked ribs and abrasions and a minor concussion. Maria says he'll be right as rain—"

This news does make me feel at least a quarter better. One of the links in the anxiety chain formerly known as my spine loosens.

"—in time for your little party at the weekend."

Aaaand that makes me feel worse. Because Brad might be at the ball, but he won't want to see me. And I don't want to see Dad. And I should be so happy right now because I did it; I'm a Breakspeare Explorer, whether I get the scholarship or not; I have Katharine Breakspeare's seal of approval and the chance to network to my heart's content in a fabulous dress Michaela officially labeled *absolutely bitchin'*. I have achieved multiple steps on my Steps to Success board, except I don't even give a damn because I've also monumentally fucked everything up.

It's possible that I'm crying again.

"Celine," Mum says, concerned. "What's wrong? Talk to me. You're giving me a heart attack. Feel my heart." She takes my limp hand and presses it to her chest, like I can feel anything through her many layers of winter clothes. "See? You're killing your mother."

"I'm sorry," I choke out.

"Don't be silly. Come now, tell me what's happened. This is a drop-off only parking space, and I can see a warden down the street." She narrows her eyes at a man in a high-vis jacket several cars away.

God, I'm being ridiculous. I take a few deep breaths and pull myself together, tucking my knees up against my chest.

"Ah!" Mum says. "No shoes on my upholstery, Celine!"

"Seriously?" I mutter. "I'm *crying*."

"I'll cry if you stain my seats. Shoes off."

I kick my boots into the footwell with great difficulty and resume my pose of desolation. Mum makes a satisfied noise, starts the engine, and speeds off with a sound of triumph as the traffic warden approaches.

My confession is delivered to the smooth, plastic face of the car's glove box. "I saw Dad."

There is a stomach-wobbling pause before Mum responds. "In a Scottish forest? On a workday? Is he going through a midlife crisis?"

I know she's trying to make me laugh so I attempt to drum

up a smile. "No. It was before Christmas. His . . ." *Say it. Stop keeping things inside to protect yourself and start sharing them to do right by other people.* "His firm is one of the BEP sponsors. He was in a meeting with Katharine and we bumped into each other. He'll probably be at the ball. I'm sorry . . . I'm sorry I didn't tell you before. I didn't want to stress you out." But that's not the whole truth. Sighing, I add, "I didn't want to tell you because my original plan was to torture him at the Explorers' Ball with my success, and I thought you might find that plan slightly deranged and be disappointed with me." My voice gets smaller and smaller as the sentence goes on, but the point is, I get it out. The world doesn't explode, I don't shrink into a hole of embarrassment, and Mum doesn't disavow me just because I'm a fool.

Another chain link of anxiety loosens a bit.

She blows out a soft breath, then reaches over and squeezes my hand. "I'm sorry. That must be the first time you've seen him in . . ."

"Years," I finish.

"What did he say?"

It's embarrassing to admit, even to Mum, that he said pretty much nothing. That, even when faced with his own child, he still wasn't moved enough to apologize or attempt to make amends. That he didn't try to get in contact afterward, that he scurried away as soon as he could and didn't look back. Again.

My throat feels tight.

"Ah," Mum murmurs.

"Aren't you angry with me? For . . . for hiding it?"

She turns to look at me for so long I become mildly concerned we might run a red light. After a moment, she says, "I did you girls a disservice when I chose your father. I should've chosen a man who would always do his duty. You shouldn't know what this feels like."

Protest rises without a second thought. "No. It's not your fault, Mum. His behavior is his choice. You can't control other people."

She smiles as she checks the rearview mirror. "Mmm. That's hard to remember sometimes."

"Yeah," I whisper. "Yeah, it is." Because even as I said the words, I knew how much of a hypocrite I am. I know my dad disappearing so completely has nothing to do with me as a person, but the hurt's still there.

"How you feel about your father," Mum begins, "and how you choose to deal with it—I cannot dictate that. It isn't happening to me. Not in the same way. So I'm sad you didn't tell me then, Celine, and I'm sad you've been alone with this, but I'm grateful you're telling me now."

My chest is tight because the truth is, I wasn't alone. I had Brad and he wouldn't leave me alone for a second, but I still tried to leave him first. "I've been thinking."

"Yes?"

"What do you think about, like . . . counseling and stuff? For me, I mean? I did some research," I add quickly, "and it doesn't have to be expensive." It's amazing what a quick Google search at the back of a bus will teach you. There's all kinds of options, and one of them's got to help, because I am sick of being like this—anxious and afraid.

"If that's what you want," Mum says slowly, "it might be a good idea. And believe it or not, Celine," she adds dryly, "we have money for important things. We are not utterly destitute."

I flush. "I know."

"Or even slightly destitute."

"I *know*—"

"Good. Maria suggested counseling to me years ago, for you girls." She chews on her lip. "I didn't think it was necessary. You seemed . . . fine. Your sister was angry, yes, but I assumed that was normal. I suppose that was unwise of me. What is normal? What is fine? I don't know." She sighs, shrugs. "We'll sort something out, baby. If that's what you want. We will."

I take a breath, and as my lungs expand my shoulders rise, looser than I thought they could be. "Thanks, Mum."

She pats my knee and shifts gears. "You said your father's supposed to be at this ball?"

"Maybe. He could be. I'm sorry." My voice peters out. I have never felt so monumentally selfish in my life. "I don't want you to have to be in the same room as him."

Mum snorts. "I would happily share a room with him to support you. But I doubt he'll be there."

I look up sharply. "Really?"

"Do you know why your father doesn't see you girls?"

I shake my head.

"It's because he's ashamed of himself. He carries this pile of guilt around, caused by nothing but his own choices. And every day he doesn't parent you, doesn't treat you the way he should, that guilt gets heavier, and when he sees you, is reminded of you, it becomes unbearable. What he doesn't realize is the difference between short-term and long-term pain. If he put up with his discomfort years ago in order to do right by you—if he had taken responsibility for his actions and tried to make it up to you—that guilt of his might have gone away. Instead, he's doomed himself to slowly die beneath it." Mum shrugs like she hasn't just blown my mind and dragged my father to filth. "George has always been good with his books, but he never was too bright. While I enjoy the fruits of my labor with two delightful daughters, I imagine his poor family is trapped in a *Stepford Wives* fan fiction that exists to protect his damaged ego." She slides me a sly look of amusement. "I mean. That is only a theory. I'm sure he's very, *very* happy."

I'm surprised, at first, to feel the laugh bubbling up from my chest. But as soon as it breaks free, it feels like the most natural thing in the world.

"If he knows you're going to be at this ball," Mum says, "I doubt he'll turn up. Too awkward. Too guilt-inducing. And if anyone realized you are his daughter and he doesn't know you . . . well. He's a partner at his firm now, isn't he? There are standards of behavior to uphold. I doubt his abandoning of you and Giselle is common knowledge and I'm sure he wants to keep it that way."

All of this makes sense, and it burns a little, but more than that, it satisfies me. I always thought it was my duty to make my father feel the weight of what he's done. It never occurred to me that he's suffering already.

I know I'm good at shoving my emotions down, letting them fester inside of me. Maybe that's where I got it from.

Which only adds to my resolve to stop.

"But if it makes you anxious," Mum continues, "the thought that he might be around, don't worry. I will tell him not to go."

My jaw drops. "How . . . how would you even talk to him?"

Mum shrugs one shoulder and flicks her turn signal, unconcerned. "I will go to his house, kick down his door, and tell him to stay away from my baby's special night or else I'll rip him a new——" She pauses and begins again. "I will motivate him, sweetheart. Don't you worry."

I dissolve into fits of laughter. Mum joins in, and for a moment I am free and light and certain that she'd really do it if I wanted her to. Mum has my back no matter what, and so does Giselle, and I don't spend enough time thinking how lucky I am to have the family I do. They are audacious with their love, and that's who I want to be. Not afraid of my feelings but fired up by them. I want to live my life with pride and as shameless as Neneh Bangura.

After all, I am my mother's daughter.

* * *

THURSDAY, 8:54 P.M.

Celine: you were right btw

Giselle✦: always am

Giselle✦: about what tho?

Giselle✦: ????

CHAPTER EIGHTEEN

BRAD

Recovering from a concussion is about as entertaining as watching paint dry. Lucky for me, I have heartbreak on the brain to spice things up a bit. When we get home, Mum puts all my stuff away (except my phone, lost that, trying not to think about it because *fuck*), and makes the bed around me really smooth and tight like she used to when I was little. I get her to do it again because I enjoy it so much.

By the time Friday afternoon rolls around, though, even the bed thing isn't making me less restless. I glare at a shadow on my duvet—the same shadow I've watched as it moved throughout the day with the course of the sun—and shout, "Mum!"

A few seconds later, she opens my door and sticks her head in, her giant bun wobbling like jelly. "What's up?"

"Can I get up yet?"

She arches an eyebrow and purses her lips in a way that means, *You're testing me.* "Do you still want to go to the ball tomorrow?"

"Yes." No. Maybe. Celine's going to be there, and I didn't finish the expedition, so I don't know why I'm even still invited, but I also know I can't stay away. I'm hooked. Like a fish. Also, I have a purple suit that looks incredible on me.

"Then stay your backside in bed," Mum says, and disappears.

"You're being irrational!" I call after her.

"Drink your Lucozade!" she shouts back. Then I hear her say, "Oh. Hi, Celine!" And the bottom falls out of my stomach.

Celine.

Here?

Crap.

"Hi, Maria," she says, her voice quieter than usual. She's right outside the door. I have this urge to check how I look but then I remember it doesn't matter and I don't care. I can't care, not if I want this constant ache to one day fade away. So I lean back against my bed's overstuffed cushions, breathe out hard, and tell myself to relax just as a knock sounds at my bedroom door.

"Yeah?" I ask, then wince at the ragged edge to my voice.

"It's . . . Celine," she says. I think she was going to say *It's me,* the way she has done for the last few months. The way she used to when I was very nearly hers.

"I have your phone," she says, like she's bartering, and I realize I haven't answered her yet.

"Yeah, okay, come in."

The door opens and she's standing there in a black and gray tennis skirt and her favorite Metallica top. There's a notebook held against her chest like a shield and she edges toward me as if I might pounce. Her eyeliner, those two butterfly wings again, is sharp. Her mouth is a blurry coral pink.

Thinking about Celine's mouth is not a good idea.

"Hey," she says.

"Hey."

Her gaze catches on my hair for a second—I took my twists down because my head aches, so it's rippling all around my face. If I was smart, I'd shake it into my eyes and never look at her ever again, but I'm trying to be mature, here.

She goes to sit down on my bed.

I make a noise like a negative game show buzzer. Clearly I'm not that mature. Her gaze flies up to mine and I know she's remembering the day I went to see her after she fractured her wrist, when she did the same thing to me. Her eyes light up with humor, her lips curve, and I'm smiling back at her before I can remember she's the reason my heart hurts so bad.

God. It's just impossible not to be Celine's friend.

She walks around to my side of the bed and gets on her knees. I am appalled. "Celine, come on, I was joking."

"Were you, though?" She arches an eyebrow.

"Well, no, but I've changed my mind, get up."

"It's okay. I'm fine here," she says primly, "since I'm apologizing."

I laugh nervously while my heart skitters around in my chest like a puppy on hardwood floors. *Stop that. It's not what you think.* "You don't need to do that, Cel. I'm sorry I . . . you know." I force the words out because I am a reasonable person, goddammit. "I'm sorry you had to watch me storm off and fall down a hill. I shouldn't have done that. We always . . . agreed it wasn't serious." The words taste like ash, but I need to say them. "Get up," I tell her. "We're good."

"We're not," she says steadily, her voice so strangely serious. I haven't been looking at her head-on because it hurts, but now I do and there's something vulnerable and solemn in her face that I don't recognize. I swallow hard. My stomach flips.

"First," she says, sliding a hand in her pocket, "here's your phone."

Of course she picked it up. The low-level panic I've carried around since losing it eases away. "Thanks. Thanks." I squeeze the cool plastic against my palm a few times to make sure it's there. I have a lot of notifications.

I have notifications from Celine?

"Second," she says, snatching back my attention, "I got you something." She releases the notebook shield and puts it beside me on the bed. I pick it up. A good-weight ring-bound notebook, which is nice, because the feeling of cracking a spine makes me want to throw up. The front cover is a symmetrical pattern of dark green leaves against black, interspersed with splashes of gold foil. It's pretty. It's very Celine, and I don't want to like that, but I do. Only, there's a name printed right in the center of the cover, and it doesn't say Celine. It says Bradley.

"You can't use screens for a while, right?" she says. "Because you're concussed. But I know you've been working on your book so I thought you could maybe keep going—and then I thought, you know, if you handwrite it, you probably won't read it back as much. And you can't just throw it away if it's not perfect. So maybe that could . . . help?" She makes an awkward I-don't-know expression that I find adorable. "Or maybe it's the exact opposite, I don't know, sorry."

I don't know either, and frankly I don't care, because my mind is just stuck on the fact that she got me this. She thought of me. Of what I'd want and what I'd need, and then she went and had it made for me because of course she did, and how the hell am I supposed to fall out of love with her if she keeps being this thoughtful?

"Brad?" she whispers.

"I . . . need you to stop," I grit out.

She flinches. "Okay. Sorry, I—"

God, she looks like a wounded puppy, and she doesn't understand. "I know you wanted to end it, but I can't just . . . suddenly change how I feel about you," I blurt out. "I'm trying. All right? Friends first. I promise. But I can't have you doing things like this or it's not going to work, so I need you to stop."

The breath rushes out of her like a crashing waterfall. "But, Brad, I don't want you to . . . I shouldn't have said . . ." She inhales through her nose and shakes her head. "God, this is so awkward—"

"Yeah, you're telling me."

She purses her pink pillowy lips, then lets them part, and words flood out. "I'm sorry I pushed you away when you didn't deserve it. I didn't even mean it. I lied. I didn't want to end things. I thought you did, which was probably paranoia because I was worried you'd notice how much I wanted to be with you, for real, and I should've just agreed when you asked me the first time, only I couldn't because I was so scared you would . . . we would . . . that it wouldn't last," she finishes, the words sputtering out like sparks from a malfunctioning machine.

My heart sags into a pile of disbelief and relief. Disrelief. "Celine."

"I'm sorry!"

"Are you serious?"

"I'm *sorry*!"

"I FELL OFF A CLIFF!"

She winces. "It was a hill. And that wasn't technically my—"

"CELINE!"

"Okay, yes, sorry!"

God, I love her. "You . . . you . . ." I think I feel another headache coming on. "Do you think you're the only one who's scared of things?"

"No," she murmurs, eyes lowered. "No."

"I don't want us to break up either! I don't want you to go to Cambridge and tutor some hot millionaire who rows and has amazing lats and fall in love with him and come home for Christmas and tell me it's just not gonna work but we can still be friends and then marry him and travel the world together saving people from capitalism!"

Celine is now staring at me, wide-eyed. "Um. Have you thought about this a lot?"

I am breathing heavily. "No," I say, pulling the blankets around me. "No. Just a normal amount. The point is, I want to take the risk because I want you. And I trust you. And you're worth it! Do you get that? You're worth it to me." And I really did not intend to essentially pour my heart all over her like this. Let's blame my concussion. At least I haven't mentioned the L word.

Celine's hand finds my clenched fist on top of the duvet. She eases my fingers apart and laces hers between them. And she looks me in the eye when she says, "You're worth it to me too."

I feel like the world's biggest arsehole. "No, I understand why you worry about these things, Cel. And I don't want to pressure you. So if we can't do this right now, it's—"

"Brad," she interrupts, "I told you once that I'd stop avoiding my feelings. I lied then. But I mean it now. *You're worth it to me.*

And I . . . um . . ." Her mouth moves, but her voice dips too low for me to hear.

I blink. "What?"

"I—" She cuts out again, like she's traveling through a tunnel on the other end of a phone instead of kneeling right in front of me.

"Celine, I can't hear you."

"Darn," she says brightly. "Maybe next time. Want to make out?"

"Yes." I put a hand on her shoulder when she moves forward. "After you speak up."

Her glower is catastrophic. "Oh my God. Fine. I LOVE YOU, okay?"

The breath whips right out of my lungs. I stare at her in shock. In the plan for our future that I developed literally two seconds ago, I didn't foresee Celine saying she loved me until a super-emotional moment such as the birth of our first child in about fifteen years. This is way ahead of schedule. I am astounded. She stares me down with a hard jaw and narrowed eyes as if daring me to say something about it. I'm about to do just that—specifically, something along the lines of *That is ideal, you absolute donkey, because I love you too*—when someone clears their throat and knocks on my open bedroom door.

We both look around to see Dad standing there with a tray in his arms, biting down very hard on a smile you could nevertheless see from space. "Er, hello," he says. "I made muffins." He raises the tray. "Anyone fancy . . ."

Celine very slowly sinks to the floor and sticks her head under my duvet.

I try not to laugh too loud. I get the sense she is mortified enough.

"Right, then," Dad says. "I'll just leave these downstairs."

I remember what Dad said before about me and Celine—how it wasn't a good idea, how it was too much pressure. If he still thinks that, well, it changes absolutely nothing, because I've decided no one's reservations—including my own—will ever stop me from going after what I want. Writing is for me, and I'm the one who makes that choice. Celine is for me, and we're making the choice to be together. If it goes wrong—any of it—I can deal with that.

I *trust* myself to deal with any outcome. I believe in me.

Still, my heart does a happy dance when Dad catches my eye, gives me an apologetic smile . . . and a thumbs-up, his hands still clutching the tray. "Help yourself when you come down, Celine." He leaves and closes the door.

"You can come out now," I tell her.

"No," she groans, her voice muffled. "No, I really can't."

"Then how am I gonna tell you that I love you too?"

At that, she pops up like a meerkat. A meerkat with an enormous smile. "Oh. Oh. *Oh*. Oh. Oh—"

I appear to have broken Celine. "Come here." I grab the front of her T-shirt and drag her closer.

"Wait! Are your ribs—"

"Don't care," I say, and then I'm kissing her. It's like birthday cake, back when sugar felt like being high. It's like laughing as you stumble through the dark under the stars. It's like Celine loving me.

She pulls back slightly, her lips—her smile—ghosting against mine. "Does this mean I'm allowed on the bed again?"

"You're allowed anywhere you want," I tell her, "as long as you're right next to me."

* * *

FRAPPES 4 ALL 💀

Minnie: Still good for tomorrow?

Jordan: 👍

Sonam: Y

Celine: yes

Brad: ???

Peter H: what

Brad: no one tells us anything

▼BREAKSPEARE BADDIES▼

Celine: hey guys

Celine: some friends from school are meeting us at maccies after the ball, if you want to come?

Raj: always up for a maccies

Sophie: yeah def x

Aurora: cute yes pls

Brad: oh THAT'S what's happening

Brad: i remember now

Celine: 😵

Brad: don't judge me

Brad: i am concussed

CHAPTER NINETEEN

CELINE

When we arrive at the Sherwood on Saturday night (just a teeny, tiny bit late), Giselle has to help me out of the backseat because my dress is so poofy. It's a good thing I'm wearing Doc Martens instead of the heels I considered, because clambering out of the car is a mission even in flats.

Mum stands a few feet away, admiring her flawless makeup in a blue compact that matches her sheath dress. She snaps it shut, looks us over, and says, "Giselle, are you sweating? What have I told you about bodily functions? Only in private." We roll our eyes while she snickers at her own joke. Then she slides an unreadable look at the side entrance to the Sherwood before glancing at me. "Ready?"

"Ready," I say, and I swear it's true. I am stepping into my destiny and nothing's going to stop me, including (but not limited to): errant fathers, Katharine Breakspeare worship, and *I love you* giddiness.

"Good," Mum says. "I'm proud of you. All right, then. Let's go." We all hook arms and storm the Sherwood like a Bangura-shaped wall. The hotel is still a maze of fancy furniture and gleaming glass pillars, reflecting us a thousand times over—Mum's skin glowing against her ocean-blue outfit, Giselle looking abominably gorgeous in her slim black suit, and me in the dress Minnie and I scoured the charity shops for. I almost gave up on finding something cute in my size, but Michaela claims thrifting is fashion magic and the perfect thing will turn up when you need it to reward you for your commitment to sustainable fashion. I might have to examine her theory on my TikTok because based on this dress, she's right.

It's an iridescent almost black but looks blue-purple in certain lights. The bodice is strapless and wrapped in layers of delicate fabric; the skirt is not full length but floofy, like in fifties films, and when I spin, it flashes the black underskirt. I have a furry shrug around my shoulders that Giselle gave me because "It'll be perfect, Celine, put it on," and—my favorite part—little black lace gloves with a single button at each wrist. The only downside to this outfit is the lack of pockets, but I've shoved my phone and some cash down my cleavage. Hopefully I won't forget it's there and worry that I'm having a heart attack when it vibrates like I did last time.

The Explorers' Ball is held in a modestly sized room with swooping ceilings and white-linen-covered tables. Perfectly round pearlescent balloons with champagne-colored confetti inside them float above us. Below, things are a lot less serene: I look out at the sea of unfamiliar faces and feel my palms prickle beneath my gloves. Parents are easy to spot—they look proud and are taking enthusiastic advantage of the free punch.

Professionals are easy to see too—they look serious and intimidating, like the future itself.

I don't see Brad.

"Maria and the boys are here already," Mum says, patting the little blue clutch where her phone lives. "Shall we look around? Or do you want to go and find your friends on your own, Celine?"

I know what she's really asking: *Do you want to separate, when we don't know if your father's here?* I take a little breath and make my choice. "You guys find Maria. I'm going to explore and, you know, network." If I can work up the nerve to approach an actual adult and sell my professional skills. Maybe that will come later in the night while we eat dinner. I know we've all been seated according to our professional interests. . . .

My stomach leaps with nerves and I decide to focus on one thing at a time. First things first: find Brad.

We separate and I wind through the crowd, spotting Raj in a dove-gray suit talking with an older lady wearing thick black-framed glasses. There's that Vanessa girl, holding court with what seems like half the professionals in the building. Impressive. There's Holly and Zion, huddled together by the punch—Zion gives me a wave; Holly offers a smoky-eyed smize—and Aurora and Sophie are waving at me from across the room. I'm practically running toward them when Katharine Breakspeare appears in front of me like the angel Gabriel—you know, mystical and too fabulous to look at. I blink like a fish to clear my eyes.

"Ah, Celine," she says cheerfully, "just the person I'd hoped to see. May I have a moment of your time?"

I agree so fast I almost choke on it. "My—Yes! Yes, of course! Hello, Katharine—er, Ms. Breakspeare—"

Her mouth twitches. "Katharine is fine."

My cheeks heat up, but I keep my spine straight. "Right, thank you."

Katharine's famous blowout is bouncing around the structured shoulders of her floor-length red gown. The gauzy fabric covers her from wrist to ankle but it's tight and constructed out of bold, slashing lines. She looks like a general. A gorgeous general with a personal stylist. I file this look away for my immensely successful future while she steers us toward the edge of the room, where a floor-to-ceiling window looks out on the streetlamp-lit square below. The thick, gathered curtains that frame the glass are a deep plum color, so vivid they almost seem alive.

"I wanted to have this conversation with you privately, before the awards begin," she murmurs. "Celine—you aren't a Golden Explorer."

I'm so pleased to be having a private chat with Katharine that it takes a moment for her words to trickle past my happy little haze. As soon as they do, I feel the smile slide right off my face. "Pardon?"

She just looks at me.

I know I messed up the last expedition. I was just so worried about Brad and so upset with myself and now I'm even *more* upset with myself because imagine throwing away a scholarship over a *boy*—

No. No, that's not what happened at all. Brad is not just a boy, he is a person—he is an *important* person—and it's okay to have feelings, even if those feelings are about people, even if those feelings come before perfection every so often. I know this. I believe this.

I also feel ABSOLUTELY SHIT ABOUT MY LACK OF SCHOLARSHIP RIGHT NOW.

Then Katharine says, "However," and there's something about that one word that makes my ears perk up like a dog's. *However* what?

Katharine is still speaking. Pay attention! "I realize," she says, "there were . . . extenuating circumstances that may have affected your performance on the final days of the expedition. I can't change your scores, but having reviewed your performance, the footage you recorded during the final expedition, and, of course, your initial application, which was really very good, Celine—"

I glow like the little lightbulb that could.

"I would personally like to offer you an internship," Katharine finishes.

I blink. "I'm sorry? An internship?" Does she want me to do what Holly and Zion and Rebecca did? Help others become Breakspeare Explorers? That's very kind of her, but I'll probably be super busy with uni and also wracked with resentment that I didn't get the scholarship, so—

"With me," Katharine says. "I know you mentioned an interest in corporate law, which is not my field, but if you're open to other avenues, I do offer summer internships to one or two students each year. Just an opportunity to shadow me and—"

Wait, what? *What??* WHAAAAT???? I am so dizzy with excitement I even think I see the curtain behind her dancing. "Really?" I ask, mortifyingly breathless.

"Absolutely," Katharine says with a little smile. "You're a remarkable young woman with an incredible educational record. And I rather enjoy your TikToks."

This can't be real except it's way too detailed for a dream, so . . . maybe it is? An internship with Katharine Breakspeare would be . . . perfect. Beyond perfect. Way better than anything with the firm I'd *hoped* to intern at because actually I'm not interested in corporate law anymore, and I'm not interested in grinding my father's firm into the dirt, but I *am* interested in getting an up-close-and-personal look at the legal superstardom that is Katharine Breakspeare—

Who is still waiting for an answer, Celine. Pull yourself together! "Wow," I breathe inanely. My heart is fizzing like champagne. "Thank you. Thank you so much. I would love that. I'm absolutely interested in other avenues. I've decided I'm definitely open to other fields and I so admire your work and an internship would be—" *An honor* seems too feudal and *my liege*-y, so I swallow my excited babble and say simply, "Yes, please."

Katharine laughs and pats me on the shoulder. I may never bathe again. "All right. I'll be in touch. Enjoy the party!" Then she drifts off into the crowd, her steps perfectly in time with the piano music coming from the corner of the room. My heartbeat, however, is not in time with anything, except maybe the speed of sound.

"Ohhhh my God," I breathe.

"RIGHT?" says the curtain, and I almost scream until Brad steps out from behind the fabric.

"Bradley!" I splutter. "What the bloody hell are you doing in the curtains?"

He wrinkles his nose and scratches the back of his neck. "Yeah, sorry about that. I was looking for you out of the window. Then I heard Katharine talking and realized no one could see me and it's like, what do you do? Step out and give *Katharine Breakspeare* a heart attack?"

"But you don't mind giving *me* a heart attack," I snort, hand still pressed tight to my chest.

"Well, you're not nearly as important to the culture. Toughen up, Bangura." But he winks and steps closer. His hand finds mine—not the one on my chest, that would be a bit scandalous, but the other one—and I can feel him fiddling with the button on my glove. "Anyway, I was hoping you'd be happy to see me."

I am. I love you. Is now a weird time to remind him? I don't know how to do this stuff like a normal person. "Um," I manage.

He laughs and it's reprehensibly gorgeous. Brad is extra handsome tonight, his hair freshly twisted and kissing the tips of his eyelashes, his skin glowing against the deep purple of his three-piece suit. "I'll just infer from the available evidence," he murmurs, his thumb stroking the bare skin of my wrist.

"You look lovely," I offer. "Even for you, I mean."

"And you," he says, his eyes soft, "look like Katharine Breakspeare's intern."

A grin spreads across my face. I temporarily forget all about Brad's hotness because *I am Katharine Breakspeare's intern*. "I do, don't I?"

"Yep." His grin matches mine. "It suits you. I knew you'd—"

A muffled *tap tap tap* sounds through the room and the music subtly quiets. I turn to the stage and curse Katharine Breakspeare's name for the first time in my life, because she's up there with a microphone *interrupting my moment*. "I think it's time we honored our Explorers," she announces, "don't you?"

Right, yes. I suppose that *is* technically why we're here.

BRAD

I hold Celine's hand all the way to the stage until we're separated by the tyranny of the alphabet. She heads toward the front of the line to stand next to Aurora, who looks adorable in a pink dress that matches her permanent blush. At least I'm next to Sophie, who is wearing *lavender* of all things (really did not have her down as a pastel girl, but she looks good).

"Hey, Romeo," she mutters as everyone's called, one by one, to the stage. "You and Celine married yet or what?"

"Pending," I murmur back.

Katharine calls up the kid in front of me.

"Are you gonna propose when we go to McDonald's later?" Sophie asks.

"If you'll take a picture of us kissing under the golden arches."

"Deal."

Katharine calls my name. After she hands me my fancy, rolled-up Explorers certificate, Celine catches my eye and beams.

I love you.

Eventually, all nine of us are standing up there, being honored or whatever, and it's time to name the Golden Explorers. I've already accepted I won't be one of them, which doesn't matter because (1) it was nice of the BEP to include me at all, since I missed most of the final expedition, and (2) when I look out at the crowd, I see my parents watching me with a pride so fierce even the most panicked and pessimistic corner of my brain can't ignore it or explain it away. Mum and Dad know what I want for my future now, and they know that, no matter what they think, I'm going to get it. But the way they look at me is still the same.

The first Golden Explorer is Vanessa, which surprises no one. The literal golden compass Katharine hands out is palm-sized and beautifully ornate, and Vanessa holds it in the air like an Olympic medal. Obviously, I'm not jealous. A scholarship would be nice, but I can do without it. I can live with roommates. I'm in a very healthy place and I'm excellent at setting boundaries.

The second Golden Explorer is a quiet, hardworking guy named Nick, who is so shocked he almost walks right off the edge of the stage. I clap for him like I did for Vanessa.

Maybe I could get a job so I can afford to live alone? I'm certainly not about to ask my parents for help, not when they have to put money toward my sister studying abroad and——

Katharine announces the third winner, Bradley Graeme, and I pause in my thoughts to clap again. No one steps forward, though. Laughter ripples through the room, and Sophie smacks me on the shoulder. "Brad."

I blink. "Yeah?"

"What's your name, genius?"

What——

I look over at Celine and she is laughing so hard, a hand over her mouth, her eyes bright and happy and . . . I think proud? I look into the crowd at my parents, sitting beside Neneh and Giselle, and they're all beaming and waving their hands at me as if to say *Go*. Then I look at Katharine, who is waiting at the podium with an amused smile and one last golden compass. She leans into the mic and says, "That's you, Brad."

Jesus H. Christ. I won a Golden Compass. I won a scholarship. I all but run over to the podium. "What? Thank you, but . . . I didn't finish the expedition! Surely I shouldn't . . ."

Katharine says into the mic, "Bradley is now explaining to me why he should not receive this award."

Celine cups her hands around her mouth and calls, "Brad. Be quiet."

Everyone laughs some more.

"It's true that, due to an unfortunate accident," Katharine says to the crowd, "Brad could not finish his final expedition. However, our team decided to average out all the data we had for his performance as a Breakspeare Explorer, and the results were undeniable. Brad scored a 4.9 on our matrix."

I. Did? WHY? HOW?

Actually, never mind. I'll take it.

Katharine's still talking. "His performance was consistently high. Therefore, we made an executive decision to honor the work he was able to do, rather than count him out based on what he couldn't complete." She hands me the compass. It's heavy and slightly warm and mine. "You are a Golden Explorer, Bradley. Congratulations."

". . . Thank you!" I manage. The next few minutes are a daze. Some closing remarks are made before Katharine instructs us all to party and we're allowed off the stage.

I stumble down the steps and head straight for Celine who hugs me—carefully, thanks to my ribs, but it still counts—in public, without a second's hesitation. Like she's just overflowing with the need to touch me. The cocoa-butter scent of her skin fills my lungs as I murmur into her neck, "I love you."

She pulls back, shock and pleasure merging in her expression. *"Brad!"* But she's grinning like she can't help herself.

"What? You started it with all the hugging!"

"People can *hear us!*"

"So whisper," I tease. Of course, I don't really expect her to announce her feelings in public like this—

But she does. "Fine. I love you, too, obviously." And then—even though we have seconds before our parents rush over to crowd us, even though our friends are already swarming with congratulations—she grabs the back of my neck and kisses me. Hard. My heart grows wings and flies away.

Me and Celine, we've been best friends. We've been enemies. We've even been a secret.

But right now?

We're everything. Anything. Whatever we want.

ACKNOWLEDGMENTS

Obsessive-compulsive disorder runs in my family, so I wasn't surprised when it finally kicked down the door of my brain, waltzed right in, and made itself at home. Upon receiving my diagnosis, I tutted a bit, panicked a bit, made several emergency cups of tea, and finally decided I'd better stick the whole thing in a book.

Which brings me to the first person I'd like to thank: Bradley Graeme, the hero of this novel, who's been dealing with OCD for years and is enviably sensible about it. I have no idea if I'll ever be as good at coping as Brad is, but I do know that writing him inspired me to take better care of myself. So . . . cheers, mate. Couldn't have done it without you.

I also couldn't have done this without the help of numerous real people. Thank you to my mother for steering me through the angsty Celine years and giving me a name to be proud of; to my baby sisters, Truly and Jade, for being delightful pudding cups; to my best friend, Cairo Aibangbee, for supporting me through multiple creative breakdowns and assuring me that I did in fact still know how to write and had not actually lost my grasp of the English language.

Thank you to Chessie Penniston-Hill for her creative (and teenage) perspective, to Aaliyah Hibbert and Orla Wain for helping me to seem Young and Hip, and to Adjani Salmon for answering my emergency spelling questions.

Thank you to the wonderful authors and literal inspirations (I know, but seriously, it's true) I've had the privilege of befriending since my career began. Therese Beharrie, Kennedy Ryan, Dylan Allen, Ali Williams, and so many more—your books, your kindness, your friendship, and your invaluable advice get me through every single project. I am so lucky to know you.

Many thanks to my incredible agent, Courtney Miller-Callihan, for always having my back, finding solutions, and reducing my professional anxiety by a solid 90 percent just by existing. (You exist in a very badass manner.)

Thank you also to the whole team at Joy Revolution who worked to make this story happen. Nicola and David Yoon, Bria Ragin, Wendy Loggia, Beverly Horowitz, Barbara Marcus, Casey Moses, Mlle Belamour, Ken Crossland, Lili Feinberg, Colleen Fellingham, Tamar Schwartz, Jillian Vandall, Adrienne Waintraub, Katie Halata, Shameiza Ally, Elizabeth Ward, Caitlin Whalen, and so many others, I am grateful for the opportunity to contribute to such an exciting mission and for having a truly beautiful book to show for it.

Thank you to the good people of Nottinghamshire and of the Trossachs for kindly not pointing out the enormous liberties I have taken with the geographical realities of Sherwood Forest and Glen Finglas (there: now that I've said that, you can't complain or you'll seem awfully graceless).

And finally, thank you to my fiancé for . . . well, where to start? For driving me six hours to camp at Glen Finglas in your crumbling Volvo, and for promptly transferring us to a hotel when it turned out camping *really* did not agree with me. For lending me entire portions of your countryside childhood, including that time you did a Bradley (although it would be more accurate to say that Bradley does a you) out in the forest. And most importantly, for bringing me approximately 12 kilos of chocolate and 78 liters of raspberry tea over the course of writing this book. *Highly Suspicious and Unfairly Cute* was powered by you.

ABOUT THE AUTHOR

TALIA HIBBERT is a *New York Times, USA Today,* and *Wall Street Journal* bestselling author who lives in a bedroom full of books in the English Midlands. She writes witty, diverse romances, including *Get a Life, Chloe Brown; The Princess Trap;* and *A Girl Like Her,* because she believes that people of marginalized identities need honest and positive representation. *Highly Suspicious and Unfairly Cute* is her debut novel for teens. Talia's interests include beauty, junk food, and unnecessary sarcasm.

taliahibbert.com

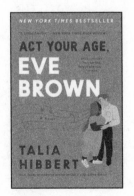